Praise for Abbie Williams

"Williams populates her historical fiction with people nearly broken by their experiences."

— *Foreword Reviews (Soul of a Crow)*

* Gold Medalist - 2015

— *Independent Publishers Awards (Heart of a Dove)*

"Set just after the U.S. Civil War, this passionate opening volume of a projected series successfully melds historical narrative, women's issues, and breathless romance with horsewomanship, trailside deer-gutting, and alluring smidgeons of Celtic ESP."

— *Publishers Weekly (Heart of a Dove)*

"There is a lot I liked about this book. It didn't pull punches, it feels period, it was filled with memorable characters and at times lovely descriptions and language. Even though there is a sequel coming, this book feels complete."

— *Dear Author (Heart of a Dove)*

"With a sweet romance, good natured camaraderie, and a very real element of danger, this book is hard to put down."

— *San Francisco Book Review (Heart of a Dove)*

Summer at the Shore Leave Cafe

a
SHORE LEAVE CAFE
novel

Abbie Williams

central
avenue
publishing

2016

Published by Central Avenue Publishing, an imprint of Central Avenue Marketing Ltd.
www.centralavenuepublishing.com

SUMMER AT THE SHORE LEAVE CAFE

978-1-77168-105-6 (pbk)
978-1-926760-92-6 (epub)
978-1-77168-054-7 (mobi)

Published in Canada

Printed in United States of America

1. FICTION / Romance   2. FICTION / Family Life

I WOULD LIKE TO DEDICATE THIS BOOK TO THOSE OF YOU WHO BELIEVE THERE IS MORE TO THIS WORLD THAN YOU CAN SEE

Prologue

We are a family of women.

In my childhood and early teens, there was the dual force of our grandmother Louisa Davis (with her denim overalls rolled to mid-calf, long white braid tucked under a battered, wide-brimmed straw hat), and Great-Aunt Minnie Davis, her older sister (who fastidiously kept her own long hair dyed its original shade of cornsilk blonde until the day she died). Both women contentedly smoked homegrown tobacco plucked from the sprawling garden behind Shore Leave, kept their nails trimmed short, could catch, clean and delectably prepare any fish that shimmered beneath the silver-blue surface of Flickertail Lake, in general disdained the company of men and were adamant about the giving of advice.

Though Gran was married for a time, long enough to produce both Aunt Ellen and my mother Joan, my grandfather reeled in his fishing line, snapped the clips on his tackle box and hiked out of Landon before Mom was quite a year old. At that time, in the late 1940s, Gran and Great-Aunt Minnie's own mother Myrtle Jean was still living and, according to every version of the story I've ever been told, agreed that Gran was better off without the thick-skulled son of a bitch anyhow. My grandfather's name? Lost to time, no doubt, though the womenfolk would tell me if I ever asked. I haven't yet, though I do know my own father's (Mick Douglas) despite the fact that he too made an early and entirely voluntary departure the summer I was eight months old and Mom was carrying Jillian.

Jilly was born when I was one year and one day old, in August of

1968; I cannot recall a time without the knowledge of her. People forever asked if we were twins, to which we sometimes replied yes, then laughed about it later, wondering if we could get away with the pranks that real twins were able to pull; we certainly resembled each other, with fair, freckled skin, long, straight hair and wide smiles, the image of our mother.

Jilly, however, had eyes of which I was jealous, very direct and intensely blue, the color at the bottom of a candle flame, framed in lashes too dark for a blonde. It was a parting gift from the father we never knew. I inherited my eyes from Gran and Mom: the Davis family eyes, a blend of gold and green, with the pale lashes Jilly should have possessed. My oldest and youngest daughters have my eyes, but my middle girl opened hers a few moments after birth and stared up at me with the eyes of my sister and my long-gone father, true indigo. Jilly always joked that the stork brought me Tish by mistake; Jilly is the only one of us to have produced a son, and likewise is the only one of us whose man was lost accidentally.

I left Landon, the only home I'd ever known, the August after high school to follow my simultaneous boyfriend of four years and husband of two weeks, Jackson Gordon, to the teeming wilds of Chicago. Trouble was I was already pregnant, a discovery made a month after senior prom, in April of 1985, and so for me Chicago's nightlife consisted of carrying a screaming infant through our tiny one-bedroom apartment, snow hurtling against the rattle-trap windows while Jackie attended freshman year at Northwestern. Flash forward a decade and a half and his high-school educated home-making wife was a step away from being a completely hollowed-out crazy woman who, after bearing three children and raising them virtually alone (not that my genes hadn't prepared me for it, really), discovered my husband screwing a lovely young colleague at his law office's otherwise prestigious Christmas party, which I unexpectedly attended. I stormed in on them going at it on Jackie's desk, suspicions horrifically confirmed; a sight so sickening I could have vomited there on the plushy taupe carpet. I wanted to kill him with my bare hands. My bare hands wrapped around a functional weapon, anyway.

I scanned the room with a vengeance, hearing Gran and Great-Aunt Minnie in my head, egging me on, telling me to grab the weighty bronze sculpture of a cat near Jackie's elbow and smash it over his cheating skull. Trouble was, I couldn't ruin that head, connected to the man whose broad shoulders I used to grip with both hands, around whose slim hips my own legs used to wrap possessively, whose hair I clutched in my hands like dark, curling treasure. Jackie straightened up, attempting to look as shameful and dignified as a man with designer slacks around his ankles and a pair of long, gleaming legs around his waist can possibly contrive. He said, "Jo, I'm sorry, I am so sorry," while I felt the earth shift beneath my feet like fresh spring mud and melting-hot blood flood my face with the heat of scorn. I had guessed the truth all along, but like a fool I refused to heed my gut instinct, Gran and Great-Aunt Minnie's most vehement advice.

Jackie was mine for so long, my connection to past, present, and future. He was the father of my children, my husband and companion in this enormous gaping mouth of a city we called home since leaving Landon. We, and eventually our daughters, lived in what amounted to a parade of ever-increasingly expensive and well-furnished properties; together we'd spent exactly as much time here in Chicago as we had in Landon. It seemed to mean something. I fled Jackie's office and hailed a taxi home, far too numb with shock to drive. Camille would be seventeen years old in just a few days, on December twenty-seventh, the baby I carried on my shoulder and nursed to sleep in the dim, multi-colored glow of our first Christmas tree, alone, as my husband hit happy hour with his college buddies. I was only eighteen then, smooth-skinned and blindly naïve, my long hair tied back in a ragged braid most days, washing dishes by hand and trudging at least three loads of laundry a day down to the basement of our apartment building, while my baby girl shrieked.

I called Jilly the moment I arrived safely in my bedroom that night, a weekly ritual. My little sister knew something was wrong before I even opened my mouth. Jilly knowing things was not unexpected; ever since we were kids, Jilly, like Great-Aunt Minnie before her, possessed a powerful sense of intuition.

"I had a dream," she said upon answering, hundreds of miles to the north of me, snug and warm in Mom's kitchen, the kitchen of our childhood with its scarred counters and farm-style sink, the solid maple table where we sat to eat when the cafe was closed. Jackie once bent me over that table on a hot summer night when we were sixteen, while my family slept, both of us further exhilarated by the thrill of the forbidden. In those days, I was the one Jackie could not get enough of.

I imagined Jilly sitting at her usual place, wool socks braced on the seat to the right, my old chair. She would have Mom's crocheted, pine-needle-green afghan tucked around her shoulders, the "Christmas blanket," and a fire would be burning in the potbelly stove, flickering orange through the small cut-out shapes in the cast iron. I imagined it all, correctly I knew, and suddenly ached with homesickness, a kind I hadn't experienced in years. The ache subdued some of the scathing anger that kept me from tears all the way home and through the crowded townhouse to my bedroom.

Jilly demanded, "What did he do?"

A scab seemed to have formed on the back of my throat, obliterating words. Down two flights of stairs, the girls and a bunch of their friends were laughing over *How the Grinch Stole Christmas* on television; the scent of popcorn and melted caramel drifted in the wake of their happiness.

"Jo, I know he did something. What is it?" Jilly's voice dropped a notch and she implored, "Tell me."

"What was your dream?" I asked, hedging, managing a shallow breath, and it was her turn to sigh. In my mind I saw Jilly's right hand lift and cup her forehead, an age-old gesture of uncertainty.

"Jackie was a centaur," she said, and I laughed, caught off guard, though her tone did not indicate a joke. She continued in a rush, "He was mounting a female horse, like, hard-core. And then I woke up. He cheated on you, didn't he? Goddamn him. Gran knew, too. That bastard!" Her voice rose in both pitch and volume.

In the background I heard our mother call, "Jillian, is that your sister on the telephone?"

"Jilly, shut up!" I squeaked. "Now Mom's going to have to know, too. Fucking *hell*." These days, I only swore this much when speaking to my sister.

"Jo, I am *so* sorry. That piece of shit. I *knew* it."

Anger slowly won out, driving the hurt and sorrow back down my throat. I snapped, "I'm glad all of you knew and no one bothered to call me!" Even as I spoke the words I imagined my mother's scolding voice: *You can't always blame the cheater. It takes two, you know.*

As if she could read my thoughts, which she accurately had too many times to count, Jilly retorted, "Jo. You could not have been blind to this possibility. That *bastard*."

I was about to respond but Jilly muttered, "*Dammit*," and in the next moment my mother's familiar voice swelled in my ear.

Mom asked, "Joelle, what is this about? Why is Jillian sitting here in the dark swearing at you?"

"Hi, Mom," I muttered. Defeat hovered like a cloud of noxious smoke and I didn't have the energy to sigh.

In the background I heard Aunt Ellen call, "Joanie, is that Jo? Hi, honey!"

"Oh, for Christ's sake," I groaned. But in our family of women, no secrets were ever kept for long, try as we might, and I surrendered to the inevitable.

Chapter One

FIVE LONG AND SHITTY MONTHS LATER, I DROVE NORTH-
west on I-94, angling into Wisconsin as the sun skimmed the surface of
the sky, melting to a golden dusk. The girls, released a good ten days early
from their private schools at my rather desperate insistence, chattered
to each other, alternately fighting over the radio station and coming up
with new and inventive ways to entertain themselves with sights available through the car windows. For a spell they played the alphabet game,
using billboards and license plates to earn points; then, as we entered
dairy country, moved to *Hey Cow*, a ridiculously simple game that involved yelling the phrase to any cows we happened to pass. The "winner"
of the game was the girl at whom the most cows glanced. I was utterly
grateful when they at last drifted to sleep, somewhere near the Twin Cit-
ies in Minnesota. At that point, the temptation to get us a hotel gnawed
at me, but we were so close to Landon that I couldn't bear not to get
there tonight. Just a few more hours…

The last mile hummed away at long last and I took the final turn
into Landon, whose population now totaled three hundred seventy, plus
four. Jackie and I brought the girls here to visit of course, every summer
of their lives, but there was something about the potential permanence
of this trip that quickened my blood and sent pin-prickles of emotion
through my limbs. The girls remained blessedly asleep, but I murmured,
"Here we are," as the most deeply familiar street of my life rolled beneath

the tires. The geography of a hometown, whether beloved or loathed, is nonetheless engraved on a person's soul.

I drove slowly, both hands hanging at the top of the steering wheel, leaning forward, the better to gaze at everything, hungry for the sights. The towering, ancient pines at the southern edge of town gave way to Fisherman's Street, Landon's main drag; at the northern-most end, Flickertail Lake was visible from the moment the sun rose, its rocky beach a brief walk and subsequent twelve-step descent from any downtown business. The beach itself curved like a clamshell, widening into soft, pale sand as it met the water of the lake a good twenty feet out.

To my right stood the Angler's Inn, the only hotel in town, with a private balcony for each of the rooms on the second floor. Jilly and I always called those "prostitute perches," then laughed hysterically whenever we spied a female guest standing upon one to admire our little hometown. The boardwalks were quiet now at such a late hour, though the windows of Eddie's Bar, a longtime fixture in Landon, just across the street from Angler's, glowed in welcome behind the Moosehead Beer light and a faded wooden shingle, painted by Eddie Sorenson decades ago, inviting *COME IN ALREADY.*

A handful of the vehicles that graced my childhood memories waited at the curb, patient as old dogs and as familiar to me as their aging owners bellied up to the bar inside. There was the immaculate red '76 Charger driven by Daniel "Dodge" Miller, who ran the filling station on Flickertail and took care of the heavy work at Shore Leave for Mom and Aunt Ellen; beside the Charger sat the once-blue, well-used '74 Ford pickup owned by my daughters' great-uncle, Nels Gordon (Jackie's only remaining relative in Landon, as his own folks passed away before Camille turned thirteen). I spied Jim Olson's rimless, rusted-out Chevy Celebrity, and our high-school shop teacher Del Christianson's pecan-brown, speed-boat sized LTD.

The last vehicle I idled past proved the newest of the bunch, Dodge's son Justin Miller's sporty silver Dakota truck. Justin graduated with Jackie and me back in 1985, and since suffered through a lengthy marriage to and subsequent messy divorce from Aubrey Pritchard. Messy in that Aubrey, lovely Homecoming Queen of Jilly's class and Justin's longtime sweetheart, cheated after Justin sustained a disfiguring injury working in his and Dodge's service garage. I didn't know the details of the divorce, mostly because Jilly hadn't known, but she did tell me about how Justin's face and neck sustained burns all along the right side. This happened five summers ago, but somehow I had not come across Justin since then. My stomach tightened with sympathy; I suppressed the perverse desire to make my way inside the warm, familiar space and see the damage for myself. Once, Justin was like a brother to Jilly and me—in summers of old, Dodge often carted Justin and Justin's little sister, Liz, to Shore Leave when he came to help out.

I realized that I'd come to a full stop in front of Eddie's and sat watching the door, while in the background my girls breathed with the soft sighs of exhaustion, both physical and emotional. After a moment, perhaps wakened by the absence of movement, Camille, with Ruthann's head on her lap, stirred from the back seat and murmured, "Mom, are we there?"

I turned to look back at my oldest daughter, whose head rested on the pillow she'd braced against the window back in Illinois. My heart, as always, tightened with the ache of a love so powerful it overrode any other in my world; I vowed I would stay strong for my girls—no matter how difficult this vow sometimes proved.

"No, sweetie, not quite," I whispered in response, letting my bare foot ease off the brake. The car rolled smoothly forward, but enough that Tish, strapped into the passenger seat beside me, snorted and began rubbing her eyes.

"Mo-*om*," she complained in a whisper. "My head hurts."

"I'm sorry, honey," I responded automatically, and accelerated to twenty miles an hour—much faster at this hour and I'd risk a ticket from the local patrol cop, Charlie Evans. I assured, "We'll be there shortly. Look, it's the lake." I gestured out into the glimmering starry night as I made a left and angled around Flickertail, where a mile up the lake road, known locally as Flicker Trail, the Shore Leave Cafe waited.

Tish, fortunately, fell for the distraction and lowered her window, allowing the sweet scent of an early spring evening into the car. The smell of the lake, so deeply ingrained in my consciousness, as familiar to me as my children's skin, was musky and welcoming. I could hear it lapping the shore to our right as the tires crunched over gravel and the headlights illuminated walls of sharp spruce and towering oaks, lacy maples and dense grapevine, decked in new emerald leaves and smelling of childhood and remembered happiness. My thoughts centered on Jackie, against my will; so often I'd driven this road with him, tucked against his strong side, my hand caressing his leg, both of us laughing…

I squelched these memories with real effort; it was like pressing on a bruise. No, more like cramming a couple of fingers into an open wound. I bit the insides of my cheeks, feeling the sleek wetness of tears on my eyeballs, glad that the darkness hid any evidence. I would not cry in front of my children again; I promised myself, fiercely, before we left Chicago for Minnesota.

"What was that?" Camille asked from the backseat, her voice startled.

"A loon," I said, listening as it wailed again from somewhere out on the lake. It was a haunting, ululating cry, almost human in its emotional intensity. "Don't worry, that's just how they keep in contact with other loons on the lake." The second I said it, another responded, farther out on the dark water.

"It gives me the shivers. They sound so lonesome, like they're lost or something. I always forget that until we're back," Camille said, and Tish cackled a laugh, twisting around to give her big sister a skeptical look.

"It's awesome," Tish said. "You're such a chicken."

Camille playfully kicked a bare foot at Tish, jostling twelve-year-old Ruthann, who made a sound of protest.

"C'mon, you guys, knock it off," my youngest mumbled. "I'm sleeping."

"And I'm carsick," Tish chimed in, helpfully. I angled a long-suffering gaze at her, and she scrunched down in her seat as if to visibly prove her claim. Tish, unlike her sisters, kept her thick curly hair cut short; the subsequent face-frame made her striking blue eyes appear even larger and more sincere. I knew her well enough to see through any of her attempts at manipulation, but people less familiar to her wiles proved easily captivated by those stunning eyes and pointy pixie chin. Her father, especially, which was the reason our fifteen-year-old sported double-pierced ears.

"Here it is," I said, immeasurably thankful, as the gravel widened and became the pitted blacktop lot of my family's longtime business. Two vehicles were parked beneath the lone streetlight at this late hour, one belonging to Rich Mayes, an elderly man I loved like a father, and who'd cooked at the cafe since my childhood; next to Rich's car sat an old black truck I didn't recognize. I thought, *Dammit. There's still a customer here.*

The cafe was a long, narrow structure, shaped vaguely like the letter *L*, with two porches, both angled to take full advantage of the gorgeous lake view, each porch constructed of wide cedar planks, now the gray of ashes from years of sun and wet feet. The cafe received a fresh coat of white paint every other June; Jilly and her son Clint took care of that now. Long ago, the task belonged to Jilly and me; I admired Jackie for the first time while painting the side of Shore Leave, around age twelve. He'd come in with his family for lunch, all those Junes ago...

I parked next to the unfamiliar truck and rolled my head slowly, first down and then back up, still hearing the rush of tires on the highway. Usually Jackie drove us to Minnesota for our annual summer visit; I reminded myself that I was determined not to think again of him for at least ten minutes. The Leinenkuegel, Moosehead, and Hamm's beer signs in the front window splashed warm tints into the night; technically Shore Leave was still open at this hour, but it was a weeknight and most of the locals retired to Eddie's. This early in the season, tourist traffic tended to remain light, but in less than two weeks that would change. From the direction of the boat landing, down the shore about twenty yards, came a yodeling cry, and I grinned in spite of myself.

"Mom, Aunt Ellen, everybody! They're here!" my little sister shrieked, and the girls began hooting and screaming in response, falling out of the car and running to hug Jillian. I climbed out more slowly, happy on the surface, where people could see. Fuck, it just sucked (there was no other way to put it) that I was coming home as the spurned woman, the jilted, separated wife, *the girl who couldn't keep her husband in her own bed*...I was gritting my teeth and stopped myself instantly. And then I couldn't help but laugh as the girls and Jilly collided hard enough to send all four of them into a heap on the grass at the edge of the parking lot. My mother's golden labs loped down the porch steps, barking at the top of their range. The girls climbed all over Jilly, wrestling to get closer to her as one of the dogs grabbed the rear pocket of Tish's shorts and began tugging.

"Joelle!" My mother hurried out the front porch door, banging the screen we'd always been bitched at for banging, wiping her hands on a dishtowel. Aunt Ellen and Rich followed in her wake, waving and calling, and I jogged forward and into Mom's warm arms, resisting the urge to burrow against her, like a child seeking refuge. No matter how much time passed between my visits here, my mom always smelled exactly the same, of Prell shampoo and rose-scented lotion, just a hint of the fish-fry batter. She hugged me close and planted a kiss on my temple before turning me over to my auntie, whose plump, freckled arms, so much like Mom's, curled me tight and snug. Rich hugged me next, and then ruffled my hair, and his scent, tobacco and aftershave, was likewise comforting, blessedly familiar.

"Looks so pretty, long like that," Rich added, indicating my hair, grinning so that his bushy white eyebrows drew nearly together over his kind brown eyes. He was as dear and solid as ever, and I felt a momentary flash of gratitude that these people, my foundation, remained here, as unchanging as the summer stars. In my teenage years, they made me claustrophobic with their concerns, driving me out of my skin with constant advice and commentary; but now, seventeen years later, I sought this place, my true home, to regroup and lick my wounds. Never mind that Jackie should –

You weren't going to think about Jackie for ten minutes, remember?

"Hi, sweetie," Aunt Ellen said, gathering me against her side. "You look like you could use a drink."

"Or a bar," Mom added, meaning dessert.

"You want a sandwich, honey?" Rich asked, thumbing over his shoulder in the direction of his kitchen.

"Not just now," I told them, although a drink sounded fantastic. "But thanks."

In the next moment my sister bolted across the parking lot, shrieking with laughter as my kids and both dogs pursued her. I turned to catch her in a hug and we rocked together before being attacked by the mob.

"Look at these beautiful girls," Mom said, claiming her granddaughters for a round of hugs and kisses. "Camille, you look so grown-up, doesn't she, Ellen? Look at that face! And my Patricia, what have you done to your hair?"

Rich caught up Ruthann in a bear hug, and then bounced her on his arm. "Ain't you grown a bit since I saw you last," he observed, and Ruthann, my baby, grinned shyly. Rich and Dodge were the only grandfathers my girls had ever known.

"Aunt Jilly, where's Clint?" Tish asked, peering around as though her cousin and best friend in Landon was hiding in the woods, purposely avoiding her.

Jilly, small and deeply tanned, her hair cropped as short as Tish's, bleached platinum from long summer days outside, gave me a look I couldn't interpret (unheard of) and then neatly caught Tish in a light headlock, knuckling her scalp. She blustered, "Not here, punk. He must not care that you guys were coming."

Tish ducked away and fastidiously smoothed her hair, contradicting, "Whatever! Where is he?"

"Inside, sleeping, along with your great-gran," Aunt Ellen answered. "He was tuckered out from his ball game today. He waited and waited for you-all to get here and ended up falling asleep on table three. Rich hauled him home to bed."

The girls giggled. "What a baby," Tish felt compelled to add. "It's not even midnight!"

"Time for these bones to head out, though," Rich said, and pecked my cheek before taking his quiet leave. He added, "It does my heart good to see you, Joelle-honey. Joanie, tell the grandson I'll see him tomorrow."

"Will do, Rich," Mom agreed, as Aunt Ellen herded the girls inside for food and drink.

"G'night, Rich," I added, following Jilly up the porch steps. Mom walked Rich to his car and the girls were already in the cafe, no doubt being plied with sweets and possibly booze by Aunt Ellen. I paused before entering and instead leaned over the porch rail, my gaze absorbing sights as well-known to me as my own body. The lake, cloaked in warm, velvet May darkness, stretched back to Landon's little downtown, where the streetlamps shone like small golden stars in the blackness.

In the other direction, to my left, Flickertail curved around a slender bend before opening into a much wider surface area, where jet-skis and motor boats whined from dawn until early evening, dragging skiers and wake boarders. The farthest shore, not visible from our porch, was similarly busy in the daylight, where fishermen tarried for hours upon end, drinking and bullshitting and doing what they loved. Though fully dark, I could see the edges of the trees that ringed the lake, from memory; if I lifted my index finger I could trace the wavering line in the air. Jilly elbowed up beside me and I rested my head on her shoulder.

"You okay?" she murmured, and I lifted my head, and sighed.

"Rich's grandson?" I asked, wishing I held a burning cigarette between my fingers just now. Years had passed since my last one, but the moment I got home, on ancient turf, an insistent craving began until I either gave in, guilted the hell out of myself, or fell asleep. I elaborated, "He doesn't have any kids, does he?" At least, none that I knew of. And I'd known Rich for exactly as long as I'd been alive.

"Actually, it's his stepdaughter Christy's son," Jilly reminded me. "You remember her, don't you? Pam's daughter who lives in Oklahoma?"

"Yeah, I guess, vaguely." A memory flickered. "Teeny bikini and big hair, like 1978, right?"

"Yeah, that's her. She stayed with Rich and Pam that summer. It seems like a million years ago now." Jilly sighed, too. "Anyway, Christy had a kid, and now he's staying with Rich in his trailer, even though Pam's gone. Mom hired him to help in the kitchen this summer. He's actually here now, having a beer."

"Dammit," I murmured, annoyed that a stranger, even a stranger connected to Rich, infringed on my homecoming. I complained, "Is he even old enough to drink?"

"Yeah, he's in his twenties," Jilly said. "And he was in jail."

My head darted to the left and I stared at her in shock. All of the mother-activated alarm bells in my head began wailing. I demanded, "What?"

"Seriously, I freaked a little bit, too, but Rich insists that he's a good kid." In response to the panicked question in my eyes, she added, "He stole a car and some cash in Oklahoma, two years ago."

I absorbed this not-so-bad-as-I-imagined information, but still felt fidgety and irritated. I could hear my daughters chattering with Aunt Ellen, their sweet voices excited and genuinely pleased; just around the corner in the bar, my family's bar, an ex-con sat having a drink, listening to them.

"Jilly, what was she thinking?" I whispered furtively, peering over my shoulder, and my sister surprised me by laughing her warm, rollicking laugh.

She unselfconsciously ran her fingers through her close-cropped hair and then squeezed my arm before saying, "It's not like you have to whisper, Jo. I don't think he has superhero senses."

Mom climbed the steps as Rich's taillights winked with a ruby flicker before he turned right and headed back into town. I accosted her immediately.

"Mom, how could you?" I demanded, yelling in a whisper, also annoyed at Jilly, for laughing at me. Jilly was a mother, but not of daughters, and that caused a distinct difference in outlook. Clint was already tall and strong, the image of Chris, his dad. He wasn't vulnerable the same way my girls were.

Mom stopped and sighed; she'd tossed her dishtowel over one shoulder and reached now into the front pocket of her overalls for a slim pack of smokes. Her silver-streaked hair was still long, caught up in a tortoiseshell clip on the crown of her head, her ears appearing sunburned in the yellow glow of the porch light. Wordlessly, she passed one to me and then Jilly, and next drew a lighter from her side pocket. She never smoked much anymore, unless under stress. I sincerely hoped the stress wasn't caused by the proximity of a former criminal. Let it be instead her eldest daughter's disgraceful and undignified return home, bearing her children and all of her dearest worldly possessions, these crammed into the trunk of a luxurious Toyota. Mom lit up and passed the small plastic tool to Jilly; I sighed and handed back the cigarette, unwilling to smoke in front of the kids. I settled for second-hand instead.

"Honestly, Jo, he's a good kid," Mom said at last, speaking quietly, blowing smoke in the direction of the lake. "Do you think Ellen or I would've hired him if we didn't think so?"

"Because of Rich," I pointed out, my voice unpleasantly contrary. "You couldn't say *no* to him, you know it."

Mom shook her head, and from my other side Jilly elbowed me. Mom griped, "Rich wouldn't have taken him in, even in honor of Pamela's memory, if he thought Bly was dangerous. Crimeny, Joelle."

"Bly?" I asked, turning to my sister.

"His name is Blythe," she informed, blowing smoke from both nostrils. Mom dropped her filter into an empty beer can on the windowsill and went inside without another word. Enough of the day and her daughters questioning her judgment, I supposed. Quietly, and yet full of teasing, Jilly added, "And she's wrong, he *is* dangerous."

I gave her a withering look but she only smiled, so Jillian. "The girls are meeting him right now," she said, heading inside, and I darted after her at these words, all of the repressed concern under the surface of my skin rushing up and into my throat. My children would not exchange introductions with a criminal without me in the same room.

"Girls, this is Rich's grandson," I heard Aunt Ellen saying. I followed Jilly through the arch separating the bar from the rest of the cafe, my lips set in a hard line. I came around the corner and blinked once, then again, noticing things as though in slow motion. My oldest daughter's radiant smile. Tish's slightly open mouth. Ruthann's hazel eyes round and glowing. Aunt Ellen and Mom both grinned up at the man I could only assume was the car thief with the ridiculously sentimental name, Gilbert's name from *Anne of Green Gables*.

He was gorgeous. There was no denying it, no matter how much older than him I must certainly have been, no matter what his sketchy past. I stopped as though having run up against a barbed wire fence and stared inanely before catching myself and darting my gaze elsewhere. My daughters certainly noticed, and were in various stages of adoration; he glanced momentarily over at me and nodded slightly, acknowledging yet another female presence in his sphere of influence before turning his attention back to my mother. He was grinning about something, grinning more with one side of his mouth than the other, a sensual mouth set in a lean face with a strong cleft chin. He towered over all of us, a dark-blond ponytail hanging down his back, navy-blue bandana tied around his forehead, the kind a short-order cook wore to keep sweat from his eyes. His eyebrows were darker than his hair, framing amused eyes, the kind of eyes that would be grinning even when he was not. Long lashes. Stubbled jaws. Hunky shoulders.

I observed this wealth of handsomeness in less than five seconds. It also proved sufficient time to set my pulse hammering before I cursed myself for a nearly-middle-aged fool. Just as I intended to introduce myself, Aunt Ellen did the honors for me, saying, "Honey, this is Rich's grandson, Blythe Tilson. Bly, dear, meet my niece, Joelle Gordon. She's just in from Chicago."

"Hi," he said just for me, warm and deep-voiced, offering a hand. I swallowed and gathered myself, smiling back at him, wishing I'd checked my reflection even once since leaving the city around dawn yesterday. I shook his hand swiftly, trying not to stare dumbly at him. His hand was warm and strong and hard. *Of course it was.*

"Hi," I said, my voice unnaturally husky, and then managed, "Nice to meet you."

"Likewise," he returned politely; surely I imagined the way he seemed to really study my face. He said then, as though in a sudden hurry, "Well, Joan, Ellen, I better head home, let you have some family time," and a gaggle of girls, including my mother, followed him to the front porch.

Only Jilly and I remained behind. She grinned knowingly, like an imp of misfortune, while I sank to a barstool and lowered my chin to my right palm. From the other room, Blythe called back, "Have a good night, ladies. Good to meet you, Joelle."

I shook my head slowly, not visible from where he stood, letting my children offer a chorus of heartfelt good-nights. The screen door clicked shut behind him and we all heard his footsteps reverberate over the porch as he headed for his truck. I hoped the girls weren't pressing their noses to the window screen.

Jilly hauled a barstool closer to mine and said succinctly, "*Told* you so."

Chapter Two

WE SAT FOR ANOTHER HOUR AT THE BAR, AND THEN MOVED out to the glider that Dodge bolted onto the planks at the end of our dock years ago. It was also the faded color of cinders, soft and worn, and wholly familiar. I sipped my fifth beer while Jilly munched a microwave corn dog. I sent the girls to bed long since; they were sharing one of the loft rooms at the top of our house, not fifty yards into the woods behind the cafe. Down by the lake in the predawn hours the air was chilly and damp, thick with the sounds of woodland and shore-dwelling creatures. I drew my knees under the faded afghan I dragged from the house earlier, after depositing my things in mine and Jilly's old room, listening now to the spring peepers and gray tree frogs chanting their ever-lovin' hearts out as they sought mates in the lush beach mud.

A thousand and more crickets harmonized; I still stubbornly clung to my childhood belief that crickets sang with their little faces pointed at the moon, rather than scraping their back legs together. Mosquitoes whined near our ears, but I kept my bare arms and feet wrapped in the wool of the blanket and felt relatively protected. Jilly, bundled in a hooded sweatshirt, sat cross-legged beside me, and for a long time we studied the fortune of stars flung out across the clear black sky; I was dizzy from both exhaustion and the beer, and would occasionally get caught up in the view, feeling as though I could detach from myself and dart up there and use the stars like stepping stones to a distant place.

"Jo, you're drunk," Jilly giggled, and I realized I spoke that last thought aloud. "You just got here, don't go leaving yet."

"Blythe is gorgeous," I muttered, and Jilly snorted, her mouth full of corn dog.

"Hell yes, he is," she agreed. "The kind you can see coming a mile and more away."

I pressed the beer can to my chest and ground the heel of my hand against my closed eyes. I heard myself say, "I miss Jackie so bad."

I sensed Jilly groping for an appropriate response. She settled for resting her cheek against the afghan over my left shoulder. I could smell the fragrance of her lavender-scented shampoo, the coconut oil from her face, the beer and cornmeal on her breath. At last she murmured, "I know. I really do."

And at that I felt even shittier, because I knew that what she said was true; she did know, and then some. Jackie and I had only lived in Chicago for a few years when Chris Henriksen died, Jilly's husband, who she loved so much and with such abandon that, in my secret heart, guarded intently, I was jealous. I loved Jackie, and believed then that I always would, but Chris and Jilly possessed something beyond that, something I could sense without directly admitting it to myself; even now, twelve years later, she had never seriously dated another man.

It was her self-inflicted punishment, her personal torture, and she lived solely now for Clint, their baby, who was only three that terrible winter when Chris fell through the ice on his snowmobile and drowned. It didn't matter what claimed his life that night: beer, the cold, the icy water or his own recklessness, he was gone. And Jilly was left behind, his devastated widow with a toddler. Eventually she'd moved back in with Mom and Aunt Ellen, who'd helped her pick up the few straggling pieces of her heart not buried with Chris, helped her raise Clint into a young man. I sighed and gritted my teeth again; what was a cheating husband compared to that? At least Jackie was alive out there.

As always, Jilly followed the trail of my thoughts almost exactly. "Don't," she whispered. "It's still horrible. And your marriage, your relationship, is dead, even if Jackie isn't."

"Jilly, don't," I moaned, hating her a little for always being stronger. I was the older sister, but she was wiser in so many ways.

"I'm sorry, Jo. I know this sounds selfish in the extreme, but I'm glad you're back no matter what the circumstances. I've missed you so much, and now I have you all to myself again. I ought to thank Jackie for it."

I laughed then, a little pathetic huff. Finally I admitted, "I knew he was cheating a few years back. I freaking knew it, but I couldn't admit it to myself."

"Like it's an easy thing to do," Jilly said. "What happened?"

But suddenly the urge to discuss my cheating spouse drained away, down into a deep well of sadness within my chest. I wanted to blame him explicitly, entirely, but that was wrong, and I knew it; the truth was, the closest thing I'd felt to desire in a long, long time occurred earlier tonight, coming unexpectedly upon the sight of my mother's new hired help. Blythe, of the wide shoulders and smoldering eyes, the full lips and easy grin. In the face of my self-doubt I denied my husband my desire for too long; what did I expect?

When Jackie and I first dated, when we were in love, I abandoned myself to him, gave every square inch of my skin up to his mouth, his tongue, his big, strong hands. We'd been wild, and tangled our bodies together making love. Jackie, who'd rubbed his face against my pregnant belly and spoken so tenderly to all three girls through my sensitive flesh, who'd cupped their tiny sleek heads moments after birth, planted bitty kisses on their smushy newborn faces. I would never share moments like that with anyone else; I would be thirty-six in August, too young to consider being without my man, but way too fucking old to start over with someone new, at least in my hurting, judgmental mind. I could hardly bear the thought of it.

Jilly tucked her arm through mine and appropriated my beer for a sip. "Jo, just take it a day at a time. That's the only way. We have all summer to talk." She stretched her slim legs and pointed her bare toes in the starlight; it was a new moon, and the stars rioted in bright, joyous rebellion. And then, almost guiltily, she whispered, "I'm so happy you're here."

"Thanks, Jilly Bean," I whispered back. "Me, too."

Even if I was here for all the wrong reasons.

❦

We straggled back to the house at some point; I passed out on the couch in the living room, the same blue-flowered piece of furniture that I once curled my baby hands around to pull myself upright before attempting a step into the wider world. Directly behind the couch the wall was sliced off on a diagonal plane, following the stairs up to a landing, where the treads next curved left and led to the bedrooms above. The house itself was silent now in the late-morning light; I could hear a rippling chorus of birdsong through the front windows, propped open to a fair, breezy May morning.

I squinted, slogging a hand through my tangled hair, enormously grateful to Mom and Aunt Ellen, who never made breakfast in the house kitchen during the summer months but instead trooped over to Shore Leave and got busy there. I imagined I could smell coffee drifting over on the air, a welcome thought despite the pain (courtesy of more alcohol than I'd intended to consume) blossoming behind my eyes. With a groan I extracted myself from the couch and climbed the stairs, pausing for a moment on the landing to study the old, pale-green wallpaper with its faded, trailing ivy vines. The house smelled exactly the same, of some indelible perfume created by all the women who'd lived within its walls for decades.

I closed my eyes and breathed deeply, inhaling my past, and then continued to the sad little excuse for a bathroom that hunkered between Mom and Aunt Ellen's rooms. Just across the hall was the room I would now be sharing with Gran, unless I decided to scrunch in with Jilly in the apartment above the garage; she and Clint shared that space. It wasn't that I minded sharing a room with Gran, but it was tempting to squeeze in with my sister to catch up on our long talks. For another moment I pictured my master bathroom in our townhouse in Chicago: a gleaming, turquoise-tiled expanse complete with heated towel racks and a tub within which it was deep enough to scuba dive. I bit my lip, hard, and entered the bathroom of my formative years.

The ancient medicine cabinet mirror caught my reflection and threw it back without a hint of sympathy for my feelings. I continued chewing my lower lip as I observed the sleepless purple smears beneath my eyes, the snarls in my hair, the shiny, sunburned skin of my nose. Good lord, had I looked this terrible last night? My lips appeared chapped. *I look like a woman who deserves to be cheated on*, I thought, wallowing in a trench of self-pity. This is what I'd degenerated to…contemplating my pitiful reflection in the mirror where I once primped for evenings out with Jackie—back when my skin gleamed tan and taut, and my eyes shone with love and excitement. The last thing I wanted to do was cry, but tears flooded anyway. God, I missed my husband.

No, I corrected myself. I missed my boyfriend Jackie, in whose eyes I could see myself as I looked in the old days, full of confidence and spirit. My *husband* Jackie was a cheating son of a bitch I'd left behind in Chicago, ideally until he chased me here to beg and plead forgiveness.

I wept, bending forward at the waist, thankful no one was around to hear this display of weakness. I leaned over the yellow, rust-stained sink where I'd brushed my teeth a thousand times and where I'd puked when I drank too much. I cried until I almost gagged, and finally sank to my knees on the shaggy green throw rug, where I pressed my forehead to the edge of the sink and breathed, shallow and shaky at first. But as the minutes ticked by golden morning light began to creep across the floor and I regained a shred of composure.

Come on, Joelle. Jesus. Get up and at least wash your hair.

Mom always said clean hair made everything easier to face. I stood in the hot water until it ran out (about three minutes) and then scrubbed my scalp with Prell (the brand of choice in this house since the 1950s), coated my face with the tingle of Noxema cream (*ditto*), and used the loofah sponge to give my body a thorough once-over.

Fifteen minutes after that, I clacked out the screen door, my hair squeaky clean and soft on my shoulders, dressed in cut-off jeans and a sleeveless green blouse. Make-up would have added untold amounts to my self-esteem, but the small zippered bag containing my cosmetics was nowhere to be found this morning. I was fortunate to locate my toothbrush. Barefoot, I gingerly crossed the gravel driveway and then made my way over the worn path to Shore Leave. Dodge must have recently mowed, because the scent of shorn grass hung fresh in the air. To my right, rising sunlight spangled the water like shifting gold coins, and I felt momentarily uplifted, unexpected but certainly not unwelcome. The air felt wonderful on my skin and in my lungs, and I drew a deep breath, smelling the lake.

"Hi, sweetie!" I heard, and smiled in spite of myself, turning to wave to Dodge, out on the end of the boat launching dock. He was a fixture around Shore Leave; a big, solid, scruffy-haired man whose black beard was now heavily salted with silver, whose infectious laughter made his stomach shake and everyone around him grin. I couldn't recall ever witnessing Dodge in a bad mood. From a distance he looked almost exactly the same as I remembered; hearty and beaming, his aviator sunglasses perched on the crown of his head.

"Morning!" I called back, blowing him a kiss. I'd catch up with him later, and he appeared busy chatting with someone ten feet below, sitting in a boat with an outboard motor.

"Good to have you home, Jo!" he yelled before turning back to whatever conversation I'd interrupted. Seconds later I climbed the porch steps and winced at the heavy smell of frying egg that met me at the screen.

"Aunt Joey!" Clint ran for me and I smiled at my nephew, catching him in a hug.

"God, Clint, you're huge!" I told him as he crushed me close. It was such an aunt sort of thing to say, but it was true. He must have grown six inches since last summer. Clint grinned delightedly at me.

"I'm so glad you guys are here!" he enthused, and my smile widened. Clint was such a dear boy, kindhearted and sincere, just like his dad had been; sometimes I couldn't believe that Clint and Tish were as close as they were. She often ate him alive, but he took it with characteristic ease. Clint appeared tan, his arms and legs lanky; Jilly's incredible blue eyes shone from his face. The rest of him was pure Chris, though; it took my breath away to see how exactly he resembled his father, from the wide, dimpled grin to the tumbled brown hair and square jawline.

Jilly was on his heels, bearing a cup of steaming coffee. She grinned, too, and gave me a quick once-over, inquiring, "You feeling all right this morning, Mama?"

I decided not to answer that, instead taking the mug, lifting it to my face and letting the steam bathe my eyelids.

"Thanks, Jills," I murmured, heartened by a sip of the strong brew as I followed the two of them into the dining room. Shore Leave was built on the spare; the best tables were of course the ones out on the porch, visible through the wide, curtainless windows; Mom claimed that cutting off the lake view was a crime. Inside, a small dining room consisted of six four-tops, eight stools at the counter, and three deep booths, not counting the row of high tops in the separate bar area; the sky-blue walls remained adorned with all manner of what Jilly affectionately called "trinkety crap," an apt description for the fishing nets, fishing poles, lures, brightly-colored tin soda signs, saw blades painted with images of lake shores in summer, the annual calendar issued by Beltrami County featuring local businesses; this month's image showcased beautiful old White Oaks Lodge, run by the Carter family on the far side of Flickertail. Shore Leave was usually July or August.

My perennial favorite wall decor continued to be the dozens of framed photos of Shore Leave in all seasons since the 1940s. I especially loved the black-and-white of Gran and Great-Aunt Minnie, taken when the two of them were in their twenties, looking like countrified beauty queens, Minnie with a cigarette caught in her teeth and Gran holding a stringer of trout. Smiles about two feet wide, happy as clams without any menfolk whatsoever. What did they know that I did not?

In the busy season, we stayed open Tuesday through Saturday from eleven to eight, Sundays for lunch, but now, early in May, there wasn't much appreciable business until the dinner hour. Locals drove or biked over from Landon to hang out on the water; I simultaneously dreaded and anticipated this particular crowd. Though I enjoyed seeing my former high school classmates, most of whom still lived within walking distance of downtown Landon, it would be difficult to explain why I was here on an extended visit without my husband. I shuddered internally, turning my attention to the kitchen, where I could hear the voices of all three girls vying for Rich's attention. I realized, on a bit of a delay this morning, that it was awfully busy back there, far more than breakfast for the family would warrant.

"What's going on?" I asked Jilly, who stood behind the speckled-white Formica counter refilling her own coffee mug. Clint reclaimed his chair at table three and poured maple syrup over a stack of pancakes around a foot tall. I looked quickly away from the food, my stomach jumping, and snagged a stool near Jilly.

"Rich said there's a party of twenty heading over for lunch today. Some guys he used to know. I guess they're at the campground and heard we serve a damn good fish fry." Jilly leaned the small of her back against the stainless steel sink near the coffee maker and took a long drink.

I sipped cautiously, glancing up as Tish's face appeared in the ticket window behind Jilly. Tish was my early riser, a true morning person, and she grinned brightly at me, visible only from the shoulders up.

"Morning, Mom. Aunt Jilly said we should be nice to you since you're hungover this morning."

I gave Jillian the evil eye. She rolled hers back at me, as Tish continued, "Grandma said we could all help out this summer in the cafe."

"Starting today, if you like," Mom called, appearing beside Tish. Mom wore a lavender-flowered blouse, hair twisted into a serviceable bun on her head. Both she and Tish sported dangly earrings made from feathers, two pairs for my daughter.

"Where'd you get those?" I asked, twirling a finger near my right ear-lobe.

"Aunt Ellen makes them," Tish informed. "Are you gonna help out today or what, Mom? There's a twenty-top at noon."

"We're here twelve hours and you're already spouting restaurant lingo," I observed, deciding not to make an issue about the earrings. I was all about picking my battles these days. I said, "Yeah, that's fine, Mom, of course I'll help."

"Better get some shoes first, Aunt Joey," Clint said, indicating my bare feet with his fork.

"Right, thanks, Clinty," I said, curling my toes over the rung of the stool.

"Here comes Gran," Jilly observed, peering over my shoulder.

I turned in time to see our grandmother come whacking through the screen door, a small, wiry woman in pink pedal pushers, her wispy, formerly-golden hair resembling nothing so much as a dandelion gone to seed. She used a cane these days, and wore thick-soled orthopedic shoes, but her voice was as strong as ever, her hazel eyes snapping as she reached with her free arm to give me a hug. I wrapped her close and hugged as hard as I dared; once plump and robust, my grandma now felt so frail in my arms, and I was not used to that. I clung for a long moment as she rubbed her hand over my back. She said decisively, "Joelle, you look good."

My heart softened. "Thanks, Gran, you do, too."

"Where's that son of a bitch, Jackson?"

I didn't even flinch I was so accustomed to her attitude; at least *this* hadn't changed. Gran, to be fair, never really warmed to Jackie, even back in our dating days. She always claimed he was too charming for his own good, which I'd resented; never mind that it was one hundred percent true. I leaned and pecked her on the cheek before replying, "He's home in Chicago, Gran. He won't be here this summer."

"How are the girls taking it?" she asked, lowering her voice. Her shrewd gaze would harbor no bullshit from me.

"Terribly," I admitted, following along at her side as she moved to join Clint at table three.

He mumbled, "Good morning, Gran," around a mouthful of pancakes, and Gran said, "Good morning, sweetheart."

I went on, keeping my voice soft, "They adore their dad. They can't see his faults."

"*Hmph*," Gran replied to this. But it was true; the girls didn't know about their father's indiscretion, though I knew Camille suspected, unwilling to swallow the story I'd concocted about the two of us needing a break. But as much as I loved my children, and desired to be honest with them, I couldn't bear to reveal that particular truth. At least, not until forced.

"Nice shirt, Gran," Jilly observed, steering the conversation onto a new path. Clint wasn't hugely observant, especially with food in front of him, but he certainly didn't need to be inadvertently informed about my husband's lover, either. Jilly asked, "Is that one Dodge got for you?"

Gran smirked, sitting up straighter so I could read the words printed across her chest. Gran loved t-shirts with slogans; this particular one announced in hot-pink script: *Everyone is Entitled to my Opinion.* I giggled.

"Speaking of the devil," Gran said, as the front porch thundered with Dodge's footsteps. I jumped up again and ran to give Dodge a big hug; it was so good to see him. He caught me up and growled into my neck, then released me for a kiss on the cheek.

"Hi, honey," he said. "It sure is good to see you coming up the lake road for breakfast. Takes me back to the olden days, you know?" His voice still rumbled like thunder in the next county.

"It's good to be here," I replied. And it was, no matter what the circumstances.

"The boy says hello," Dodge went on, referring to Justin. "He was heading out on the lake this morning."

"How is he doing?" I asked. "I haven't seen Justin in years."

Dodge opened his mouth but Gran filled in, living up to her shirt, "He's in a bad place, Jo, real bitter. He can't get over his accident."

To my surprise, Dodge didn't argue. He sighed and accepted the coffee Jilly held out to him, saying, "Thanks, honey." He sipped and then added, "Lou's right, Joelle, much as I hate to admit it."

Gran pursed her lips in satisfaction at these words, then said, "We haven't seen much of the boy around here lately," and with those words her knowing look pinned Jillian to the wall. My sister, I was startled to see, busied herself with the coffeepot, not returning Gran's look; Clint studied Dodge with his blue eyes full of questions.

"How bad is it?" I asked, directing the question at Dodge, but again Gran jumped in to answer, "Justin is still a handsome devil. But the scarring is hard on his vanity. He's not himself these days. You'll just have to see for yourself, Joelle."

Ruthann burst through the swinging door between the kitchen and dining rooms and scampered over for a hug. She was young for her age, with a sweeter disposition than her big sisters; at twelve, neither Camille nor Tish would have been overly willing to hug me in public. I snuggled Ruthie while Dodge ruffled her long, curly hair. Tish reappeared and Gran began to badger her about her earrings, and it was off to the races for another day.

By twelve-thirty, Shore Leave was packed to the gills with fishermen. I donned a blue server apron over my shorts, reprising my role as server along with Jilly and Camille. Tish helped in the kitchen while Mom and Aunt Ellen took care of seating and bartending, respectively. I fell right back into the ebb and flow of waiting tables, even enjoying myself in the familiar space, bantering with Rich's buddies as they ordered mugs of beer and fried fish sandwiches. Jilly and I took care of the porch crowd, letting Camille handle the indoor tables, which weren't as busy; she was still getting used to the whole waitressing gig. I watched her surreptitiously as she worked, marveling anew at how lovely and grown-up she looked, my prim, intelligent, dreamer of an eldest daughter, her dark curls held back in a barrette, her cheeks flushed and her eyes merry. It struck me that at her age I'd been with Jackie for nearly two years, spending countless hours in the backseat of his car and in his parents' basement, drinking cheap wine and listening to Billy Squires and Van Halen, making love in every conceivable position known to two teenagers in the early '80s.

Oh Camille, I thought, my heart constricting with an ancient ache. I was so very glad she'd yet to have a serious boyfriend; I couldn't bear to imagine my girls doing the things I'd done. Done...and enjoyed very much. That in itself was one of the most profoundly difficult realities of being a mother, reconciling the old self with the mother-self. The sexless, dull, rule-spouting mother I'd most surely become. The worst part was I would give almost anything to go back to the old me, at least for a weekend.

"Can I get this without cheese?" a man at my elbow asked, pulling me from my wool-gathering. It was bright and sunny on the porch, with little wind, and Flickertail Lake gleamed like a polished blue agate under the radiance.

"For sure," I told him, transferring a pitcher of iced tea to my left hand and collecting his plate. "I'm sorry."

"Nothing doing, honey," he said, catching up his beer and returning to a story in progress at his table. I headed for the kitchen, using my rear to open the outer door, and eased through the throng of people and up to the ticket window.

"Rich!" I called, clacking the fish sandwich onto the high metal counter. "I need a number five, no cheese!"

"Coming right up," someone said, and I startled slightly as Rich's grandson Blythe appeared from around the corner and into my line of sight. He was so tall he needed to duck to meet my eyes. My heart began pounding my breastbone like a fist and I found myself momentarily tongue-tied. How humiliating.

"Thanks," I finally managed.

"Busy out there," he observed, taking the plate and turning to the grill while I remained motionless, unable to tear my gaze away. Holy hell, he was handsome. Because his back was to me, I studied him longer than prudent, taking in his faded jeans, worn almost smooth over the back pockets. His hair was probably almost as long as mine when undone, currently tied low on his nape with a piece of twine. The bandana was still wrapped around his forehead, though he'd shaved since last night. His shoulders were so wide under the sky-blue Shore Leave t-shirt that a yardstick wouldn't be enough to measure them. The pale color of the material allowed for the play of muscles across his back. I bit the insides of my cheeks, hard.

"Jo, two headed for ten!" Mom called over the din as she walked a couple out to a porch table.

I refocused with effort, reprimanding, *Joelle. You are pathetic right now. Beyond pathetic.*

"Coming!" I called, and turned away abruptly, almost crashing into Camille as she refilled two sodas at the drink stand.

"Hi, Mom," she said.

"Hi, love," I replied. "You hanging in there?"

"Yeah, it's fun," she responded, with sincere enthusiasm. Her gaze suddenly darted over my right shoulder and instantly her cheeks heated. I didn't have to turn around to know that Blythe was back in the window.

"Number five, Joelle," his deep voice announced.

I turned, acting indifferent, and said, "Thanks," for the second time. I didn't mean to meet his eyes; it was a complete accident. Our gazes collided for an intense moment...how could he look at me so knowingly? I grabbed the new sandwich and turned away, as flustered as though he was able to read my mind.

By evening I'd earned over seventy dollars in tips. Jilly, Camille, and I sat at table one, rolling silverware for tomorrow, with Camille gloating that she'd also pocketed quite a bit of change. Clint, Tish, and Ruthann were out on the paddleboat, Mom and Aunt Ellen chatting with Rich on the porch, enjoying after-dinner smokes. Gran was snoozing at the house, Dodge had long since headed home, and Blythe was...I tried to pretend I didn't have the slightest notion that he remained in the kitchen, brushing down the grill and getting a last load of dishes washed.

"What a pretty sunset," Camille observed, nodding her head at the windows.

"You can say that again," Jilly agreed, hands flying as she rolled napkins around flatware.

I glanced up, drinking in the marvelous view. How many times had I watched the sun melt into Flickertail Lake? Enough to realize that I would never tire of the sight. The lake shone satin-smooth, a gleaming cerulean in the last rays. The only disturbance on the water was the paddleboat; we could hear Tish and Ruthie shrieking and Clint laughing as the sound carried over the static surface of the water. The sky itself was awash in a rosy tangerine, the air mellow as evening descended.

We rehashed the unexpectedly busy day before Camille said, quietly, "Mom, Dad called today."

My heart snagged on something sharp. I felt Jilly's gaze but met Camille's when I looked away from the window. Infusing my tone with nonchalance, I asked, "Did you get to talk to him?"

Camille shook her head. She'd slipped the barrette from her hair and her dark curls hung to her shoulder blades. Her blue work shirt was undone past three buttons, allowing for a tiny glimpse of nude-colored bra beneath. Obviously she didn't realize that it was showing, and I was about to tell her when she said, "No, but Ruthie did."

"Well, that's good," I allowed, my voice unpleasantly brusque. I felt suddenly sweaty and confined, as though my blouse spontaneously shrank. Hoping to change the subject, I said softly, "Hon, I can see your bra," and indicated the gaping button.

"Ruthie said he misses us," Camille added, fastening her shirt without missing a beat, undoubtedly unaware of the guilt she heaped on my head with her words.

"I know he does," I replied, throttling the resentment in my voice down a notch. "He can call anytime he wants, you know that. And you can call him, too." As per tradition, I insisted on an electronics-free summer, and the girls obeyed without too much complaint. The only exception was our cell phone, which I hadn't even unpacked yet.

"Will Dad come up here this summer?" Camille pressed.

I wasn't prepared for these questions yet; we'd been in Landon for less than forty-eight hours, for heaven's sake. Using my special nickname for my oldest, coined in her toddler days, I said, "I don't know, Milla, I really don't."

Camille sensed she was crossing the border into unknown territory and backed off. I knew she was dying to press the issue, but I'd been unusually reticent with her in the past few months. I hated it as much as she did, but I didn't know what else to do; as much as I wanted to smash my husband's reputation (and skull) to smithereens, I didn't want the girls to know he'd cheated. It was too humiliating.

Nodding at the calendar hanging on the wall near our table, Camille said, "That's a really pretty place."

"White Oaks," I confirmed, grateful for a new conversational vein. "It's right around the lake. Bull and Diana Carter run it now, but it's been in Bull's family for generations. Since the 1800s, at least."

"Really?" Camille's dark eyebrows lifted as she studied the photograph with renewed interest. She harbored aspirations of becoming a history professor. She suggested, "Maybe we could visit? Do the Carters ever come in here?"

"Only all the time," Jilly said, grinning. "Bull and Dodge are cousins, you know, Milla. You'd probably recognize the whole Carter family from past summers."

"Do they give tours of the lodge?" she asked, leaning forward and abandoning her silverware-rolling.

"I'm sure Bull would be more than delighted to show you around," I said. "He lives for talking about his ancestors."

"Just ask Diana," Jilly giggled.

"God, Mom, that would be so cool," Camille gushed. "Is the whole place from the nineteenth century, or just parts of it?"

"I don't know exactly–" I started to say, but then saw Blythe come from the kitchen and head straight for us. My heart flared to life as swiftly as a stick of dynamite. He stopped at our table, leaning against the only empty chair, curling his big hands around the top. I pretended to be occupied, my blood afire as I saw him grin at us from the corner of my eye.

Jilly said companionably, "Hey, Bly, you outta here for the night?"

His grin widened as he looked Jilly's way, and I suddenly found myself studying the line of his jaw, darkened now with a day's growth of whiskers. His forearms were tan and strong and sinewy, braced against the chair back, lightly dusted with dark hair. As much as I wanted to kick myself, I would be lying if I said that a wild pulse didn't beat low in my stomach at the very sight of him.

"I'm headed into town, actually. I thought I might see what's shaking over at Eddie's." Eddie nearly always featured live music on Fridays, and Blythe's deep voice was so very appealing. For a split second I allowed myself to fantasize that I was seventeen—*no, make that eighteen*—and that I could willingly accompany this gorgeous man to the bar, where we would drink and dance and flirt, and then…

I mentally bashed my forehead on the tabletop in front of me. *Joelle Gordon, you have absolutely lost your mind*, I reprimanded, harshly. Far too long since I'd had sex with Jackie. Obviously not once since the incident at the Christmas party. Much more time since we'd made love like we used to…hot and heavy and fantastic. In all those years of marriage I scarcely even *fantasized* about other men, so consumed with wife- and motherhood. It was clearly the dearth of sex, catching up with me at last.

But then, to my amazement, Blythe looked directly at me and added, "You two would be more than welcome to come with me. What do you say?"

If Jilly was as overwhelmingly tempted by this request as I was, she did a marvelous job of hiding the fact. She said, "I know, that was fun the other night, wasn't it? But Jo, you're probably pretty tired, huh?"

Damn you, Jilly, I telegraphed her fiercely. And what did she mean, the other night? I would grill her later. But I knew she was actually just giving me a delicate out. I almost ground my teeth together before saying what I knew I must, what propriety demanded. Offering an impersonal smile I said, "Maybe some other time. Thanks, though."

Blythe appeared unruffled. "I'll hold you to it," he told me, and his lips were full and soft as he held my gaze for a fraction of a second, with the merest suggestion of heat. I was sure I wasn't imagining it, and darted my eyes away.

"See you," he added before leaving; all three of us watched him go, and then continued to study him through the window as he bid the older folks good-night. Mom actually slapped him on the butt as he said something to make them laugh, and I was absurdly jealous of her.

Camille said, low, as he disappeared into his truck, "Oh my God, he's hot."

Jilly and I exchanged a quick look (the sister kind that actually amounted to an in-depth conversation) at the reverence in her tone. Shit, this must stop right now; my own fantasies were insane enough. I would absolutely not allow my impressionable young daughter to consider going down that road with a full-grown man, and an ex-convict, no matter how handsome and tempting he was.

"Milla, goofball, he's got a girlfriend," Jilly said, keeping her tone intentionally light. She conceded, "I know he's cute, though."

A girlfriend. Of course he had a girlfriend…and I mentally thanked Jilly for mentioning her. "Milla-billa," I added, in keeping with the nicknames. "He's a man. Isn't that sort of, you know, grody?" I borrowed a word she'd once used with laughable regularity.

And, to my utter relief, in the next instant my girl was back. She giggled at the word and said, "What*ever*, Mom. Hey, can I still go out on the boat for a while? It's not too dark yet, is it?"

"Of course, just yell and Clinty will paddle them back to shore," Jilly told her.

Camille bounded from her chair, untying her apron, hurrying out into the gathering dusk. I was watching her, marveling again at how lovely she was, so close to being a woman, when Jilly said, startling me, "I had another dream, Jo."

Jillian and her dreams. At times during our lives I'd been compelled to laugh over them, but then she'd have one that was eerily precognitive, and I'd shut the hell up. Jilly was observant. Her sense of knowing, of the future, was strong, there was no denying; Great-Aunt Minnie had been similarly gifted. I felt a chill ripple up my spine, but kept my tone light as I asked, "Another one?"

"Yes, but this time you were the horse being mounted." Although her words were seemingly ridiculous, her beautiful face was wreathed in somber lines. She let this sink in before she added, "And Jackie wasn't the centaur."

My heart thrust hard, but still I tried to tease her, "Jilly, what's with the horse thing?"

"Joelle, you know who it was, I can tell." My little sister reached and caught my hands in her smaller ones, warm and soft, and gripped my fingers tightly. "I can't see it all, but it's dangerous, Jo. Please just think about that."

I looked deep into her indigo-blue eyes, this woman that I knew (and who knew me) far better than my husband, better than even my children. I lied, "I don't know what you mean, Jills."

Mom was coming into the cafe, Ellen on her heels. Jilly broke the contact of our hands and said, answering my earlier question even before I could ask it, "We played pool at Eddie's the other night, that's what Blythe meant. With Justin. I mean, Justin and I played pool, that is." She paused to draw a breath and then said, "And you *do* know what I mean, Jo, you're a bad liar."

Chapter Three

WE OVERRAN THE TINY LIVING ROOM AT JILLY AND CLINT'S place above the garage an hour later, the kids giggly and sunburned, tussling over the limited couch space; Clint battled Tish for the lone bean bag chair. Jilly and I made popcorn while the kids fought for control of the television remote, and to my relief she didn't mention her dream again. Although I knew it wasn't for long - Jilly kept no opinions from me, which I both appreciated and dreaded. No matter how many years passed, the sense of ease between us never wavered.

Watching my little sister flit, butterfly-like, around her warm, overcrowded kitchen, it finally dawned upon me how wrong it was to be physically separated from her for so long. How had I survived? I was just about to voice this thought when there was heightened commotion from the living room, followed by a giggling scuffle between Ruthie and Tish. The atmosphere among the kids was pure carnival; I remembered well that feeling after a blissful summer day spent on the lake.

"Hey, Mom! *Hitchhiker III* is on!" Tish yelled, dodging Ruthann's attempt to steal the remote. "Can we watch it? Please?"

"No way!" I yelled, sticking my head around the edge of the half-wall that separated the two rooms. "That's a horror movie."

"Awww, come on, Aunt Joey," wheedled Clint, and I almost relented; it was nearly impossible to refuse Clinty. His big blue eyes and all.

Jilly came to my rescue, adding firmly, "Clint, no way. That's the scary time-traveler one, where the hitchhiker gets trapped in the past. Ruthann will have nightmares for a week."

"Nuh-uh!" protested my youngest from the direction of the couch.

"Hey, *Sex and the City* is on!" Tish crowed. "Ooh, it's a good one!"

"Patricia, I'm taking that remote away," I warned.

Tish yelped as Clint bashed the back of her head with a crocheted throw pillow. Tish attacked, inadvertently dropping the remote, and Ruthann dove for it, exclaiming in triumph. Camille was draped over the back of the couch, doing leg lifts with her head propped on her left hand.

"Mom, hurry with the popcorn!" she called. And then, "Ruthie, stop on that one!"

I rejoined Jilly, muttering over the sound of popping kernels, "We're just indentured servants to them," and she handed me an ice-cold glass with a salty rim.

"Here, drink up."

"But it's not Saturday," I protested, taking a deep swig anyway. Saturdays were the traditional margarita night for the Davis women.

"I know, but this is a special occasion," Jilly clarified. She drew me to the small table with its four mismatched chairs, teasing, "Sit. I'll get our rotten, ungrateful kids their snack."

She returned moments later, her own drink in hand, and settled across from me, with nothing but a pair of salt and pepper shakers that looked like mallard ducks between us. Those particular ducks had graced this table for the past decade; I was struck with a sudden memory of sitting at this very table in the terrible days after Chris died, trying with everything in me to comfort Jillian, though nothing could have offered her solace back then. My heart clenched at the remembrance of her pain.

"Jilly," I whispered, and could have sworn that something like guilt flickered over her face. She studied me, her blue eyes intently focused, an expression particular to her, though I'd never been as adept at reading Jilly's thoughts as she did mine. Jilly possessed an uncanny ability to sense things, particularly the future. Both waking and sleeping, a mysterious connection linked her to this inexplicable knowing. The problem was, the knowing happened randomly, without warning, and could not be forced. She referred to these flashes of insight as 'notions.'

The television was blaring, the kids talking over one another and scarfing popcorn, and no one but I heard her as she asked, "So what happened?"

We talked on the phone since Christmas, of course. But I'd been gripped in a painful clutch of emotions, alternating between anger, denial, depression, and exhaustion, unable to carry on a lengthy conversation. It took me months to find the courage to leave the house with the kids, and even then I'd done so under pretense of visiting my family in Minnesota. Jackie should have been the one to move out of our townhouse, but he'd stayed, albeit in a separate room; I was admittedly terrified by the thought of losing him, even when I wanted to claw out his eyes. A daily struggle, a long stretch of months since Christmas, waiting for summer and the temporary escape it offered. I sighed, scraping one hand through my tangled hair.

"I let him go, I guess," I finally said. I took another deep drink of the sweet golden froth; tonight I'd just have one drink before cutting myself off. I could not give in to abject alcohol abuse, no matter how tempting. I confessed, "I knew it was happening. It started about five years ago, best I can tell."

"Why then?" she asked, concern and sympathy crossing paths over her delicate features.

"Jackie got a new assistant around then," I answered, picking up the girl duck salt shaker and turning her around and around in my hands as I told the story, running my thumb over the bright blue stripe on her wing. I elaborated, "He would come home talking about her, this girl named Lanny." Even now I wanted to spit out her name like a bad grape. "He talked about her so much, and I thought he couldn't be possibly be that obvious. I was just being suspicious of nothing, right? And then I met her." My voice dropped ominously and Jilly's eyebrows lifted.

"Slutty, nasty, grody, right?" she asked, and I smiled with grudging humor.

"No, of course beautiful, and young. Long eyelashes, long legs, tiny skirt. Jackie was obsessed, I could tell. But it took me years to admit it. I knew he was cheating, I *knew* it, Jill, but I did nothing. I'm a total coward." I set down the duck and reclaimed my drink. Jilly waited calmly. I continued, feeling tears prickle, "See, the thing is, Jilly Bean, he used to look at *me* that way. I know he loved me once. We were totally in love."

"I know you were," she agreed softly. "Anyone with eyes could see it."

"People change, you know? I used to think that if we'd stayed around Landon, Jackie would never have strayed. But now I'm not so sure. He doesn't look at me the same way anymore."

"Don't be a martyr, Jo, c'mon. You're still gorgeous, and desirable, and all of the things that you've always been. Don't give me any crap about it being all your fault." That was the Gran in her, coming out. My mouth twisted wryly as I considered voicing this thought to Jillian.

Instead I said, "I don't really think that, honestly. But it's not all *his* fault either, I can at least acknowledge that."

"Mom is going to hound you about getting back with him, forgiving him. She's already plotting. She always liked Jackie."

"I know," I groaned. "And Aunt Ellen and Gran are in the exact opposite camp."

"Of course. Gran thinks good riddance."

I contemplated my sister's tan face, pixie-like chin and small, pointed nose. Her eyes were the blue of an August afternoon on Flickertail Lake, sincere upon mine. "What do *you* think?" I finally asked.

"Like I said last night, Jo, I'm just glad you're home. Fuck Jackie, for now, anyway," she said. Her tone grew serious as she tapped her drink on the table with every other word, for emphasis, "But don't go fucking anyone else until you're sure he's the right guy. No rebound fucking, okay?"

I giggled in spite of myself. I knew she didn't want me to get hurt, didn't want me to make a complete fool of myself, fantasizing about a much younger man; a much younger ex-convict, for that matter. I would forcibly rein in my attraction to him from this point forward. *Forcibly*, I repeated, as the kids invaded the kitchen, requesting drinks, and our conversation was shelved for the moment.

Hours later I led my drowsy children along the dew-damp shore to the big house and then up the steps to the third-level loft, where I left them to their own devices for getting into pajamas and then bed. I crept back down the tiny wooden staircase and eased open the door into Gran's room, which I used to share with Jilly. Gran's snores met my ears from where she lay curled on one of the twin beds; I tugged the quilt higher over my grandmother's shoulders, tenderly smoothing her hair as I knew she'd smoothed mine a hundred thousand times in years gone by, before slipping out of my clothes, too exhausted to find my own night-shirt. Naked, I curled beneath the covers of my old twin bed. I swore my pillow still smelled the same, a combination of my old perfume and hair spray, just faintly of cigarette smoke, the scents of my teenaged years forever trapped in the faded cotton fabric; I drifted to sleep wondering if this was the first step toward inevitable insanity.

May drifted into June. The days grew longer and the air hotter, and we were all incredibly fortunate for the proximity of the lake, which al-lowed relief from the increasing humidity. In the garden behind the cafe, the tomato vines climbed like green monsters up their stakes, and the stargazer lilies and wild roses bloomed in splendid clusters of oranges and pinks; in the morning air, their sweet scents flowed like a magical elixir. I woke each day to a chorus of wrens, who'd industriously built a mini-city in the birch tree outside my bedroom window. And Shore Leave became ever busier as the fishing season blasted into full swing.

I was happy on the surface. The familiarity of place and the pres-ence of family infused my soul like a comforting balm. The girls settled into routine, helping out occasionally during lunch, but mostly having fun with their cousin on the lake, canoeing, fishing, swimming, paddle-boating and clam-digging to their hearts' content. They met several of the other local kids as the weeks slipped past, and I was grateful for this distraction. They talked often to their father, but were so busy filling him in on the details of their active days that they forgot to mention me; Jackie didn't ask and I didn't offer, and so I hadn't heard my husband's voice in almost a month. While at the cafe, I was very careful to replace my intense attraction to Blythe with a sort of false bravado. I actually just avoided him whenever I could, and when it was necessary to talk I fronted a cheerful, almost deprecating attitude that I quite hated.

But it was either that or admit to things I had no right acknowledging.

It was just that Blythe was so very difficult to avoid, there every day in the kitchen, working beside Rich, joking with everyone, good-natured and calm. If I found my gaze lingering too long on him, I chastised myself and recalled that (among other clear issues requiring reflection, such as my status as a still-technically-married mother of three) Blythe was in a relationship, though he never mentioned this girlfriend. And I could not pretend I didn't notice him studying me sometimes, too—not outright, but instead the same way that I attempted to surreptitiously peek at him. There was an undeniable undercurrent—a sense of *knowing* between the two of us that I could not rationalize, or even explain.

It just *was*; not that realizing this changed anything. I still knew what was best, and that was to continue avoiding any interaction other than as fellow employees at my family's business.

As the metaphorical, ironic cherry atop the whole situation, my girls adored him. Tish, especially, the only one of my daughters seemingly immune to romantic nonsense of any kind, and who made fast friends with Blythe, sometimes working with him and Rich in the kitchen during lunch rush. My middle daughter cheerfully tied her curls beneath a bandana just like Blythe's and took up a spatula. Each evening her clothes and skin retained the scent of cooking oil, but Tish remained undeterred.

"Bly is super funny, Mom," she told me as we walked over the gravel to the house from the cafe, late one night during our second week in Landon. Ruthie and Camille trailed us, giggling over something.

"'Bly?'" I repeated, pausing as carefully as I could to draw a breath; just speaking his name made my pulse race, a reaction which served again to stun me. I hadn't experienced such intense flutterings over a man since— well, since my husband, back when we were in high school.

"That's his nickname," Tish explained importantly. "He said I should be a lawyer, Mom, since I always question everything he and Rich tell me. Like yesterday I told him that no one should just *accept* what another person tells them, and he was all like, 'Kid, I'd hate to go before a judge against you.'"

"Like you didn't already tell him you want to be a lawyer," Camille contradicted, from behind us. "You tell everybody that. Maybe we could get you a tattoo so people would know before you even start talking."

I knew Tish longed to follow in Jackie's footsteps and work in law, and she was prone to informing people of this desire; I bit back a smile. I sincerely hoped that each of my girls continued to college, no matter what professional field. Jackie and I always encouraged them in this direction, beginning with their private school educations.

"Well, it'll be way more exciting than teaching history," Tish said breezily in response, referring to Camille's choice of career path. "And I would never get a tattoo. How *tacky*."

"There's plenty of history right here in Landon," I said, hoping to redirect a potential round of bickering between Tish and Camille, and then remembered I had something to tell my oldest. "Milla, I forgot to tell you—Bull Carter was in here this afternoon and said he'd love to show you around White Oaks."

"Oh, Mom, really?"

I smiled at the anticipation in her voice.

"What's White Oaks?" Tish asked.

"It's a lodge just around Flickertail," I explained.

"Why do you want to see it?" Tish demanded of her sister.

"Can I come?" Ruthie asked, but her sisters were too busy picking at each other to answer.

"What's so great about some old lodge?"

"I just want to see it," Camille explained.

"Sounds boring," Tish concluded.

"Shows how much you know," Camille threw back. "It's got history attached to it. It was built in another century. You wouldn't understand." And then, unable to resist the urge to further stir the pot, "You need to *shower*, Tish. I can still smell the fry vat all over you."

"Maybe I will, maybe I *won't*," Tish singsonged, and I was reminded of Jilly and me at those same ages, tormenting each other. I felt a little guilty that all three girls were crammed into one bedroom when they were accustomed to having their own spaces. If Tish chose to torture her sisters and refused to shower, their entire loft would smell like the cafe.

"Patricia," I began, with a warning note, but Ruthie interrupted.

"Mama, can we have some ice cream when we get home?" she wondered, always the peacemaker, and I waited a step to allow her and Camille catch up with us; even Tish stilled her footsteps so we could walk four abreast over the gravel path.

"Of course, sweetie," I told my youngest, taking her hand into mine, so happy she still allowed this.

And I reflected that I could get through just about anything on Earth, as long as my girls were near me.

Chapter Four

After that first time, Blythe didn't ask Jilly or me to accompany him to town; maybe Rich talked to him about the inappropriateness of that, even though I couldn't imagine Rich doing so. And it was apparent that dear Rich thought the world of his step-grandson. I hadn't yet driven into Landon for any bar-hopping (and with two bars in town, it's not as though there was too far to hop), too exhausted at the end of each day to do more than hang out on the dock with Jilly, sipping a beer. It wasn't until a lazy evening in the second week of June that she finally talked me into going over to Eddie's; I was tired of making excuses, and so that evening we managed to sneak the golf cart away from the kids and drove it around the lake to town.

The scene at Eddie's was mellow, the usual for a Monday night. Jilly and I were greeted with open arms (literally, as he swept each of us into an affectionate hug) by Eddie himself, who then proceeded to pour us a draft on the house. I opted for a Leinie's, Jilly a Schell, and we chatted for a bit with Eddie and the ever-present Jim Olson, his best friend and, as we'd concluded long ago, Eddie's Platonic Life Partner. Jilly coined the phrase years ago when we decided, in middle school, to be each other's if we never found our true loves. Both men were long married, with grown children, but apparently found the most happiness in one another's company, down here at Eddie's little bar.

"Jo, you look beautiful," Eddie told me, his eyes crinkling at the corners as he grinned. "And Jillian, you too, darlin' girl. You Davis girls are all such beauties. Just like Joanie and Ell twenty years ago."

"Thanks, you big flatterer," I told him, grateful Mom and Aunt Ellen weren't with to hear this drunken compliment. I stole a long sip and muttered, "This hits the spot."

"Jackie coming up later in the month?" Jim asked from the far side of Jilly. He leaned against the bar to industriously apply chalk to the end of a pool cue.

"Yeah, yes, he probably will," I lied, then took another long drink, in hopes Jim would abandon this line of questioning.

"Well, have fun, ladies," Jim said, and then made his leisurely way to the pool table, where his drink waited. Eddie joined him minutes later, leaving us in relative peace. The radio above the bar was tuned to the local country station, out of Bemidji. An older couple sat at the far end of the bar, chatting quietly. I sighed and ran one hand over my hair, which felt vaguely unfamiliar as it hung past my shoulder blades. For most of my motherhood career, I'd kept it shoulder-length or in a tight ponytail. It used to shine as golden as Jilly's from the endless days spent on the lake; a shade or two darker, these days.

"Jo, it's so good to have you back home. I swear it feels like no time has passed," Jilly reflected, nudging me with her shoulder. "It seems like the old days."

"It does, kinda, doesn't it?" I observed, though in the old days I possessed loads more confidence, a good tan, and much perkier breasts. It seemed so petty, so ridiculous, when I thought of it that way; but, I justified, my self-esteem had taken a huge hit and my pre-baby figure would have added untold amounts to my current outlook. I sighed for a second time.

"Stop that," Jilly admonished, and I caught her eye in the Pabst Blue Ribbon mirror above the bar. She gave me a look, blue eyes narrowed, and I turned to face her, smiling in spite of myself.

"Okay, you're right, no more self-pity," I allowed.

"You want to do a couple shots, maybe go dancing? Scare up some trouble?" Jilly teased.

"Yeah, all the people we'd scare up trouble with are probably home with their kids," I said.

"Or already in bed," she joked. "It is a Monday, after all."

"It's good to be working again," I said. "Truly, it gives me something to do so I don't have to think. I don't know how I got through the last five months since Christmas."

"You're a Davis at heart, remember that," Jilly said. "We get by on our own." But her voice was sad, beneath the surface. I debated asking what was bothering her; I could tell something really was, but I sensed it was not the time to acknowledge that I knew something was wrong. Instead I gently nudged her shoulder with mine, attempting to nonverbally communicate that I was here for her.

"I know, I know," I said at last, then admitted, "I'm not very good at getting by on my own, though. I'm slowly starting to realize how much I depended on Jackie. God, I don't even have any friends in Chicago, at least not any of my own."

"Why not?" my sister asked, studying me. She swirled the remaining beer in her glass, slowly, as though beginning a hypnosis routine.

"I don't know, motherhood, maybe. It's so easy to blame that. All these years I've been so busy mothering and running around for them—not that I mind—but it's hard to have a life."

"I mind!" Jilly interrupted, and I giggled. She went on, "Clinty is demanding as hell most days, and he's a teenager, who's supposed to be at least partially self-sufficient. I can't imagine dealing with three teenagers at once."

"Even if Chris was still alive?" I asked. I was the only person, other than Gran, who would have dared to ask her such a thing.

Jilly blinked and then her gaze shifted up and to the right, back into time. She said quietly, "Chris wanted at least six kids. He always hated being an only child, remember? I always wished Clint had some cousins on the Henriksen side."

"Chris's mom is still alive, right?"

"Yeah, but she's not in great shape. Chris was born when they were in their late forties."

"I remember that they were pretty old. I guess not everyone begins bearing children in their teenage years, like our family," I joked, only sounding a little bitter. It's not as though Jilly or I conceived those babies without help, after all.

"Right," Jilly laughed. "But hey, our kids have turned out all right. The girls seem totally happy to be here. I love hearing them chatting with Ellen and Mom in the mornings. And Tish is a great help to Rich, you know."

"I know, Rich was telling me that last night actually. Tish loves helping them. She ties on a bandana just like…" And for only a fraction of a second did I pause over his name. "Just like Blythe, and then gets right to work."

Jilly giggled. "We're going to get cited for child labor." And then, her gaze lifting over my shoulder, she murmured, "Speaking of the devil."

"Huh?" I asked, but my internal radar began humming and as I turned on the bar stool to see the front entrance, I already knew who was coming into Eddie's.

Blythe grinned widely, effortlessly, to see us, and my heart stopped beating and began thrashing. I swallowed once, unable to tear my gaze away from him; because I was closest to the door, he claimed the open stool beside me, his eyes never moving from mine as he sat, with easy masculine grace.

His hair was tied back, as usual, though he was not wearing his customary bandana—the first I'd seen him that way. He had a high forehead, edged by his slightly wavy hair, which was a honey shade of brown. His eyebrows, by contrast, were thick and slightly darker, as were his enviable long lashes. I'd never been so close to him before, as the bar stool beside mine put our faces about eighteen inches apart, and my breath was tight and shallow. His eyes shone dark blue, with flecks of gray throughout his irises, giving them a smoky appearance. I observed all this quickly, before forcing myself to turn away, though it seemed to me that a space heater had taken up residence against my left side, burning up with him so close.

"Hi, Bly," Jilly said comfortably; in my foolish preoccupation, I almost forgot my sister was there. Apparently she felt free to use his nickname, too.

"Hi, you two," he said, with obvious happiness to find us here. "So, you don't come out when I ask, huh? Am I interrupting a ladies' night?"

"Nah, we just needed to get out of the cafe for a while," Jilly said, doing all of the conversing while I sat, tongue-tied and overwhelmed by the fact that Blythe was so near that if I shifted my left knee just a few inches it would come into contact with his right one, clad in his usual faded jeans.

"I was driving home and saw the golf cart out front, thought I'd say hey," Blythe explained, leaning both forearms against the bar. The position made his biceps and wide shoulders appear even more powerful. Eddie waved hello, and moved as though to get him a drink, but Blythe called, "I got it, Ed," and so saying, rose and leaned forward over the bar, helping himself to a can of soda. He sat back, comfortably, and cracked the top on the can. He observed, "You guys managed to steal the golf cart from Clint, huh?"

"Yeah, he left it unguarded for a second and we nabbed it," Jilly teased.

"You two planning on getting wasted, or what?" Blythe joked back, grinning again.

"Tempting," I said, finally speaking up. "But no, we were just too lazy to walk."

Blythe turned his gaze fully upon me and my body absolutely radiated with warmth and light. I took another very long drink and almost drained my glass. He went on, watching me, "Is it good to be back home? Jilly told me that you never really liked living in such a big city like Chicago."

And what else has she mentioned? I took a moment to wonder. Then I replied, pleased that my voice sounded normal and not at all breathless, "Yeah, I miss it here. You never really get over where you grew up, you know?" I braved a look into his eyes. I hoped my cheeks didn't appear as broiling-hot as they felt. For the love of all things holy, we were just having a conversation.

"That's true," he said, still a hint of a grin hovering around his mouth. "And it's so beautiful here in Landon. You guys are lucky to have this place to come home to."

"You're from Oklahoma?" I asked, loving this excuse to continue looking at him. Holy hell, he was handsome. And leaning just slightly nearer to me, as if he couldn't wait to hear what I might say next. Despite the fact that we'd worked in the same space for a month now, I had tried so honorably to avoid a one-on-one conversation with him; I was overwhelmed by the foolish desire to make up for the lost time, longing to ask Blythe everything about himself.

"I am, born and raised. It's pretty there, in its own way, but I can't get over all the lakes up here. It's beautiful."

"It really is. I'm glad my girls get a chance to be here and experience some of that, away from Chicago," I agreed.

"Your daughter Tish is a big help to Gramps," Blythe said. "She told him yesterday she wants to learn to cook like a chef, and can she practice with us? She's a hoot. And a hard worker." He spoke with just the slightest drawl in his deep voice. It was *so* sexy. Everything about him was, dammit. I felt as though my clothes were too tight, surprised that sweat wasn't trickling over my temples.

"Yeah, she loves Rich, he's like their grandpa, too," I went on, hardly aware of what I was saying. I refocused and added, "And thanks for letting her help out. She loves being in the center of things."

"Well, the girls could all teach Clint a thing or two about work ethic," Jilly said. "He's lazy as hell. Even Ruthie helps with rolling silverware."

"Aw, it's summer," Blythe defended. "He's got the rest of his life to work, right?"

"He can quit asking me for money then," Jilly said, and nodded at my empty glass. "Jo, you about ready for another one?"

"Yeah, thanks," I told her.

She hopped nimbly to her feet and called over to Eddie, "I'm grabbing two more, k?"

"That's fine, sweetie," Eddie called back.

Then Jim said, "Jillian, you got to watch this shot," and she rolled her eyes but good-naturedly collected both glasses and ambled over to the pool table.

I now sat alone at the bar with Blythe. He remained angled in my direction, and I made myself speak, asking the first thing that popped into my mind. "So, how did you get your name, anyway?"

He laughed, a warm, deep, wonderful sound. I felt it vibrate in my belly; I struggled to keep breathing at a regular pace.

"No one here has asked me that yet," he said. "It's kind of a strange one, I know. It's my dad's name, and one that's always been in his family. How about yours?"

"Oh, Mom put together her and Ellen's names," I explained. "She thought it was an original, but I have met other Joelles before."

"It's so pretty," he said easily, and I swore his eyes were teasing me, daring me to misinterpret him. There was a merriment about him that was almost addictive. "Joelle what?"

"Thank you," I said. "And it's Joelle Anne."

He sat still, just watching my face, and my heart throbbed. Surely no one had ever looked at me with such absorption. I was unable to move my gaze from his, and asked, "So, what's yours?"

"Edward," he said, a smile nudging his lips. "After another ancestor on my dad's side. There have been lots of Edward Tilsons in our family, I guess. That was *almost* my first name."

I giggled just a little, explaining, "I can't picture you as an 'Ed.' It just doesn't suit you."

"Right?" he said, giving me a wink. Oh God, he had a good wink; I almost fell from the barstool, and then could have laughed even more, at my own foolishness. He added, "It's so good to talk to you, Joelle. I've been wanting to. I kinda thought you might be avoiding me."

I felt lost in his eyes as I whispered, "No. No, of course not."

I might never have dragged my gaze away from him if not for Jilly's tinkling voice floating back in our direction.

She asked, "You want the same thing, Jo?"

I nodded, keeping my eyes from Blythe, with real effort. So my attempt to keep my distance hadn't been lost on him.

"How about you, Bly?" Jilly asked.

"I'm good with the soda," he replied, and Jilly filled two more drafts for us, sliding one across to me.

"How is it going, living with Rich?" she asked Blythe, sipping her beer behind the bar, leaning against the far counter like she did at Shore Leave.

"Good, actually. His trailer is just like Mom's, back in Oklahoma, so it feels like home. And he's is such a good guy. I love him like family," Blythe said. "He does so much for my mom and me, always has."

"I don't remember Christy ever coming back up here after that one summer," Jilly said.

"We didn't often. I think I might've been about five the last time," Blythe responded. "Mom likes it in Oklahoma since that's where Dad always comes back to look for her."

"That sounds familiar," I said, referring to my own mother and Mick Douglas. "But our dad never got back the Landon way."

"Yeah, sometimes I think we should try to hunt him down on the Internet," Jilly said. We'd discussed it before, but it was only ever talk, and Jilly and I strongly disagreed on the subject.

"No, I say let sleeping dogs lie," I said.

"Okay, Gran," Jilly teased, and I held up my right hand in defense, the other curled around my beer.

"Can you just see a man trying to help Mom and Ellen run the cafe?" I laughed at the very idea of my independent mother putting up with a husband. It was something I'd not inherited from her, long dependent on Jackie.

"Now that's a picture," Blythe said, and he nudged me companionably with his right shoulder, sending my heart cartwheeling. I felt Jilly's speculative, observant gaze.

"True," Jilly acknowledged. From outside came the elongated moan of a train whistle, on the tracks just north of town. Jilly listened for a moment, then asked, "Jo, remember that night Jackie and Justin hopped the train on a dare?"

I shook my head slowly at the memory, wondering why she'd bring this up right now, other than the fact that we just heard a train. I said, sarcastically, "No, I'd forgotten."

"What happened?" Blythe asked.

"They would have been fine, probably, but Jackie slipped and fell off the train, and then Justin freaked out and jumped off to see if he'd been hurt, and they both wound up in the hospital," Jilly explained.

For me, the most vivid memory of that night was my fear that Jackie was badly or permanently injured; I flew into that hospital room with my heart in my throat and cradled him to me, sobbing. It was only a few weeks before the fateful prom night during which we ended up conceiving Camille. I never confessed to anyone that I'd been secretly thrilled to be pregnant with Jackson Gordon's baby, beneath the fear and terror about telling everyone the news, because it meant that Jackie belonged to me, and me only, from then on. God, I'd been so stupid and naïve; so blind.

"I've hopped a ride on a train a time or two," Blythe was saying, drawing me back to the present. "But I never did fall off. Grandma Pam always said my guardian angel worked overtime."

"From the stories I've heard Rich tell about you, she's right," Jilly commented, and he grinned again, shrugging his shoulders and then draining the last of his soda.

"Well, I'll let you two enjoy the rest of your night," Blythe said, rising to his feet and putting a couple of dollar bills onto the bar; I was probably imagining that he seemed reluctant to leave. He angled a quick look at Jilly and then his eyes came to rest on me. I leaned my right elbow on the bar and held his gaze, my chin tilted high; he was so tall. He added, his tone light but his eyes intent on mine, "Call over to Gramps' place if you need a ride, all right? I'll come get you."

"Thanks, buddy," Jilly said and I pulled myself together.

"We'll be good," I told him, all shivery and hot and trying not to let it show.

"See you tomorrow, then," he said, and walked out the door with his shoulders shifting so amazingly beneath his t-shirt. Moments later I heard the sound of his truck firing to life and only then realized I still stared after him. I turned back to find Jillian watching me with her arms folded like an irritated schoolteacher.

"What?" I muttered.

"Jo, Jo, Jo," she said, sounding exactly like Gran. And then, "Let's get home. Enough excitement for tonight, huh?"

It rained that night, a steady downpour through which thunder rumbled and lightning backlit the curtains at regular intervals. I told myself this was why I couldn't sleep, not because of my thoughts that kept circling back around to Blythe sitting so close to me at the bar. Again I played over our conversation, whispering his name, a longtime family name that now belonged to him. And then I would curl around my stomach and just manage to drift into a restless sleep before thunder would grumble and my eyes would flinch open yet again.

I'll come get you, he'd said.

Forget it, Joelle, I told myself, in misery as I lay restless and sensitized, longing for what was not mine, and could never be mine. *Forget these feelings. No good can come from them.*

My thoughts ran darker as the minutes crept past. I thought of all the old stories that Gran and Great-Aunt Minnie used to tell, of the curse that plagued the women in our family; the notion that all Davis women were destined to lose the men they loved.

It's bullshit. You've never believed in the curse, remember?

Then explain why none of us have our men.

Explain that.

But I could not explain, and my heart ached too much to continue trying, at least for tonight.

Chapter Five

A few days later, Landon's Trout Days, our official hometown celebration, opened with a fish fry, parade, and street dance. And that was just the Friday lineup. The girls were beside themselves with excitement Friday morning; Clint planned to drive them into town for the parade, courtesy of the golf cart. The girls wore what had become their summer uniforms: jean shorts and tank tops over their swimsuits, curly hair tied up in high ponytails. Camille, however, was currently clad in a bikini top, one slightly on the skimpy side, a garment I didn't recognize as part of her wardrobe. I sat with Aunt Ellen and Gran at table three, sipping coffee, watching my girls make their way into the cafe and debating whether or not to say something about Camille's mostly-bare torso. Gran, however, took the decision out of my hands, gesturing with her cane and wondering aloud, "Camille, what's that dental floss around your chest?"

Aunt Ellen hid a smile in her coffee; I watched, ready to do damage control if necessary.

Camille knelt near Gran's chair and hooked her wrist over the back of it, giving her great-granny a winning smile. For a second she looked exactly like Jackie—that smile. She said, "Gran, it's just my bathing suit."

Gran harrumphed, not one to be easily charmed. "Well, one tug on those strings and you'll be bare as an egg from the waist up, girl. It's indecent."

Ruthie came to give me a kiss but Tish laughed, loving every moment of Gran scolding her big sister. Camille shot me a look that clearly asked for help. I sighed, torn between Gran's authority and my own. At last I said, "Bring a shirt along, sweetie, just in case."

"I was going to anyway," she let me know, sounding the slightest bit defiant.

"Fabulous," I replied, matching her tone with an edge of sarcasm.

The girls took off with Clint minutes later. I was mildly concerned that her older sisters wouldn't keep an eye on Ruthie, but then reminded myself that she was twelve, not a toddler, and was headed into Landon, not downtown Chicago. Jilly and I ran wild all around Landon, the lake, and the acres surrounding Shore Leave since the summer we were seven and eight. Probably even before that. Besides, I planned to join them after the lunch crowd came and went, nostalgic for the Trout Days decorations that hadn't changed since I was a kid: the huge plaster replica of a rainbow trout, the nets, lures, and poles strung between all the local businesses, the scent of fish and cheese curds frying. It would make a native Chicagoan cringe and run in the opposite direction; fortunately my girls spent enough time here to refrain from being judgmental.

We watched as the four of them, Clint and Tish in the front, Camille and Ruthie in back, clung to the roll bars as Clint hightailed it down the gravel road. I could hear their laughter through the screen door and open windows, and sighed, depression momentarily crushing me as I contemplated how long it was since I'd laughed that way. I mentally scolded myself for being so morbid, and Aunt Ellen commented, "It seems like yesterday that was you and Jillian."

"I know. It's scary how fast time flies," I agreed, shoulders sagging. I bolstered myself with a sip of the strong coffee.

"Things will get better, Jo," Gran said, elbows braced on the tabletop, her own mug just inches below her chin as she studied me. It was uncharacteristic of her to be so optimistic. I waited too long to reply, feeling the familiar sting of unshed tears, and Gran went on, "I hear you crying at night, sweetie, just like that sad song on your radio that we hear again and again."

I had to laugh at that, staving off the tears. Of course she meant the Dixie Chicks, who I loved and listened to religiously, even still. "Gran,"

I said, setting my coffee on the table and leaning to kiss her cheek, with complete affection. "You're funny. And I'm sorry if I wake you, really."

She rolled her eyes at me. Mom breezed through the swinging kitchen door and handed me a fresh apron, officially signaling the start of the work day. But by four-thirty in the afternoon I was done with work, sitting on the dock waiting for slowpoke Jilly. I'd managed to sneak home for a shower and emerged feeling just slightly renewed, wearing a sundress, albeit a plain cream-colored one. My bare legs were submerged to mid-calf in the lukewarm lake water. My hair hung loose and damp and I was enjoying watching a pair of sailboats out on the lake, the sounds of laughter and merriment from Trout Days drifting across the water. When the dock began shuddering with the impact of an approach, I called back, "Took you long enough!"

A man laughed at that, and my head jerked around. For a second my heart stuttered in my chest; the angle of the sun distorted my vision and I was certain that Jackie was walking my way. A fist seemed to seize my throat and I clutched the boards at the end of the dock with a hard, startled grip. Then in the next instant I realized that it was not Jackie at all, but only Justin Miller, wearing dirty jeans and a work shirt, with his name stitched across the pocket. He said, "Well, about sixteen years, I'd say."

He approached to within a couple of feet and regarded me in silence, while I took in the familiar—his wide-legged stance, strong arms, and thick black hair—and the unfamiliar—his terribly scarred face. From a certain direction anyone would consider him the best-looking guy they'd seen in a long time; straight on, the damage was intense and resembled something from a Halloween mask. I found myself gaping and immediately glanced away, then immediately back, sure he would know I was uncomfortable. I finally spit out, "Well, hi, Justin, long time no see."

His full lips curled into something resembling a grin. He knelt and our faces were suddenly at the same height. I turned more fully around, bending one knee against the dock and struggling to find something to say. I managed, "How are you?"

His no-nonsense expression was at least familiar, this man who'd been like a brother to me and Jilly in the old days; Justin had always been especially fond of tormenting Jilly during those long-ago summers, calling her 'tomboy' and 'Jill the pill.' As a teenager, Justin ran wild, known for his outrageous sense of humor and boldness; I remembered him cajoling the guys to race their trucks with his, and I remembered him slamming beer and yelping in victory during football games, also one of Jackie's longtime buddies. For a moment I sat steeped in memories of those bygone days, rendered mute.

Justin's face appeared cross-hatched with ropy red scars all along the right side. The outside corner of his right eye was pulled slightly down, giving him an unintentionally menacing look. The scarring continued down his neck and into the unbuttoned collar of his work shirt. He said, "Fucking great, how about you?" but his tone held no malice. I felt one corner of my lips lift in a smile, suddenly at ease with him.

"Me, too. In fact, this last year has been really amazing," I said.

He adjusted his position and caught one wrist in the opposite hand, forearms braced on his knees, asking, "Jackie is still in Chicago, huh?"

I figured Dodge already told him everything anyway; the two of them had always been close.

"Yep," I agreed, without elaborating. "I brought the girls for the summer."

"You usually do, right?"

"Yeah, they love it."

"Funny I haven't seen you around before now."

"I know, it's Landon, right? But we don't usually stay more than a couple weeks."

Such surface conversation, while his eyes seemed to be telling me something much more complex. It was odd being engaged in a multi-level communication I wasn't sure he intended. It struck me that he'd lived through a divorce, and that Aubrey cheated on him; he knew exactly how I felt. Not to mention that the entire town of Landon knew about Aubrey's cheating. He asked quietly, "Longer this summer, though?"

Something caught in my throat, so I nodded instead of answering. He went on, "Dad is glad you're home. He misses you a lot around here.

Jillian, too. She's been so excited for you to get here." And on my sister's name, his voice held a note of...something. My eyes snapped back to him, instantly on alert for a sign of what that might mean. But maybe I was imagining things.

I moved my gaze to the dock, embarrassed that I found it difficult to keep looking at his scars, instead studying the unchanging wood grain, with its knot holes and wavy lines. I said, "I miss everybody here, too."

Justin rose abruptly, back to his full height. I shaded my eyes with one hand and returned his gaze; it was much easier with distance between our faces. He said, "Well, it's good to see you. You and Jilly going to Trout Days later?"

"We're headed there now, actually."

"See you around, Jo," he said companionably, and then turned and walked away; I suddenly noticed Jilly, clad in a bright yellow sundress and looking smoking-hot, approaching from the cafe. Justin's footsteps faltered at the sight of her, but only for a second; I tried to read my sister's expression, to see if she sensed something amiss, but she was cheerful-looking as ever, offering him her most dazzling smile.

"Hi, Justin," she called, and he lifted one arm in a brief wave. She then directed her smile my way and stopped on the bank, planting her hands on both hips. "Come on, Joey, I'm sick of waiting for your ass!"

"Oh for the love, Jillian," I grumbled, hiking down my dress and standing. My wet bare feet left slim prints along the boards of the dock; I leaned and grabbed my sandals by the heel straps.

"You wanna walk or take my car?" she called as I made my way over the grass.

"Let's walk, do you mind?" I replied. I saw Justin climb into his truck up in the parking lot; he began driving but then braked suddenly as his dad called over to him. For a moment they spoke, and then he drove away.

Dodge turned back to the cafe and caught sight of us. He yelled, "Have fun, girls, don't break too many hearts!"

"I don't think there's much danger of that," Jilly called back.

Mom appeared on the porch and teased, "Back before midnight, girls."

"Hardy *har har*," I responded. "Seriously, Mom, I turn into a pumpkin way before that hour. I'm old!"

"If you're old, then I don't want to think about what I am!" Mom grumbled.

"You guys are coming over later, right?" Jilly asked Mom. We always closed after lunch during Trout Days; no one ventured out of Landon during the festivities, even the scant mile it took to get out here.

"Sure, we couldn't keep Gran from the dance," Mom joked, lighting a smoke.

Jilly and I made our way along the lake road, dappled with shadows from the maples, oaks, pines, and grapevines that grew thick enough on either side to make it seem as though we traversed a glowing green tunnel. Flicker Trail was so familiar I could have walked with a bandana over my eyes; instead I ambled along beside my sister, happy that we were in no hurry and could enjoy the luxury of walking barefoot (I still carried my sandals) beside the lake. It lay to our left in a clear blue expanse, calm as sheet of sapphire silk where no boats broke the surface. The sun in a cloudless sky danced over the water, twinkling in an ever-changing light path, tempting as always, as though you could climb out there and walk along its length.

"So I talked to Justin," I told Jilly.

"So I gathered," she responded.

"His face…"

"I know. It's hard to get used to, at first." Her voice was very soft.

"I always think of him as so carefree. And he and Aubrey seemed so in love, back when."

"We were all carefree back when. God, if only," Jilly said, and hung her head back, walking for a few steps as she stared straight up at the treetops. Her voice sounded strangely reedy as she said, "Aubrey tried to keep their marriage going, I think. I mean, from what I've heard. But it couldn't have been easy. He's so bitter."

"Yeah, but who can blame him?" I felt a flash of defensiveness for

Justin. "He gets scarred up and then she cheats. Shit. But she always craved everyone's attention." I hadn't intended to sound so bitchy, and if that wasn't me projecting my own experience onto the situation, then I didn't know what was.

Jilly didn't disagree, saying quietly, "That's true."

"What exactly happened? Do you know?"

To my surprise, Jilly was completely silent. When she spoke, her tone was unreadable. She said simply, "No."

I peeked carefully at her, confused by such a short answer. She did not look back at me, and so I asked, changing the subject, "So, how's Clint looking forward to tenth grade?"

We were discussing our children's respective future plans fifteen minutes later as we came out from under the canopy of trees and onto Landon's main drag, Fisherman's Street. The music grew steadily louder, as the atmosphere would undoubtedly grow more raucous as the evening progressed. The air was redolent with the smell of the fish fry; vendor's booths were set up along the street, festooned with colored lanterns, fishing lures, plastic trout and blue garlands meant to resemble waves.

Near the lake, a local band called Untamed set up their equipment on the pavilion for a show later tonight. Eddie Sorenson and Jim Olson were putting on an impromptu show at the moment, sitting on a bench under an enormous weeping willow whose branches trailed into Flickertail Lake, plucking along on their respective guitar and banjo. Picnic tables were jammed with families; kids ran everywhere, most wearing foam fish heads that fit like headbands over their sweaty hair. I felt a small pang, remembering my own girls at those fun ages of seven, eight, nine…big enough to have some independence, but still with enough of a child's heart to hold my hand, wear a foam fish head without restraint or fear of embarrassment.

"Joelle Davis!" I heard, and turned toward the familiar voice of Leslie Gregerson, a former classmate. But today I was prepared for questions. I wasn't about to let anyone see the real me, the aching one. I could project the happy, smiling Joelle that I used to be, the one everyone remembered; Jackie's Perky Girlfriend. Hopefully they weren't instead remembering Slut Who Got Pregnant on Prom Night.

"Hi, Leslie," I said, and we hugged briefly; her hair smelled exactly like I remembered.

"You look great, Jo," she said, and then smiled warmly at my sister. "Hi, Jilly, you know I think that about you, too."

"Thanks, Les, same to you," I said; it was funny how after a few moments around people you knew as teenagers, no matter how much they'd physically changed, you suddenly just saw the person you remembered. Despite the extra pounds and much shorter hair, she was still the girl I'd known since grade school.

"These are my kids," she said, trying to grasp the shoulders of a couple of boys as they darted by, with no luck. "How many do you and Jackie have now?"

"Three girls," I told her. "They're here somewhere, with Clint."

"Oh sure, I've seen them today. I was wondering where Clint found a couple of girlfriends."

"He's a lady's man," Jilly teased, rolling her eyes at Leslie. "At least, he's beginning to think he is."

"My oldest will be thirteen this fall," Leslie said. "I'm not ready for a teenager!"

We chatted for a few more minutes before heading farther into town; I wanted cheese curds, and to lay eyes on my own kids. Of course we were waylaid about a thousand times along the way, and so the sun had almost disappeared behind the pines by the time we found the kids, confirmed they were fine, and then threaded through the crowd, all the way back to the picnic area. In the gathering dusk, Landon appeared magical. Twinkling white lights began winking on all around the pavilion dance area. Someone lit the hanging lanterns that adorned the trees, and sparklers crackled everywhere as kids found grown-ups with lighters in their pockets. It became imperative to keep your elbows close to avoid getting burned by a stray spark. Untamed was about ready to get rolling on the stage.

I sighed, mostly in pleasure, and joined Jilly and my youngest daughter at a picnic table; Ruthann elected to stay with us for a while. Minutes later Mom, Gran, Aunt Ellen, and Rich found us in the crowd. I tried as unobtrusively as possible to determine if Blythe had accompanied them, but to my extreme disappointment he was nowhere to be seen.

It's for the best, Jo-elle, I reminded myself, emphasizing the syllables of my name as Mom did when angry with me, but some of the magic seeped from the evening anyway. I scooted down the bench seat to make room, and then saw Liz Miller, Dodge's daughter, making her way through the mass of people. Dodge was with her, carrying a kid piggyback, while Liz carted two more with her.

Dodge led her to our table. Liz looked frazzled, and I extracted myself from the picnic bench to hug her as Dodge introduced Ruthann to Liz's triplets.

"Joelle, hi," she murmured, drawing back to smile at me. She was little, and looked just like I remembered her mother, Marjorie; Marjorie and Dodge divorced many years ago. She added, "It's so good to see you!"

"So, three kids at once, huh, Liz?" I teased her, and she made a face, half sheepish, half proud.

"Yeah, these are my rugrats. Do your girls baby-sit?"

I laughed, and suddenly Clint, Tish, and Camille all converged. Our picnic table was far too small to accommodate our group, so I told Camille (who was wearing her tank top now, I noticed with relief) to take the kids to a separate one within eyeshot. Ruthann and the triplets seemed to be getting along, and Ruthann, who'd collected a king's ransom in parade candy, shared her loot with them. Twilight descended and stars sparked in the navy sweep of the sky. The band did a quick instrument check and then launched full force into some good old-fashioned country music. Because talking was impossible with the noise, Jilly leaned practically into my ear to be heard. She asked, "You having fun?"

I nodded, sincerely. She grinned back at me, looking young and beautiful with her short hair and stunningly-blue eyes. She'd worn a little make-up: mascara, lip gloss and some eyeliner. She mouthed the word *good*.

Mom hauled along a cooler and began passing out beer to the adults.

I snagged one, and then a couple of soda cans for the kids, and headed across the way to deliver them. I snaked through the crowd and deposited the drinks for Clint to distribute; the melted ice clinging to the cans left the front of my dress damp and sticking to me.

"Dammit," I muttered. I paused to pluck at my dress, and it was then that a big, warm hand caught my elbow from behind.

I somehow knew it was Blythe even before I turned around. He let go of my arm almost instantly, now that he'd gotten my attention, but my skin burned as though he still touched me. For a moment, with the music pulsing and people swirling all around us, we were a little island of stillness, only our gazes making contact. My heart seemed to be trying to keep rhythm with the foot-stomping beat, battering my chest.

Blythe smiled, leaning closer to me, and I went shaky and weak-kneed, like he was about to kiss me. He was not, of course, instead just attempting to be heard over the noise.

"Hi," he said, his voice melting over me, sending shivers spiraling through my ribcage and along my spine.

Hi. My lips formed the word, but no sound emerged. I stared up at him, suddenly hyperaware of my own body...the way my breasts and belly ached to be pressed against him, how my fingertips curled against my palms to avoid reaching...

His eyes held steady on mine in the glow of the twinkle lights strung around the dance floor, smoky-blue and good-humored, echoed by the grin lifting one side of his mouth a little higher than the other. His t-shirt was dark and he filled it out the way an apple fills its skin.

He touched my elbow again, however briefly, and said, "You look really good," and all appreciable breath lodged in my throat. Shockwaves exploded outward along my skin from that point of contact.

I whispered, "Thank you."

At long last I managed to shake myself free of his eyes and said, loudly, "We're over here!" indicating the direction of our table with my head.

He followed me, close behind, and I was forced to admit that my self-imposed avoidance, though perhaps pitifully admirable, helped me in no way at the moment. No matter how much I wanted to squash the desire

I felt for him, it was there nonetheless, swelling within me, begging to be acknowledged. As we approached the group I caught Jilly's gaze, and her eyes narrowed just slightly, certainly recalling her advice to me about the dream, the centaurs and the mounting…and my insides seemed to liquefy just thinking the word *mounting* with Blythe a foot away from my body.

No one else noticed a thing; how could they? I was a much older woman. Blythe was young and he was incredibly handsome, and he was off limits. *Period.* I knew all of these things, but as Mom tossed a beer at him and he slid onto the bench with long-limbed grace, I was aware of absolutely nothing else. He claimed the seat kitty-corner from me, beside Dodge, and proceeded to have a conversation with him. I kept my eyes away, but from the edge of my vision I noticed every movement he made. When Jilly leaned over I cringed, sure she was going to chastise me, but instead she asked, "You wanna go dance?"

Most of the mobile population of Landon was already dancing to the music; it was the kind of beat that made it impossible to remain sitting for long. I nodded, then gulped the last of my beer, and she grabbed my hand and then Liz's. Liz protested, but no one denied Jilly, and moments later she edged us into the crowd. I saw the kids watching and waved them over; Camille, Ruthann, and the triplets came willingly, but Tish made a face at me and stayed at the table with Clint. Within four songs I was drenched in sweat, laughing, stomping and twirling in a huge circle that expanded to include our entire group. When Todd Kellen, the lead singer, leaned over to the mic and called, "Let's slow things down a bit, folks!" I groaned along with just about everyone else.

I fanned myself vigorously, realizing Jilly had disappeared as though into thin air, and accepted a beer from Liz, who'd dashed back to our picnic table and Mom's cooler, when Justin Miller appeared through the crowd and asked, "One for old time's sake?"

I shrugged acceptance, slightly drunk, popping the top on another beer.

"Does it matter if we don't have any old times, exactly?" I teased.

He smiled and said, "Hell, no."

I slid my left arm comfortably over his shoulders and he took my right wrist in his left hand so I wouldn't be forced to abandon my cold beer. The song began and I was surprised to feel so at ease with him, despite the fact that our dancing embrace put his disfigured face so close to mine, his scars livid even in the fairy lights. His shoulders felt like iron beneath my arm. He asked, "My face doesn't freak you out too much, huh?" and though his tone was light, I sensed the vulnerability cloaked within the words.

"Shit, Justin," I heard myself say. I racked my brain for what Gran would say to set him at ease while remaining truthful. "Of course not. Yeah, it's a shock. But you're still you."

I felt an almost imperceptible release of tension under my left arm as his shoulders eased a fraction. He went on, "I know, but I've had five years to get used to it. And I'm still shocked when I look in the mirror sometimes."

I lifted my chin to study him full in the face. He'd changed into a clean shirt and different jeans. The scars looked so raw, so painful to see. He appeared to be studying something over my shoulder as I perused his face.

"Jackie's in love with someone else," I said then, out of nowhere, surprising myself. It was the first time I'd voiced what I knew in my gut.

He didn't act shocked or embarrassed. Instead he admitted, "Jilly told me that he cheated. But nothing about that."

I pressed my lips tightly together, presumably to block out any more startling confessions. But then I babbled on, "I haven't told the girls. They don't know anything about him…" I paused before adding quietly, "About him fucking around."

Justin said, "No kid should have to know that about their dad."

"Even if it's the truth?" I snapped. I sounded so terribly bitter. But he grinned slightly and shifted so I could take a drink from my beer.

"Let Jackson explain himself," Justin suggested. "He was always a smooth talker. Let him talk his way out of this one." Almost immediately he said, "I'm sorry, Jo. I know how much that sucks."

"I know you do," I said. "I'm sorry, too." I wanted to mention what a selfish, self-centered bitch I'd always thought Aubrey was, but I couldn't put that into words without the risk of offending him. And I felt oddly better, the music and the stars and my slight buzz all combining to make me realize that I was actually feeling better overall. Despite what I just admitted about my husband, I didn't feel the burning sting of tears making their way into my nasal passages.

"Yeah, well, what do you do?" he murmured rhetorically, gazing again across the crowd, in the same direction.

The music stopped and we stepped apart simultaneously. He said politely, "Thanks for the dance, Jo. And I am sorry about Jackie."

"You're welcome," I replied. "And thanks."

He asked suddenly, "Would you mind…"

"Mind what?" I persisted when his voice trailed away.

Justin's gaze was fixed straight across from where we stood, the direction he'd kept looking while we danced, and I looked that way to see Jilly in her sexy yellow sundress, sitting at the picnic table with Blythe, seemingly unaware that Justin studied her so intently, without a hint of a smile on his face. Justin's dark eyes were as serious as I'd ever seen them. But just as quickly he snapped his gaze away from her and drew a deep breath. He muttered, "Never mind."

And before I could say another word, he disappeared in the opposite direction.

Chapter Six

DESPITE MY SNIDE REMARK ABOUT TURNING INTO A PUMPkin, we didn't make it back to Shore Leave until after one in the morning. Mom and Aunt Ellen loaded the girls into the station wagon, and Clint offered to haul Jilly and me on the golf cart. So that's how I came to be clinging to the roll bar on the backseat, drunk again despite my better judgment, singing along with my sister and her son as we followed the wagon's taillights along Flicker Trail.

Clint sings a pretty darn good Kenny Chesney, I thought as we bumped over the gravel. Though, he managed to hit every pothole on the trail.

"Clinty, watch it, dammit!" I yelled at him as our butts flew about a foot off the vinyl seats yet again.

"Sorry, Aunt Joey!" he yelled over his shoulder.

The parking lot came into view and Clint roared (as much as one can roar in a golf cart) into it and came to a neck-snapping halt. I punched his shoulder and Jilly laughed as he yelped, "Ow!"

"Toughen up!" she teased him, and Clint loped around the cart and caught me in a playful headlock, rubbing his right fist into my hair and creating a fabulous rat's nest.

"Clint, you little shit!" I blustered, and heard Rich laughing as he parked Mom's car.

My girls came running, whooping and laughing to see their cousin destroying my hair. At last he let me go and I laughed, too, unable to help it, though I went after Clint with fingers curled into claws. He darted away, full-steam toward the lake. Tish and Ruthann followed, and moments later, inevitably, given the mood of the whole evening, there was a shriek followed by a splash. In the next moment Tish, who'd presumably just surfaced, let out a scream that would have done credit to a victim in *Hitchhiker III*. The night air was so calm that anyone still partying at Trout Days would be able to hear every word we spoke out here, let alone blood-curdling screams. I hoped no one was currently calling the police to report a possible homicide.

"*Clint!*" Tish screeched.

Ruthann yelled, "You better run!"

Camille murmured, "Uh-oh."

"Make waaaaaay!" Clint yelped instead, and there was tremendous splash, as though he'd belly-flopped. To my relief, Tish began laughing, instead of launching into one of her infamous rages. Despite her age, my middle girl was still a hell of a fit-thrower when she felt she'd been wronged. Camille headed for the dock as Mom leaned to help Gran from the front seat of the car. Mom still drove the ancient station wagon that we'd been hauled about in as kids, the very vehicle Jilly and I used for our driver's license exams.

Gran called in her squawky voice, "Watch out for rattlesnakes, you kids!"

"God, Gran, that's so mean!" Jilly yelled over her shoulder as she jogged after Camille.

Gran chuckled. I was about to follow Jilly when headlights sent twin beams across the parking lot and I immediately recognized Blythe's old black truck. He must be stopping out to bring Rich home. Of course he was. I watched as he parked and climbed down from the cab, my insides humming with what could only be described as joy.

I thought, *He's here, he's here, he's here!*

It was then that I heard Camille cry out, "No no no no no!" in rapid succession, and Clint hee-hawing in typical adolescent-boy laughter as he tossed her into the lake.

"I could hear you guys all the way along the trail," Blythe commented, loping over to join Rich and Mom. Aunt Ellen helped Gran up the porch steps.

"Joelle, go get those kids out of there before someone gets hurt!" Mom commanded in her bitchiest tone, as though I were solely to blame for Jilly's son's obnoxious behavior.

"I'll help," Blythe offered, and so I waited while he joined me. I felt positively tiny as he headed to my side; if I stepped close enough to him, my nose would touch his chest. He was backlit by the lone streetlight in the lot but I could see the grin on his face. My belly felt weightless as I smiled back, wide and warm.

"Good to see you again," he said, and I almost reached to take his hand into mine.

You're drunk, I reminded myself.

"This way," I said instead, almost shyly.

We reached the dock just in time to see Clint run and hurtle off the end, arms and legs wind-milling. There was a gigantic splash, followed by more laughter. Judging from the number of sleek wet heads bobbing around in the lake, both Jilly and Ruthann had joined the swimmers.

"Mom!" Tish called, noticing me and Blythe as she treaded water ten feet out. "Get in!"

"Oh, no," I said. "You guys get *out!*"

Clint leaped athletically onto the dock and made for me, curving his shoulders menacingly.

"Dammit!" I said, turning to evade him and blundering right into Blythe. Some wicked male force emanating from Clint infected Blythe, and he grinned devilishly and actually picked me up, continuing to the end of the dock.

Before I could react to the fact that I was being held in his incredible arms, Blythe put his lips almost against my ear to murmur softly, "Sorry, Joelle," and then neatly launched me into the rippling black water.

My own shriek rang even louder than Tish's. We were going to get a visit from Charlie Evans, police officer, in about five minutes. I surfaced and blew water out my nose (so attractive) and then moaned, "My shoes!"

Blythe sat calmly on the end of the dock, near his own discarded shoes, legs dangling in the water as he laughed; he'd rolled up his pant legs.

"You too, Bly!" Tish yelled at him. "C'mon!"

He grinned at her and replied, "No way. I'm wearing jeans!"

"You're forcing me to do this!" she warned him, swimming for the dock. Ruthann joined her and they approached him, dripping wet and giggling.

Blythe spread his arms wide and shook his head. "Give it a go, then, girls," he teased them.

Tish war-whooped and began shoving at his back. Of course he didn't budge an inch.

"Milla, help us!" she implored, but Camille, though laughing, instantly shook her head. Ruthann gamely gave it a try, but they hadn't a chance. Blythe shifted slightly, caught Tish by both arms, and deposited her into the water. She surfaced with a splutter and began tugging at his legs. Clint executed a graceful cartwheel off the end of the dock, nearly knocking Blythe across the head.

Jilly swam over to me, sleek as an otter, and murmured, "What a night."

I slipped off my sandals and chucked them to the shore, one at a time, as Blythe finally gave in and with a roar cannon-balled into the water. My girls yelped with delight as he surfaced and began trying to dunk them. From fifteen feet away, Jilly and I observed, up to our necks in lukewarm liquid. A smile played around my sister's mouth. She asked, "Remember when we used to skinny-dip out here?"

I giggled. "Of course. Me and Jackie used to, too."

"You haven't lived 'til you've done it in the lake," Jilly agreed, slicking back her hair with both hands. "Chris used to tell me that I couldn't get pregnant if we were in the water."

"I remember you telling me that. What a turkey."

"He always hated using a condom," she said.

"Jackie, too," I murmured. Which was why we'd been teenaged parents. I thought suddenly of how Justin had been about to ask me a question involving my sister and debated telling her, right now under the stars.

Maybe when you aren't drunk, I thought next. But I was curious as hell about it.

Jilly laughed, watching as Blythe sent Ruthann flying into the air. Beside him in the water, Tish begged, "Me next, me next!"

"God, they miss their dad," I said. I knew it was true. If Jackie were here, he'd be pitching them into the air, playing with them in the lake on a gorgeous summer night, letting their happy chatter make its way into his heart. The bitch of it was Jackie was a really good dad; not a doubt in my mind about how much he loved our girls. But he wasn't here…and I was pretty damn sure that I knew where he was on this same hot June night, back in Chicago. Probably just getting Lanny out of her panties on the cream-leather designer sofa in our front room. My husband with all his charm, his familiar smile…his strong hands…everything that used to be mine.

I made two fists and slammed them viciously against the surface of the lake. Jilly responded to my splash by flipping around and letting loose a volley of kicks, soaking my face. I ducked under the water and swam blindly, revisiting what I'd confessed to Justin, just earlier this evening. Keeping my eyes closed, I stayed under until my lungs burned, sinking into a sitting position, letting the water fill my ears and listening to the amplified rhythm of my wounded heart. Because what I'd acknowledged earlier was true…and no matter what I felt, my husband loved somebody else.

Twenty minutes later we clambered up the shore, wet and shivering, Clint and Tish still bickering about something. Mom and Rich sat on the porch having a smoke, illuminated by the muted yellow glow of the outside light. Moths flapped madly against the glass cube encasing the bulb, and about a million mosquitoes whined around our ears; we were sure to be pockmarked with bites by tomorrow.

"Kids, come have some cocoa," Aunt Ellen leaned out the door to invite. My girls, Clint, and Blythe, apparently considering himself one of the kids, all scrambled inside. Jilly helped herself to a smoke from the pack on the table between Mom and Rich and sank, dripping, onto the third chair. I leaned against the railing and inhaled deeply, crossing my arms over my freezing and very alert nipples.

Mom, reading my mind, leaned and grabbed two sweatshirts from the window ledge, tossing one to me and one to Jillian. I shoved my damp, goose-bumped arms inside and zipped it all the way up. Scraping my wet hair over one shoulder, I gave in and shook a cigarette out of the pack. The first drag made me cough a little. On the next I blew smoke out my nostrils, letting the old familiar bad habit relax the tension between my shoulder blades.

"You two have fun?" Rich asked, grinding out his smoke and leaning back with one ankle caught on the opposite knee.

"Yeah, it's great to see everyone," I said, and that was true enough.

"Mom!" came an accusatory voice from inside.

I muttered, "Shit," and moved for the ashtray, but it was too late. Tish appeared momentarily at the screen door, hot chocolate mug wrapped in her hands, and looked pointedly at my fingers. I crushed out the smoke.

"I know, it's just this one," I defended, though there was no excuse; Tish rolled her eyes before heading back inside the cafe. I deserved it; I'd been setting a terrible example for my girls this summer, separating them from their dad, drinking and sleeping late, letting my mother and aunt cook them breakfast, and now smoking. I felt instantly deflated, like just plain giving up. Maybe I should march into the cafe, find Blythe, shove him against the bar, rip down his jeans, and proceed to give him head. It wasn't as though I could do much worse at this low point. For a moment I almost smiled at the naughty absurdity of my thoughts.

"Here, Joelle, you look cold," Blythe said, ducking out the door carrying two mugs. My eyebrows lifted in complete surprise as I accepted one of these from him. He grinned at me, drenched in lake water, long ponytail dripping down his back, standing only a few inches away. A flush spread across my face; I could sense Jilly watching us, but didn't dare look her way.

"Thank you," I whispered.

"Ellen said you love hot chocolate," he elaborated, sipping from his, eyeing me over the rim.

"I do," I agreed, caught off guard by his sweetness, doubly guilty considering what I'd just been imagining doing with him.

"Time to head for the hills," Rich said as he bent to kiss Jilly's cheek. She murmured sleepily, "G'night, Rich, love you."

"Good-night, honey," Rich replied, and stepped around Blythe to give me a good-night kiss, too. Then he put his hand on Blythe's back in a grandfatherly gesture and asked, "You about ready?"

Blythe nodded but didn't look away from me.

Jilly rose, yawning, and banged through the screen door into the cafe. Mom emptied the ashtray in the trashcan around the side of the cafe. Rich headed down the porch steps and Blythe and I were allowed a few unexpected seconds nearly alone. His eyes were unreadable, serious for the first time all evening. I thought about how warm his hand felt when he caught my elbow earlier. I thought again about getting him out of his jeans, though I couldn't be completely certain that my cheating husband wasn't at the root of that.

He said softly, "See you tomorrow, Joelle," and my name on his lips did things to my insides, lovely, desirous, melting things. And suddenly it wasn't about Jackie at all. I wanted to respond, but nothing came forward. I stared up at him and wanted him with an intensity that seared through my body. Something crackled in the air between us, stronger than ever.

"See you," I finally whispered, and Mom approaching from around the far side of porch brought me instantly to reality. Blythe drew his gaze from mine.

"Good-night, Joan," he said politely to Mom, setting his empty mug on the table and then following in Rich's footsteps. I watched, unable to stop myself; Mom went inside and the screen door clacked shut. Just before Blythe reached his truck he turned back and caught me staring after him. He lifted both forearms, bracing them atop his head, his feet falling completely still. My gut instinct was to run straight to his arms, but because I couldn't do that, I blew him a kiss. I did this without thinking, without considering how stupid I probably seemed, but he grinned, wide and joyously. He pretended to catch my kiss, then pressed it to his heart.

Chapter Seven

MORNING SUNLIGHT FELL ACROSS MY FACE AND I SNUG-
gled my jaw into the pillow, thinking, *I'll see him today! I'll see him as soon
as I get to the cafe! He caught my kiss!*

Joelle, stop this, I thought next, rolling to my back and slapping the
pillow over my face. I was thirty-five years old. I was reading too much
into things. Far worse, I was obviously using Blythe as an outlet for
both my bottled-up sex drive and my desire for revenge on my husband. There was no way that anything could happen between us. When
it came down to it, I didn't even know exactly how old he was. He could
be twenty. Good lord. Fifteen years younger than me. And didn't he have
a girlfriend, like Jilly mentioned? What the hell? With these sobering
thoughts in mind, I showered in ice-cold water as a sort of penance for
my thoughts, Puritan-like, and brushed my hair with vigor.

As usual, I was rolling out of bed at about ten-thirty, as though a
teenager with no children of my own. That must end today. And, as responsibility and duty required, I would sit down with the girls this afternoon and explain some things about their dad and me. As I walked along
the sunny shore to the cafe, I considered Justin's advice from last night.
Letting Jackie explain his actions was not a bad idea…but it seemed
cowardly, as though I couldn't face our daughters with the truth. Then
again, Jackie was the one who'd put me in this position. And the bastard
was a smooth talker; Justin was right on the money there.

As though my thoughts conjured him up, I heard a voice call, "Morning, Jo," and looked over to see Justin in the parking lot, just climbing

from his truck. I changed direction and strolled over his way, glad to see him despite everything else crowding for attention in my mind.

"I've been thinking about what you said last night," I told him, catching up as he moved some gear from the cab into the bed. He was in his dirty jeans again, his work shirt, and a Minnesota Wild ball cap.

He slammed the tailgate closed and asked, "About what?"

"About Jackie, and about him talking to the girls. But I feel like he'd mess it up, say the wrong thing. Or spin it to his benefit."

Justin lifted his hat, swiped at his unruly hair and replaced it. He asked, "Would they believe what he said?"

"Yeah, they worship their dad." My tone suggested that I might possibly resent this fact, and I hurried on, "But I don't mind that. I'm glad they have a good relationship with him. I just don't want that shattered, you know?"

"Won't they have to know sooner or later?"

"I know," I said, and didn't have to sigh.

Justin straightened and ordered, "Enough moping. Let's go get some coffee, huh?"

"I wasn't moping," I complained, sounding like Tish in a bad mood.

"You are," he said, over his shoulder.

I jogged to catch up with him, smacking his arm much as I smacked Clint's last night.

"I don't remember you being so judgmental in high school," I said. And then I pestered, "Hey, what did you want to ask yesterday?" I almost prompted him with the words *about Jilly*, but could already see the tension in his posture and was more intrigued by all of this than ever.

"Forget it," he said, and his voice sounded hoarse. He all but stomped up the porch steps and I stood there watching, thinking, *You wish I'm just going to forget it, Miller!* Inside the cafe it smelled like coffee and sweetbread, the air full of animated chatter despite everyone's late night. Mom, Gran, Dodge, and Aunt Ellen were crowded around table two, while Clint attacked a pile of bacon, eggs, and a football-sized cinnamon roll at table three. My girls were lined up at the counter stools with sticky fingers, working their way through a pan of gooey caramel rolls. But Jilly, as Justin and I both immediately noticed (I could tell), was conspicuously absent.

What's up, Jilly? I thought, willing her to hear me. *I* will *get to the bottom of this, you know.*

I made for the coffeepot while the conversation swelled to include Justin, who pulled a chair from Clint's table, swung it around backward, and straddled it. I filled a mug and surveyed my girls, who sat there giggling about something. Tish wore the double set of feather earrings again, all four of which twirled merrily as she spoke. Camille's long hair was arranged in a twist, a purple pen stuck behind her ear, her lips shiny with gloss. Ruthann's curls hung in two braids, making her look more like my baby than ever; she wore earrings, too, I realized with a start, but then recognized the pair as one from Gran's clip-on jewelry collection, which Jilly and I always played with as kids. All three wore neon-tinted jelly bracelets surely gifted to them by Jillian, relics from our middle school collection.

"Good morning, Mom," Tish said with a sarcastic edge. I knew she was mad at me for smoking. I took a sip of my coffee, evading, then reached for the sugar bowl, at once distracted by the sight of Blythe's black truck rolling into the parking lot. My hand twitched in response to my increased pulse, and sugar spilled all over the counter.

I'd blown him a kiss last night.

And he'd caught it.

"Good morning," I murmured in response, tearing my eyes from the incredible view out the window, that of Blythe stepping from his truck and into the sunshine. "Did you guys sleep all right?"

"Yes, and Mom, Dad called this morning," Camille informed me, lining her forearms beneath her breasts on the counter and regarding me with somber hazel eyes. Her long lashes were extra thick with mascara; I reminded myself that she was seventeen and entitled to wear make-up. She said, "He asked me to have you call him."

Again I sipped my coffee to avoid responding. Blythe and Rich were coming across the parking lot now.

Ruthann asked in a small voice, "When is Daddy coming up here, too?"

"Mom doesn't know," Tish said, surprising me. I regarded her warily.

"Tish is right, honey, I don't know," I told Ruthann. All three of my girls sat staring up at me from their stools; three pairs of eyes wide and curious, appearing suddenly much younger than their years. My heart panged with uncertainty. Blythe opened the screen door and called good morning to all of us; I pretended that I did not notice him looking my way. I said softly to my daughters, "Hey, I promise we'll talk tonight, okay?"

Tish pursed her lips as though to disagree, but Camille spoke up, cutting her off. "That's fine, Mom, sounds good."

Aunt Ellen approached the counter and nodded at the spilled sugar, asking, "So, which one of you is falling in love?"

"What?" asked Tish.

"The sugar," Ellen replied. "Whoever spilled it is next to fall in love."

The girls were nearly identical in their perplexity. Ruthann piped up, "It was Mom, Auntie Ellen, who spilled the sugar. But she's already in love," my youngest earnestly explained. "With Daddy."

Her innocent words were a blow in the chest. I forced a laugh and said, "That's right, Ruthie, now where's my apron?" and with that pathetically transparent non-sequitur, began my day.

"You want to head over to the street dance again tonight?" Jilly asked as we refilled the salt shakers after the lunch crowd came and went.

"Yeah, maybe," I said distractedly, messing with a stubborn metal lid on the salt at table three. "Jackie wants me to call him today. I haven't actually spoken to him since before we left. I'm such a coward," I concluded, finally settling the cap in place, salt grains prickly on my fingertips.

"Oh, *whatever*, Jo," Jillian responded. "A coward?"

"No, I'm afraid what he wants is a divorce," I admitted, keeping my eyes on my task. A divorce, and what that would mean for our family, our home, everything, was more than I could bear to think about, let alone discuss. For once Jilly didn't make a smart-aleck comment, but instead squeezed my hand.

After a moment, during which we worked in companionable silence, she murmured, "If you do get divorced, you sure as hell better stay around here."

Late afternoon, I tried Jackie's cell and office phones with no luck, and was not receptive to the idea of leaving a message, despite his warm, familiar voice suggesting I do so after the beep. Our townhouse was the final number, and I let it ring and ring; when at last the machine picked up I heard Camille's recorded voice, with a painfully cheerful lilt, "You've reached the Gordons, and we'd like to know you called, so leave your information."

I squeezed my eyes closed and squeezed the cell phone even harder, my hand slick over its length. God, we'd been happy, once upon a time. Back when Tish and Camille seemed tethered to me by an invisible cord, following me everywhere, their dark curls restrained in pigtails, plying me with a million questions an hour. In those days I'd carried Ruthann in a baby sling and Jackie would come home to find us elbow-deep in pasta or bread dough, cooking something fun for supper. It hurt so much to think that my girls would never be five years old again, or ten. My baby would be a teenager on her next birthday, my oldest an adult.

"Jackie, it's me," I said to his voicemail, keeping my voice light with extreme effort. "Call when you get a chance."

At that moment I heard my two oldest come outside onto the porch. Their sweet voices preceded them onto the dock, where I sat on the glider, and I turned to watch them head my way, both dressed in cut-off jeans and tank tops, Camille's a lacy, spaghetti-strapped, carnation-pink affair, very feminine, and Tish's pitch-black, decorated with neon-green squiggles. I wondered if she'd grabbed that from Jilly's closet; it looked vaguely familiar, and circa 1984. They were obviously coming to have the talk I'd promised at breakfast, and I craned my neck looking for Ruthann to come running behind them. I'd envisioned us sitting on the bed in my room late tonight, in our pajamas, with a single lamp lighting the space, along with a gallon of ice cream and four spoons. But I couldn't put them off yet again.

"Hi, guys, where's your sister?" I asked as their footfalls trembled along the dock. Instead of joining me, they paused a few feet away and made no moves to sit down.

"Inside," Tish said briefly.

"Can we head over to town?" Camille asked. She let her gaze dance across the water in the direction of Landon. I could tell she'd taken great care with her hair and make-up. By contrast, Tish wore zero make-up, and further, I could tell she was wearing her sports bra under her blouse, embarrassed by her breasts, which required a D-cup these days, same as mine. Camille and Ruthie were slightly more petite, built like Jilly, and my tomboy Tish wasn't any too happy about her swelling chest. I bit my lower lip to restrain an amused smile. Tish was curvy as ever; I wanted to assure her that someday she wouldn't mind this fact *quite* so much, but didn't dare voice the thought just now.

"I think we should talk," I finally responded, and observed two nearly identical expressions of dismay move over their faces.

"Mom, we'll talk when we get home," Camille insisted. "Is that all right? We want to go to the street dance. Clint is driving the golf cart over."

Across the lake I could hear the laughter and commotion, music and the snap of an occasional firecracker. I felt the weight of desolation press against my breastbone as I contemplated their lovely, eager faces, ready to head into Landon for an evening of fun, while I sat here and tried not to think about how I was waiting by the phone for their father to call me back.

"That's fine, girls, have fun." I relented without a fight. "Is Ruthie coming with you guys?" *You coward*, I berated myself. But at least this way I could wait to hear what Jackie said before I decided what to tell the girls.

Tish shifted impatiently, standing on the outside edges of her feet, curling them against the boards of the dock, before saying, "She's staying here with Grandma."

"Be careful, please," I told them, reaching out my hands. They knew what I wanted and leaned to let me clasp their faces for quick kisses, Tish rolling her eyes as she allowed the affection. Camille kissed me back and I felt tears threaten again; my daughters looked so grown-up, so beautiful. What I really needed was a good long cry. Not because I felt sorry for myself, not that. Of course not that.

I watched them hurry across the parking lot to the golf cart; Clint kept inching forward so that Tish couldn't quite manage to climb inside. I sighed a little as they finally peeled away, their laughter cascading back to where I sat. Maybe this way we could have our heart-to-hearts when they were home, in my room as I'd originally pictured.

"Jo, you getting hungry?" Mom leaned over the porch rail to call down to me, and I nodded in response, bracing my hands on my thighs to stand.

Aunt Ellen, Mom, and Gran sat at one of the outside tables, watching the sunset color the sky a rich rose-pink. Aunt Ellen had burgers going on the little charcoal grill we kept on the porch; Jilly emerged from inside with four beer bottles hooked between her fingers. She saw me and called over her shoulder, "Ruthann, grab your mom a beer, will you, honey?"

Ruthie appeared seconds later, a Shore Leave apron tied around her waist, curls still arranged into braids. I kissed her freckled cheek as she brought me a beer. "Thanks, miss," I said, smoothing a palm over her soft hair.

"You're welcome," she responded, before jogging down the porch steps to throw a tennis ball for the dogs. I plunked onto the chair near Gran and wilted, relieved that it was just us girls for the evening.

"Jillian told us about the divorce," Gran said without preamble, taking a long swallow of her beer.

I shot my sister an evil look; she gave me the *What do you expect? It's Gran* eyes I knew so well.

"We aren't getting divorced yet," I muttered, and drained the neck of my bottle. The beer was icy cold and flavored with honey, and just what

I needed at the moment to settle the tension lodged at the back of my neck.

From the left, Mom reached to pat my knee and said, "Oh, Jo, I'm glad."

Ellen's back was to us as she stood at the grill, but she looked over her shoulder to contradict, "Joanie, how is the girl supposed to trust Jackson ever again?"

Gran asked me the same question with a pointed expression. Ellen's hazel eyes brimmed with empathy and she said, "Jo, I just don't feel like Jackie deserves you. Not anymore."

"Not ever," Gran added. She raised a small, wrinkled hand to stem the flow of words that my expression surely hinted was coming. "Joelle, he was the best-looking boy in Landon, I admit it. Those eyes, and his easy way of talking. I know you loved the boy. But re-examine the man, honey. You are better off without him. You know it."

My gaze moved away from the truth in hers, flitted over to where my youngest child was laughing in the slanting evening sunlight, engaging Chief in a tug of war with the ball in his mouth. Ruthie was many yards away, safely distant from our conversation. The sun glinted over her shining dark hair that was just like Jackie's.

I felt like I might pitch forward into a faint; my vision wavered, my head spun. But a minute passed and I didn't. Instead I looked back to the table of women who loved me, who would do anything for me, as I would for them. They all watched expectantly, three pairs of golden-hazel eyes and one pair of indigo blue. Mom's lips trembled a little; Jilly's pixie chin tipped down in determination, her lips pressed tightly together.

"I know you're right," I exhaled at last. Gran nodded with asperity. Mom's shoulders fell, but Ellen poked her with the end of the spatula. I whispered, "But it hurts so fucking much."

"Oh, sweetie," Mom murmured, cupping her palm over my knee again.

"Hey, it's Saturday," I said, as though just realizing it, my voice only slightly choked. I needed badly to change the subject.

"Then you and Jillian better get your asses into the kitchen and whip up some margaritas," Gran said.

Chapter Eight

THE FULL MOON WAS A SILVER STUNNER IN THE EBONY SKY. From across the lake, Trout Days roared in characteristic, catastrophic full swing; it was classic rock at the dance tonight, and so "Old Time Rock and Roll" bounced across the water, as clear as though the band was jamming on the porch at Shore Leave. Amazingly, Ruthann lay sound asleep on the ancient porch swing, her snores keeping it engaged in gentle motion, the dogs curled on the floorboards beneath her.

The rest of us, the Davis women, were deep into our third pitcher of drinks, the pitcher a relic as dated as the glider. Many thousands of frothy, golden-yellow, tequila-laced drinks had flowed from its smooth pewter belly. We each claimed our own special glass. Mine was a rippled green-glass goblet with a slender stem, one that would look more appropriate holding jellybeans on a dessert table, but it was what I'd used for this purpose since I was a teenager; Ellen and Mom had always looked the other way, as long as Jilly and I stayed home on our Saturday margarita nights.

"This is the kind of moon that we were under when I first met Mick," Mom was saying, in her classic drunken ramble down memory lane. She leaned back and studied the stars, though they were dim in contrast to the brilliant moonlight washing over our hair.

"Gran, were you ever slutty?" I asked her comfortably, slouching low in my chair, truly curious about the answer. Mom slapped at my shoulder for asking such a question.

Gran, also more than a little sloshed, snorted a laugh and then grew dewy-eyed in the light from the single candle lantern adorning the middle of the table.

"I was," she responded with relish. "Your granddad turned me into a loose woman for a time. If you think Jackson is good-looking, you should have seen him. My, he had a way with his hands."

We all laughed, and Aunt Ellen said, "Aunt Minnie used to say he had a lazy eye, remember, Joanie?" and Mom snorted a laugh, almost sending margarita out her nose.

Gran huffed and responded drily, "No, more like a roving one. He couldn't stay with just one woman any more than he could stay in one town. Your pa was a wanderer. I would have given about anything to hear from him one last time. But I never did."

"Oh, Gran," I said, with nearly-slurred sentimentality, though I'd heard this story about a million times before. I reached for her hand, but she snorted and wouldn't allow me to comfort her.

"No, there's no point crying over spilled perfume, just like that song you like says," Gran grumbled at me.

Jilly asked, "Mom, Clint wondered once if you had a picture of Mick anywhere. Do you?"

Mom continued to study the sky, her gaze dreamy. She said, "I have our engagement picture somewhere, and a few from that summer. He liked to take pictures more than he liked to be in them."

"I wish I had more of Chris," Jilly said then, surprising me. She didn't normally speak of Christopher when she'd been drinking. She went on, "He would be turning thirty-five tomorrow." She glanced at her watch and then amended, "Today, actually."

There was no trace of self-pity or even sadness in her voice; her tone was utterly matter-of-fact, but we all stilled and everyone's gaze settled on Jillian, just as they'd settled on me in my time of need earlier in the evening. Jilly tilted her chin into one shoulder and held the position, clutching the margarita glass to her chest. She said softly, "I just can't stop thinking of him tonight, guys, I'm sorry."

For once Gran was gentle-voiced. She murmured, "Jillian, it's natural, love."

Jilly pressed her mouth hard against her shoulder. I felt my heart pang for my sister; all summer I'd been so busy wallowing in my own problems, selfishly. And she was hurting…time hadn't much dulled it for her, I knew, and my heart constricted again. I loved her so much.

"Jilly Bean, we love you," I said, voicing my thoughts. "We love you so much."

She nodded without speaking. Across Flickertail Lake the music stopped and the night sounds around us were instantly amplified; Ruthann, who'd slept through the last two hours without a flinch, suddenly sighed and shifted restlessly.

"I think it's time for bed," Jilly whispered.

"Do you want to take a walk, Jilly Bean?" I asked, standing with only a little tipsiness and moving around the table to cup her head in my hands. I smoothed her soft, short hair. Aunt Ellen leaned to kiss her cheek, then Mom, before they moved as one to help Gran.

My sister caught my right hand in hers and pressed it to her face. Then she said, "No. Thanks though, Jo."

She helped me cart Ruthann over the path to the house, where we giggled at the difficult process of hauling her inert body up to the third floor. So much for all three girls sitting on my bed for a good long talk tonight. Ruthie mumbled, "I like hearing the drums, Mama," as we tucked her into bed. I bent and kissed her soft round cheek, murmuring, "I love you, honey," and then followed Jilly back down the stairs. Outside, under the full moon, we stood side by side and studied the sky. Mosquitoes whined and buzzed around us, and I slapped at one on my ankle. It was impossibly still, creating the sensation that we were on a sound stage rather than outdoors; the splendid, spotlight-quality of the moonlight only added to that impression. It would be the moment in a play when the lead character revealed a truth or insight.

"Are you worried about the kids? Should I head to town?" I asked at last. I wouldn't drive after consuming so much tequila, but I could certainly walk over to Landon. I craved a walk anyway; my legs were restless, my spirits unsettled. The air seemed electric, unresolved.

"Nah, they're fine, Clinty will bring them home now that the music is done," my sister said. She gave me a long look, seeming resigned. She whispered, "'Night, Jo." And then she turned and made for her apartment, one floor above the garage, without another word.

"Good-night," I called after her retreating figure, feeling a little abandoned. The porch was empty, too; Mom, Ellen, and Gran came in to bed while we carried Ruthann upstairs. I noticed the candle lantern flickering and moved to blow it out, finding Chief still dozing on the porch as I climbed the porch steps, leaving the house in quiet darkness behind me. He thumped his tail and I knelt to rub his shaggy head.

"You wanna take a walk, boy?" I asked him, and he got immediately to his feet, tail flopping like a flag in high wind. Chester, our other lab, must have gone home with Mom. The night air was warm but I pulled the rubber band from my ponytail, letting my hair act as a sort of neck-shield from mosquitoes. I leaned and blew a breath at the candle flame, releasing a tendril of smoke into the night air, and then slipped on the tennis shoes that Mom left on the porch earlier in the evening.

"Come on, buddy," I muttered to Chief, and started for Flicker Trail, hoping I might spy the kids returning from Trout Days. I knew they were more than old enough to navigate the wilds of Landon without me, but it was late, and I was a mother. I couldn't help but worry.

I walked slowly along the familiar path in the darkness, occasionally kicking at a piece of gravel, imagining Jackie at my side on this same stretch of road, holding my hand, encouraging a detour to find a sheltered spot between the trees to make love. I recalled laughing and gasping as I clutched the slim trunk of a maple, bent over, jeans bunched around my ankles, with Jackie behind me, clutching my hips and hurrying to come before we got caught, or too bug-bit. It was a wonder I hadn't gotten pregnant long before senior prom; it was a wonder I hadn't realized back then how we always seemed to end up having sex before anything else, that this was Jackie's number one priority. I sighed then, my gaze falling to the ground, where the ivory moonlight spilled between the trees and created faint leaf-shadows at my feet. The truth was I didn't want to think about Jackie at all; I wanted to think about

Blythe. I wanted to think about Blythe Edward Tilson pressing my kiss to his heart.

Where are you tonight? I thought. *I haven't seen you since you worked at lunch. What are you doing right now? Am I crazy for even wondering?* And I realized painfully, *Yes. And you're probably with your girlfriend, anyway.*

In the next moment I heard the sound of an engine and headlights beamed from around the bend. I was sure it was the kids on the golf cart before I realized it was a much bigger vehicle; its lights bounced over me and Chief and then Blythe braked his truck just a few feet away, his window rolled down. My body seemed to pulse, an electric current of pure and simple need.

You're here! Drunk as I was, and unguarded, I smiled at him with complete joy.

His face lit with an answering smile. He said, "Well hey there. Isn't it a little late for a walk?"

I wanted to say, *I was just thinking about you. I'm so happy you're here, oh God, Blythe, you don't even know.*

But instead I said, "I was worried about the kids."

"Actually, that's why I'm headed over," he said. "The kids want to stay and watch the fireworks. Jim Olson's shooting them off over the lake. I tried calling the cafe, but no one answered."

"Oh," I said, genius-like. "I forgot about the fireworks. Thanks."

He asked, "Do you want to go and watch the show? I'll drive you."

I did, so very much. But I was afraid that if I climbed into his truck the way I was feeling right now, it wouldn't be a good idea for anyone involved. What if I surrendered to the urge to straddle him and dig my fingers into his long hair?

I heard myself ask, "Do you care if Chief rides along?" and nodded at the dog, as though the lab would keep me from doing anything that I should not.

Blythe laughed and said, "Of course not."

I walked around his truck and watched as he leaned to open the door for me. Chief bounded into the tiny backseat, while I climbed more slowly, settling onto the worn seat, absorbing the gift of this time alone with him, with Blythe. The truck smelled like leather and like him. Warm and faintly of cologne, just a hint of something really good. I kept my gaze fixed straight ahead as he reversed and cranked the wheel to head back into town. He drove with his right hand at six o'clock, the other resting lightly on his left thigh.

Blythe turned to look at me from two feet away, and I braved a peek in his direction to find him grinning. My heart splattered against my ribs. He asked, "Did you by any chance pour tequila over your head this evening?"

I heard myself giggle, and asked, "Is it that bad?"

"Saturday margarita night," he understood.

"How do you know about that?" I asked, somewhat astonished.

"Gramps, of course," he replied easily, as he slowed down to turn back onto Fisherman's Street.

The festivities were still going on, lights twinkling, everyone heading for the beach now to claim seats for the fireworks. Blythe drove to the end of the street and parked, and moments later he, Chief, and I made our way along with the crowd. It felt strange walking with him, heady and exhilarating, as though we were a couple. Again I wondered about his girlfriend, and contemplated what she must look like, and if I knew her—she must be from the Landon area. I scoured my drunken mind for images of local girls, and in my foolish preoccupation tripped over an abandoned bottle. Blythe caught my arm in his hand and kept me safely upright.

"Shit, thank you," I told him, embarrassed as hell. He kept his hand curled around my bare upper arm a little longer, studying my profile.

"Anytime," he responded gently, and stroked lightly with his thumb. It was just a flickering touch, but my breath caught. As we started walking again, Blythe stayed just slightly nearer than before, and I was aware of him along every inch of my skin. *He caressed me*, I couldn't help thinking, marveling at this fact. I could not be imagining that touch for anything but what it was, and my belly went weightless with equal parts desire and wonder.

I suddenly realized, *He doesn't have a girlfriend. Jilly was just saying that to try and protect me.*

The beach appeared mobbed in the moonlight, kids still running everywhere despite the late hour. I peered around in vain, searching for my own, but a resounding crack signaled the first of the fireworks, and there was no hope of finding them now. Above the lake, the air exploded in a firebomb of sizzling red sparkles. Cheers absolutely erupted and Chief barked excitedly. Blythe took charge and said, "Come on," leading us through the crowd and to a lone picnic table close to the trees.

It was darker here, slightly away from the rest of the crowd. No one claimed this table because its position allowed for a slightly impaired view of the fireworks over the lake, but I didn't care. The only fireworks I was interested in were occurring inside of me. We sat on the table, bracing our feet against the bench seat. I sat first, allowing Blythe to choose the distance between our bodies; he moved close, his left arm brushing my right. I felt faint and thrilled, terrified and joyous, all swirled together under my breastbone. As the fireworks shot up and over the lake in a continuous radiance of shimmering color, Blythe turned to look at me. He said, leaning close to be heard, "I'm so glad I found you walking."

I couldn't look at him even though I wanted to, my entire body humming and my cheeks practically blistering. I cupped my hands around my bare knees, trying to still the trembling. He allowed no quarter, following these words with a soft, "Thanks for coming with me."

How should I respond? *You're welcome* seemed absurd. I wanted to say, *Blythe, if you only knew what I fantasize about you, if you only knew what I am feeling right now...*

His hand, his strong, warm hand rested against my lower back then, lightly, skimming the edge of my worn blue t-shirt, and he trailed his fingertips along the skin bared there. We were virtually alone, anonymous here in the darkness of my hometown. I couldn't help but gasp a little; his touch sent such trailers of pleasure through my limbs. He felt the trembling in my body, I was certain. Still I couldn't look at him, because if I did I would give in and kiss him, and then all I would want was to make love until I couldn't walk.

"Joelle," he whispered, gently tucking hair behind my ear before pressing a soft kiss to the side of my neck, and I was done for with that touch from his beautiful lips, which I'd watched for weeks now, had dreamed about opening over my nipples.

I lifted my chin just a fraction and he brought his mouth to within an inch of mine, his other hand moving to press against my belly in a wide, warm length. I moaned, softly, leaning into him and then he kissed me, a lush, open-mouthed kiss that sent me melting against him, my hands moving to curl around his huge, hard shoulders. Somewhere within me, where the last bit of my sanity attempted to make a valiant stand, I couldn't believe I was doing this.

Oh God, Blythe, Blythe, I thought, as he suckled gently on my lower lip and wrapped his big hands around my waist, letting his fingers slip beneath the fabric of my shirt to tease my bare flesh. His tongue stroked mine, his mouth more inviting than anything I had ever known. We kissed and kissed, and he moved his hands slowly up my waist, cupping my breasts as I arched my back to invite this, his thumbs finding my nipples beneath my bra. He drew lazy circles over them while his mouth plundered mine and it felt so good. So necessary.

When he drew back I almost collapsed against him, my eyes closed, lips still parted. His words brushing my skin, he said, low and husky, "I've wanted to do that since the night I met you, Joelle."

My eyes flew open. I regarded him with something close to stun, held securely in his arms.

"Don't look so surprised," he laughed, nuzzling warm kisses along my jaw, stroking my loose hair with both hands. I was liquid and fire, all at the same moment. He whispered, "You haven't noticed how much I wanted this moment to happen, huh?"

Still I couldn't form words. I came slowly to my senses and grew suddenly terrified that someone might have spied us…I was still a married woman whose daughters were in this crowd, after all. But the fireworks were still exploding and no one could see us where we sat.

I finally managed, "But how can you…how can that be?"

"What do you mean?" he asked, holding me close, caressing my waist.

"I'm…you're…" I found I couldn't articulate the problem of the difference in our ages.

"Because I'm younger?" he finished for me.

I nodded at last.

"I'm twenty-three," he clarified in his deep voice, though I hadn't asked.

Twelve years, I thought miserably. *I am twelve years older than him.*

"And I've been in jail," he added, soberly. "Gramps said you knew."

"Yeah, I know," I said softly. I wanted to tell him it didn't matter, but of course it did. So many things mattered, but then he kissed me again, and all things reasonable flew swiftly away. For that beautiful moment I let him saturate my senses and kissed him back with total abandon, sliding my hands over his hard torso, down to the vee of his bent legs. He moaned a little, thrilling me…I hadn't heard that sound from a man in way too long, and I wanted it, absolutely craved it. He shifted to accept my left hand as I slid it over the zipper on his jeans, pressing against the ridge of incredible hardness. I wanted him inside me, and that meant I must stop this right now.

"Joelle," he said heatedly, as if somehow sensing my thoughts about stopping this; he crushed me closer, reclaiming my mouth, the interior of his sweet and sleek against my tongue, our hands all over each other, urgent and intense. The last volley of fireworks, the grand finale, was happening now, I could tell, the sky above Flickertail Lake absolutely soaked in bursting color, the full moon like a beacon in the background. As the noise died out and the smoky scent of black powder filled the air, I forced myself to draw slightly away, even though I kept my arms around him. I was shaking and Blythe murmured, "Holy *God*, woman."

"You're so good at that," I whispered, still all shivery.

Blythe grinned at me, hardly an inch away, then tenderly kissed my chin, my jaw, my lips one last time. He whispered, "Can you meet me sometime this week?"

Yes, oh yes, yes, yes…

We can't…this is so wrong…I can't possibly…

"I will," I promised, as we got to our feet and I tugged at my shirt, smoothed my hands over my hair with trembling fingers. Chief wagged his tail, waiting dutifully for me. I patted the dog's head and tried desperately to pull myself together. Blythe rubbed his hand over my back, briefly resting his palm low on my spine.

"Good," he said simply. "Let me know."

We joined the crowd, just two more people who'd enjoyed the fireworks, and hadn't walked more than twenty yards before I intercepted Clint and my girls, tangled in a big bunch of laughing teenagers.

"Hi, Mom!" called Tish, waving and grinning at me, uncharacteristically giddy. I wasn't three feet away before I caught the beer on her breath.

Dammit, this was just what I deserved right now.

Camille detached herself from the group and hurried to my side; if she seemed surprised that Blythe and Chief were both with me, she hid it well. But I was suddenly too angry at Tish to care what anyone might notice. My oldest read my face and instantly began laying the groundwork to cover up for her sister; I knew this technique all too well. Hadn't I used it to cover for my own younger sister a million times in years past?

"She's not drunk, Mom," Camille said right away, but I could see that Clint was, and then I was even more infuriated. Oh, the irony of parenthood. It was a whole new experience to be on this side of the equation, the angry adult who saw clearly what was going on, then immediately projected all of that wrongdoing into a lifetime of potential crime and heartbreak for her daughters and nephew.

"*Goddammit*, Camille," I said. I felt like the world's biggest hypocrite. Blythe, who could have easily distanced himself and headed for his truck, instead moved through the crowd of kids and caught Clint in what appeared to be a brotherly headlock.

"Come on, little buddy," he said, easing Clinty away from his friends, who were hooting and acting obnoxious.

"Mom, she just had one beer," Camille persisted, dogging me as I clutched Tish's upper arm in one hand and propelled her after Blythe and Clint.

Clint leaned on Blythe for support and they made it to the edge of the beach, where the sand gave way to grass, just in time for Clint to double forward and spew vomit in a wide arc. His friends instantly ratcheted up their teasing laughter and commentary, and I yelled in their direction, "I know *all of your parents!*"

"God, Mom!" Tish yelped at me, horrified.

"You are grounded with a capital *G*," I informed her through clenched teeth, meanly pleased to see the group of rowdy kids disperse like ants at my words. I curbed the urge to yell something else after them. The smell of boozy puke hung thick in the air as we caught up with Clint and Blythe. This was a recreation of a hundred thousand of my own teenage nights.

"Hang in there," Blythe told Clint, keeping an arm around the boy's waist, supporting him.

"Mom, I'm sorry," Camille said, breathlessly, probably figuring that as the oldest she was in the most trouble.

"I am in no mood to deal with this tonight," I told my girls, and then took pity on Clinty, who was clutching his belly and groaning softly. I released Tish and patted my nephew's spine.

"Sorry, Aunt Joey," he managed to whisper before another wave of retching engulfed him.

"Not as sorry as you'll feel in the morning," I said, and then to Blythe, "Thank you."

Five minutes later we rounded up the golf cart, which Camille elected to drive home, with me supporting Clint in the backseat, Chief on his far side. Tish rode in front with her sister, eyes forward, an angry set to her shoulders. I bid Blythe a totally platonic and apologetic farewell, insisting that he didn't need to drive us back to Shore Leave. He offered three times, and I could sense his reluctance to walk in the opposite direction, over to his truck but without us. His gaze lingered on me as I herded the kids into the golf cart, and despite the anger churning through me, I let just the thought of meeting him later this week (because surely I couldn't really meet him) fill my soul with a buoyancy unknown to me in a very long time.

Chapter Nine

ONCE IN OUR PARKING LOT, I HELPED CLINT FROM THE golf cart and up the porch steps, unlocked the cafe with the key hidden under a window shutter, and proceeded to brew a pot of coffee. The girls settled their cousin at table three, where he tucked his head into his bent arms and groaned again. Both girls were edgy and I allowed that, not speaking or looking at them as I worked with quiet efficiency, toasting a few slices of bread for myself, spreading peanut butter as my gaze wandered to the kitchen, where Blythe worked. He, Blythe Edward Tilson, wanted to kiss me since the night we met. My hands trembled yet again as I attempted to pour a cup of coffee for Clint. Never in a million years would I have guessed it, especially that first night.

Even Tish's eyebrows were quirked with anxiety as I slipped the mug in front of Clint, then leaned back against the counter between two stools and regarded the three of them with my arms crossed. Camille sat chewing her thumbnail, mascara smudged under her eyes. Tish was obviously stone-sober by this point, watching me as warily as a mouse would a cat, tipping her chair back on its hind legs.

Finally I ordered, "So tell me about tonight."

Tish plunged in, her voice contrite, "Mom, we were just having fun."

I rolled my eyes and asked, "What have we talked about *so many times?*"

Camille said, "It's not like that, really. You know we don't drink, Mom, but Clint's friends had all this beer, and a bottle of whiskey. Tish just drank one beer, seriously. I only had a sip, I don't even like beer. And the whiskey smelled like paint thinner, it was disgusting, but the guys were doing shots."

I sensed she was telling me the truth and said, "Well, that explains Clint."

He groaned at the sound of his name, and mumbled, head still cradled in his arms, "Aunt Joey, *please* don't tell Mom."

"You are shitfaced drunk, young man," I observed, forcing a stern tone—Clint would be so hungover tomorrow it was probably punishment enough, but for good measure I added, "Tell me why this won't happen again, or I will go and wake up your mother this moment."

Clint lifted his head at that, wincing at the motion, and said, "It won't happen again, I promise, Aunt Joey."

I finally sat down across from my nephew and took one of his hands in both of mine. His hands were big, and all knuckles. I folded his fingers into mine and said quietly, "Your mom would die if anything ever happened to you, you know that don't you?"

Clint's eyes welled, and my own responded at once, but I blinked back the tears and whispered, "It's your dad's birthday, and so you need to be extra good to your mom tomorrow, okay?"

He wiped his eyes with his free hand, and I knew he was truly sorry. He whispered, "I will, I promise."

I suddenly pictured Christopher, perpetually good-natured Chris, leaning over this same table, teasing my sister, chatting with Gran, drinking Dr. Pepper from a can; Clint looked so much like him. I could still hear Chris's easy laugh and almost shuddered at the pain of the memory. The girls fell silent, motionless, alternating between studying Clint and me, not entirely certain what I was thinking but sensing its seriousness. They had never known their uncle; he was robbed from our lives so early. It was so fucking unfair.

Tish took advantage of the calm to reenter the conversation with a vengeance, asking, "Mom, where is Dad this summer? Can you please just answer? Why is he being so weird when we talk to him on the phone?"

My future lawyer, who would accept nothing less than a straight answer. I regrouped and said, "Tish, I meant to talk with you, all of you girls, earlier tonight."

"No time like the present," Camille murmured, but not in a snotty way, still worrying her thumbnail between her front teeth.

I gulped and then plunged headfirst, even though Clint listened avidly, too.

"Girls, Dad and I are separating. He's been seeing someone else," I said, and released a sigh that bubbled up from the bottom of my heart.

A force field seemed to spring into existence in the air surrounding us. I battled the urge to get up and escape to the house, to avoid the stunned pain in their eyes, the avalanche of questions I could sense coming; just a little pebble-sized ice chunk now, but…

Tish cried breathlessly, "What? Who?" She gained momentum and demanded, "Is it someone we know? Mom, how come you didn't tell us? Dad's having an *affair*?"

Camille directed her gaze at the tabletop and spoke quietly, but I heard her even over Tish's brimming anger. She said, "I knew it, Mom, I knew it."

"You knew?" Tish stormed at her big sister, betrayed all over again. "How come *you* didn't say anything? What in the hell?"

I asked, "You guessed? Oh Milla, I'm so sorry, I should have—"

But she interrupted, finally looking up and into my eyes, whispering, "No, I saw him. And that stupid woman he works with."

My heart stuttered painfully.

"Where?" I managed to ask, thinking, *Don't let it be at home, oh God, please…*

"They were at Gioco's," she said, naming a popular Chicago restaurant. "I was walking by with Payton and Cara, and we saw them. They were holding hands. It was last Thanksgiving break." Tears gushed over her face and I moved quickly, taking her into my arms as she gave over to weeping.

"Oh, sweetie," I said, stroking her soft, curly hair as I hadn't in ages, a part of me grateful that she let me comfort and hold her just now—two things she'd not much allowed since her advent into the teen years.

"Mom, I should have told you," she choked out, pressing her face against the belly of my t-shirt and sobbing even harder, and I damned Jackie for putting her through all of this.

"No, no, don't think that," I reassured, planting a kiss on the crown of her head. Tish simmered down and lowered her face onto her arms, reminiscent of Clint's earlier pose. He, poor boy, sat with both hands wrapped around the mug of cooling coffee, eyebrows drawn into a look of total discomfort. Well, that couldn't be helped now.

"I found out around the same time," I told Camille, as her sobs eventually subsided to shaky gasps. I reached to cup my other hand around Tish's bent head, patting her. I confessed, "I didn't know what to do. I haven't felt better until we came here, to tell you the truth."

Tish asked, her voice muffled, "Are you guys getting divorced?"

I bit the insides of my cheeks and at last admitted, "Probably, honey."

Camille began weeping again and exhaustion dragged at my limbs. But I couldn't surrender to bed just yet. I gently rocked my oldest side to side.

Tish observed, "Ruthie is gonna be really upset, Mom." She lifted her face and I saw that her eyes brimmed with moisture, but she continued staunchly, "Can we move here, then?"

"I don't know, honey, I really don't."

Clint chimed in at last, adding, "That would be *so* great, Aunt Joey. Mom would be so happy. I would, too."

I caught sight of the clock over the kitchen pass-through; quarter to two, and I was about to collapse. Camille sniffled and sighed, sounding like a little girl, and then pulled gently away, knuckling her eyes.

"I'm ready for bed," she said through a plugged nose.

"Aren't we all," I agreed, and dumped the rest of the coffee into the sink.

Alone in bed twenty minutes later, my face scrubbed clean and coated with moisturizer, I allowed myself to revisit kissing Blythe. Immediately my belly seemed poised at the top of a roller coaster, soaring, and I curled around it, cupping my breasts and caressing my nipples with my thumbs, scarcely able to believe that Blythe, gorgeous, hunky, young Blythe Tilson, held and kissed me like that.

Joelle, I despaired, angry and so aroused, conflicting emotions rioting within me again. Despite the aching tiredness weighting my body, and the emotional upheaval I'd been through with the girls, I longed for his hands back on my body.

When the cell phone on my nightstand suddenly buzzed with an incoming call, I startled as though someone had smashed a gong at the foot of my bed. Heart clanging, I groped for it, thinking it was Jackie finally returning my call. But the number was one I didn't recognize. Softly, so not to wake Gran, I whispered, "Hello?"

"Did I wake you?" came a deep voice. It sounded like he was smiling and my heart pounded even more fiercely.

"No, actually," I murmured, pulling the covers over my head like a naughty child, snuggling up with the phone, with his husky voice.

"Is Clint all right?"

"Yeah, he's okay. I just got them all to bed."

"How about you?" he asked next, definitely smiling. I exhaled in a trembling rush and Blythe added, "I can't stop thinking about you."

How could this be real? I marveled anew, and heard myself admit, "I'm thinking about you, too."

"I'm glad," he responded. "When are we meeting this week?"

My blood hummed with the thrill, the disbelief of it all. I dared to confess, "I wish you were out in the parking lot right now."

I heard him inhale. He whispered intently, "Oh God, I can be there in five minutes." He said at once, as though worried about offending me, "I'm kidding. But soon, then."

"Yes," I whispered back.

"Good-night, Joelle," he said, low and sweet-voiced, and I trembled all over again.

"Good-night," I murmured, and hung up, then rolled to my back and smiled, wide, up at the dim ceiling.

Chapter Ten

THE NEXT MORNING I WAS JOINED IN THE BATHROOM BY my period, earlier than I'd expected it this month. *Fantastic,* I thought, brushing my teeth and glaring at myself in the mirror. Talk about a reality check. It was an obvious sign that I should not be entertaining the thought of amazing sex with Blythe. Or, for that matter, any man who was not my lawfully-wedded husband and father of my children. As the hot water of the shower poured over me minutes later, I leaned into the spray, both hands pressed flat to the tile, torn. *Head versus heart…*I knew what I wanted to do, and what I must do, and they were so very opposite. I held my breath until my lungs nearly burst, keeping my face within the water, until it finally ran cold.

Outside, the air was thick with June humidity, the sky leaden as I made my way to the cafe, angry at myself for being so fluttery; I debated what to wear for nearly twenty minutes. My hair hung loose and soft over my shoulders, and I wore mascara at this ungodly hour of the morning. But I was also simultaneously crackling with anticipation at the thought of seeing Blythe. Would anyone suspect? What if I stared at him too long and Mom wondered? Or Jillian, more likely. Mom loved us, but she tended more toward the oblivious than the observant. My sister would smell a rat long before our mother.

"Good morning!" Jilly called from the porch, where she sat sipping coffee. I studied her closely as I climbed the steps, but she didn't appear too stressed out (considering that today was Chris's birthday, I took particular notice), nor was she looking at me knowingly. The memory of

Blythe's kisses burned so strongly in my mind that I felt as though my lips were branded and would surely betray me to anyone looking.

"What time did the kids get back last night?" she asked, motioning with her head for me to join her. I did, commandeering her cup for a sip.

"Late," I hedged. I knew Clint would be feeling miserable enough this morning without me tattling on him. He'd been sincerely sorry last night, I knew.

"How about you?" Her tone seemed deceptively innocent.

Shit. She suspects. I sipped again, biding my time, but when I met her gaze, Jilly was staring off across the parking lot. I turned to follow her eyes, my heart suddenly awake and throbbing, but it was Justin and Dodge pulling in for breakfast, not Blythe. Not yet.

"Hi, girls," Dodge called, his sunglasses pushed up on his forehead. Justin, his own shades still in place, followed behind, silently.

"Morning, guys," I said, smiling at them. Dodge lumbered inside, calling hello, while Justin paused at our table. I gave him the once-over and asked, "A little under the weather this morning, Mr. Miller?"

He winced and said, half-kiddingly, "Don't ask."

"I saw you heading into Eddie's last night, buddy," I said. I hadn't said anything because I'd been with Blythe, but decided against mentioning this particular fact.

Jilly snapped her gaze back to me; she'd been quietly assessing Justin's face. She asked, "You went into town?"

There was no point lying. I wouldn't be telling the whole truth, in any case. I admitted, "Yeah, I saw the fireworks."

Her lips parted to ask another question, but to my relief the screen burst open and Ruthann bounded out, the cordless phone from the counter in her right hand.

"Mom, it's Daddy!" she said breathlessly, sounding happy and excited, catching me right the hell off guard. If I was apprehensive to tell my two older girls about their father and me, I was downright terrified to inform Ruthann. I stared at the phone in her hand as though it was a spider she'd caught and held out for me to touch.

Jilly's golden eyebrows crooked in concern and Justin pushed back his sunglasses, revealing blood-shot brown eyes, also sympathetic. Ruthie wiggled the phone at me, smiling. I finally reached to accept it and Jilly said with forced brightness, "Ruthie, come with me and let's get another muffin, huh?"

I walked directly back down the porch steps I'd just climbed, and made for the dock. I put the phone to my ear and said, affecting a cheerful tone, "Hello?" Questioningly, as though I didn't know who was on the other end.

"Hi, Jo," said my husband, and his voice was as familiar as always. Not so warm anymore, though.

"Hi," I said again. I waited, but no tears threatened.

"How's the summer going?" Jackie asked, and his voice sounded slightly deeper than normal, as if there was something stuck in his throat; I couldn't quite read the emotion present in his tone.

"Great," I replied, reaching the end of the dock, too restless to sit. The sky appeared the color of an old tin teakettle, and as I watched, a blue-white flash of lightning sizzled in the west. Seconds later a low grumble resonated from the same direction. I clarified, "Fantastic, actually."

"Great," he said, sounding relieved now. He cleared his throat and then added, "Sorry I didn't call you yesterday. I got your message."

I waited silently, not about to help him out.

"The girls sound happy," he observed after a pause. "I miss them around here."

"I know you do," I allowed. He was a good dad to them, I couldn't pretend otherwise.

It began to sprinkle and I shivered, but was not about to return inside right now.

"What's up, Jackie?" I finally asked. Lightning threatened again, more brilliantly than before.

"Jo," he said in his lawyer voice, a much different tone now. "I am going to get married."

All of the breath seemed to leave my lungs. Thunder rolled through the sky, rumbling like the indignant rage coming to a boil inside my chest. Heavy raindrops peppered the lake. Keeping my voice tightly controlled, I said, "I hate to tell you, but you're already married."

"Dammit, Jo, don't be like this. You left me. It's over between us."

Despite the fact that I knew this to be true, it still hurt like hell to hear Jackie speak so bluntly. Anger coiled like a living thing inside of me; I could not help but picture Lanny's long legs wrapped around his hips as he did her on his office desk. I hissed through clenched teeth, "I left because you *cheated on me.*" I refused to add, *You fucking asshole.*

"And I'm sorry I hurt you, Jo," he fired right back. "I never wanted to and I am goddamn sorry. But I can't change how I feel. I love Lanny. I'm going to marry her."

I felt kicked in the gut. This was my children's father talking to me like this. But it was no time to feel sorry for myself, not right now. I clung to the shred of pride afforded me by Gran's genes. "You'll be happy with that slut, I'm sure," I said, spitting out the words. Rain fell heavily now, and I should probably be worried about getting electrocuted, standing here with an antenna phone in my grasp, hair plastered to my neck. I yelled, "You two fucking deserve each other!"

"Jo, for Christ's sake!" he said. "It doesn't have to be like this!"

"Really, Jackson, how should it be?" I demanded. There was no chance anyone up in the cafe could hear me, what with the thunder.

"What is that noise?" he asked then, sounding perplexed. "Are you washing clothes?"

"No, it's raining, you moron," I said, descending now into name-calling. So much for keeping my cool.

"Nice, Joelle, let's be like this," he said, drippy with sarcasm. "I'll call later when you're not being such an unreasonable bitch!"

"Bitch?!" I shrieked. "*Unreasonable!* How dare you!"

But he'd hung up. Without thinking, I whirled and threw the phone as hard as I could into the lake. I closed my eyes, tipped my head back and let the rain wash over my face, much like I'd done earlier in the shower, as though I could somehow be washed clean of all disappointment, all mistakes. *If only.* At first I thought it was thunder making the dock tremble violently, and felt a flash of fear, my eyes flying open. But in the next second, warm, strong hands wrapped a raincoat over my shoulders; Blythe gently turned me around to face him.

He was such a welcome sight, even as angry and shredded-up as I felt right now. His hair hung in a ponytail, bandana in place, shirt clinging to his huge shoulders in the downpour, his somber blue eyes holding mine. He leaned close to say, "Come on, Joelle, you need to get out of the rain."

I heard the tenderness of my name on his lips.

"Thanks," I whispered, and let him lead me back into the cafe.

Five minutes later Jilly herded me into the passenger seat of her car, the two of us suddenly bound on an impromptu trip to the Walmart in Bemidji. Mom claimed to need a dozen things that we couldn't possibly buy at the co-op in Landon. Figuring she was being helpful by offering a distraction (clearly they all knew I'd been talking to Jackie), Mom practically shoved Jilly and me out the door.

"You know, we've had that phone since we were in high school," my sister said, sounding serious. "I was kind of attached to it."

"I didn't mean to chuck it," I said, half-resentfully, watching the drenched landscape flash by out the window, the southbound lane heavy with traffic: trucks hauling boats with outboard motors, cars with luggage racks strapped on top, enormous RVs loaded with families heading back to Minneapolis after a weekend of camping.

"So, what did he say?" she pressed.

I hadn't been exactly forthcoming after Blythe opened the door to Shore Leave for me, his eyes on my face. I sensed his reluctance to go to work as though nothing had happened between us last night, without so much as being able to talk privately, but we didn't have a choice. Ruthann was eating breakfast at the counter (the three older kids were certainly still in bed) while Jilly worked to keep everyone involved in conversation, attempting to ignore me as politely as possible. My instinct was to retreat to my own bed, but then Mom trumped up the necessity of a trip to the supermarket, and Jilly summarily forced me into the car.

I looked over at my sister, wanting suddenly to tell her everything about last night, and how amazing it was kissing Blythe. About how I felt crazy with longing to meet him this week, and make love all night.

Again, just the thought made my stomach light as cottonwood puffs on the June breeze. The last thing I wanted to discuss was my cheating husband who wanted to get remarried. Stalling, I said, "I'm sorry about the phone, Jills."

"Fuck the phone," she said, rolling her eyes. "What did Jackie want?"

"He wants to marry Lanny," I said, pressing four fingertips to my forehead.

"Really," Jillian said, her voice ripe with scorn. "Well, let him. What a bastard."

"You know, he really thinks he loves her," I added, not sure if I was sticking up for him or just torturing myself. "And you know what, I hope he's happy. She just better be good to the girls when they visit, or I'll kill her with my bare hands."

Jilly angled a glance my way. She said carefully, "You seem okay with it."

I shrugged, looking back out the window. I was still wrapped in the raincoat that Blythe brought me on the dock, and snuggled into it a little more, hugging myself. I was totally unprepared for Jilly's next statement.

"Jo, I made love with someone," my sister whispered, and my head whipped around as though magnetized to the opposite side of the car. Jilly kept her gaze fastened out the windshield.

If it's Blythe I will come unglued, I thought, irrationally, my heart clanging. I could hardly form a word past the ball that had suddenly lodged in my throat. But Jilly continued, still looking away from me, "With Justin."

All of my tension drained abruptly, replaced by surprise. And then I thought, *Of course*.

Her voice low and intense, she rushed on before I could speak. "He and I sat on the dock one night, just about a week before you and the girls got here. It was Saturday margarita night and we were talking about old times. Oh God, and then we kissed."

"And?" I pressed, poking her in the ribs.

"He was so passionate. It was amazing, Jo, oh God, it was so good."

"And?" I asked, and applied my pointer finger to her ribs a second time, for good measure. I was thrilled at these revelations; to the best of my not-inconsiderable knowledge, Jilly hadn't made love with anyone since Christopher.

"Ugh, don't," she bitched at me, flinging an elbow in my direction. "And nothing. I don't know why I tell you shit!"

I knew she wasn't really angry, so I bent my finger and flicked her earlobe. Just to pester her, I added a third, "And?"

She whispered, "We made love right on the dock. I mean, Justin spread out his shirt for us to lay on first, and then…Oh God, Jo, but now I—"

"Jilly, don't beat yourself up," I interrupted, laying off the teasing, knowing she was upset because of Chris. I knew how much she loved her husband, and I knew she still felt like she was cheating on him, even over a decade later. I insisted, "You *know* you have a right to be happy."

She shook her head vehemently. "It's not that, truly. Oh God, making love with Justin was so incredible, so *right*, I can't even describe it. I didn't feel guilty about Christopher, it wasn't that. It was afterwards, the next day I mean…Justin was angry at me, actually *angry*, thinking I… took pity on him."

"He said that?" I cried, louder than I'd intended.

"He didn't have to," she said softly, finally turning to look at me. "When I saw him after work that day he was so remote, and when I got him alone he told me I didn't *owe* him anything, and that we'd made a mistake by making love."

"He did?" Just as swiftly, I was furious for her. "What the hell?"

"He's protecting himself, don't you see?"

Suddenly the little things I noticed between her and Justin made far more sense, puzzle pieces falling into place.

"It's been terrible. He hardly shows up at the cafe anymore," she said. "No one suspects anything, so please don't say a word. Well, Gran suspects. And I guess Blythe does, too…"

"He does?" I asked, surprised at this revelation.

"Yeah, he's hung out with Justin and me a few times, when he first got to Landon back in April. He said something at Trout Days, he was all like, 'Nice try,' when I tried to act like I didn't care if Justin was there or not."

I realized I couldn't appear to care so much about what Blythe thought. I steered the conversation back to safer territory, saying, "Well, I suppose now I can tell you that Justin wanted to ask me something about you that night. He was staring at you while we danced, but then he disappeared as soon as the song ended. It makes sense, now." I added, "I hate that he's hurting you this way."

"He's not hurting me," she insisted. "I mean, he is, but not how you mean. He's just so afraid of feeling something for me that he's purposely pushing me away."

"But he could at least listen to you, believe what you say," I said. "It's all because of his scars."

"Well, *yeah*," she said, emphasizing that I stated the obvious.

"Would you want to date him? God, that's crazy to think about you and Justin after all these years. What would Clint think?"

Jilly said softly, "Clint loves Justin, he always has. And I want to date him, I want to see where a relationship between us would go, more than about anything. That's what was freaking me out last night. Today is Christopher's birthday but all I could think about this morning was that I was worried about Justin drinking too much last night."

I floundered for a response, not wanting to say the wrong thing. I finally concluded, "That's all right, you know."

"All I can think about is Justin, and it's been that way for a long time," she said with an air of confession, sounding so guilty that my own troubles seemed pale, even ridiculous, in comparison. And I had far more to be guilty about, when it came down to it. She whispered, "He was *so* passionate that night, it was so beautiful. We couldn't get enough of each other, we made love five times, oh God, at least. And then he…oh, Jo, he let me touch his scars. It was almost more intimate than anything else."

I felt a sharp pang for her, imagining the scene as she'd described it, Justin letting down his guard that way, and then turning from her the next day.

"You know I like Justin," I said. "I always have. He's a good guy who's been through a lot of shit the last few years. But if he can't acknowledge the truth about how you feel, about how *he* feels, if he's that bitter..."

"But I haven't told him how I really feel," Jilly protested in a painful whisper. "I just *want* him, I want him so fucking much..."

I knew that feeling well—hadn't I been torturing myself over Blythe, the exact same way?

"*Jillian*," I interrupted again, hearing the depth of feeling in her voice. "You have to tell him the truth."

She shifted gear, slowing as we took the exit onto Paul Bunyan Drive. She sighed and then changed the subject, inquiring, "Do you really want to go to Walmart?"

"Yes, I need tampons," I said.

Chapter Eleven

By EVENING THE STORM CLEARED OUT, LEAVING THE AIR
washed clean, fragrant with June roses and pine needles. The sun appeared beneath a lingering ridge of cloud, casting jeweled light over the
lake. The dull gray that permeated everything since morning was instan-
taneously shattered by the rays, igniting emerald and sapphire and topaz
fire on the surface of the water.

Jilly and I did double duty at the cafe after getting home from Bemidji; with Trout Days over, the usual crowd reappeared at Shore Leave.
Rich and Blythe were busy in the kitchen and every time I sent an order
back, I had an excuse to look at Blythe, to smile into his eyes (as long as
no one else was looking), and bask in the warmth of his gaze in return. I
was only distracted from him for a few minutes, when Tish, Camille, and
Clint, all three lounging down by the dock, were joined by a teenaged
guy I didn't know; that in itself wasn't alarming. The fact that he wrapped
one arm in a familiar way around Camille's waist and planted a kiss on
her temple, however, was.

The porch tables were overloaded on this resplendent evening, loud
with the chatter of customers admiring the lake; I stood with a tray of
beer balanced over my left forearm and just by chance observed this
exchange from my vantage point. Camille turned to face this guy, laughing with him in a private way that suggested she knew him pretty damn
well; I watched as he linked their fingers, gliding to the rail for a better
view before I realized I'd moved. The mother in me wanted to march
straight down to the lake, grab this kid's ear and demand a few answers,

but the four-top expecting their beer called over to me, and I was forced to wait until the rush died out. Besides, I reflected, I harbored no desire to embarrass my daughter; what I felt most strongly just now was plain and simple hurt, similar to the throb of a new bruise on your shin bone. Why hadn't I heard about Camille's boyfriend from her? Or from Tish? Tish was my middle child, my future lawyer, a self-appointed informant. I tried not to let a feeling of betrayal overwhelm my sensibilities.

"Jilly, who is that guy who got here earlier?" I asked the moment her section calmed.

"What guy?" she asked, craning her neck to check out the crowd still seated both in and outside the cafe. "One of my customers?"

"No, that guy outside with Clint and the girls," I elaborated, dragging her to a window, pointing at the four of them playing fetch with Chief and Chester.

"Oh, you'll never believe who that is," she laughed.

"Who? You know I hate guessing," I complained, watching him intently.

"It's Ben Utley's little brother," she said, naming a classmate of ours from high school.

"No kidding?"

"His name is Noah," she said. "He must be eighteen or nineteen, now...he doesn't normally hang out with Clinty..." Her expression shifted from speculation as understanding dawned. She pursed her lips as my daughter and Noah collided, laughing, and struggled playfully in the evening sun. She murmured, "*Ohhhh.*"

"*Right,*" I said, and accepted that I sounded a little too much like our own mother.

"You want to go meet him? Just let me grab another round for ten and then I'll introduce you."

I followed Jilly outside, my insides hopping with anxiety. Camille, to my knowledge, had never actually had a boyfriend. And I always trusted, *blindly* apparently, that even if Camille didn't immediately confide in me, Tish would give away the news for the simple joy of pestering her big sister. But my girls were clearly just as protective of one another's secrets as Jilly and me.

"Noah, this is Camille and Tish's mom, my sister Joelle," Jilly said after we joined them on the shore. The dogs scattered as Clint chucked the tennis ball into the lake. Camille looked just the tiniest bit apprehensive as she observed me openly assessing Noah Utley. He was a younger version of his brother Ben, who I'd known fairly well in high school; same lanky build, same light scattering of freckles across the summer tan on his face, close-cropped golden hair and baby-blue eyes. Almost angelic-looking. He smiled easily at me and offered a hand.

"Nice to meet you," I murmured, shaking with him. Camille, just behind his shoulder, sent me a warning with her eyes; she was not oblivious to the tone in my voice, an expert at hearing between the lines of my words. Noah appeared innocent enough but he was really good-looking, a charmer as I could already tell, and had no doubt been trying to talk my daughter out of her bikini since the beginning of June, without me suspecting a thing. *Jeez, Joelle,* I reprimanded. *When did you become such a hag?* I forced myself to remember that not all teenagers behaved the way Jackie and I used to behave.

"You, too," Noah said pleasantly.

"How are your parents?" asked Jilly. "I haven't seen them out here in a while."

"Fine," he responded, now directing his smile in Jilly's direction. A man of few words, then.

"Ben just took over for Curt," Jilly told me. Curt was Ben and Noah's father, a dairy farmer near Landon since the time of Gran and Great-Aunt Minnie's salad days.

I asked, "What are your plans, Noah?"

Camille with the warning look again.

Noah asked, innocently, "For tonight or do you mean, like, life plans?"

Ha, ha. What a joker. My mind was at once flooded by a noise like that of a small plane's engine just before the crew began yelling *mayday.*

"Mom, we were hoping to take out the paddleboat," Camille jumped in, her tone just shy of outright pleading.

I decided, though reluctantly, to back off; it was apparent that Clint and Tish planned to accompany the two of them, and if any two people could stop romance in its tracks, it was my nephew with his hee-hawing laughter and Tish with her sarcasm.

"Go, have fun and don't stay on the water past dark," I told them.

"Thanks, Mama," Camille gushed, trotting out her oldest name for me. I tried to pretend it was not any sort of manipulation. She leaned and kissed my cheek, and I was assaulted by a rush of tenderness, thinking of holding her as she cried last night. And I found myself wondering what Noah knew about her feelings. Did he know more than me? Did Camille tell him things? Was he aware of how she was hurting this summer, that her dad was all but choosing another woman over his family?

"You, too," I told Tish, reaching for her, and she grumbled but allowed a quick hug, before the four of them ran off, pursued by the dogs.

An hour later the crowd at Shore Leave dwindled to two bar tables and an older couple from Landon, chatting with Aunt Ellen and Jilly as they all sipped gin-and-tonics, another favorite summertime drink. Mellow, rose-tinted clouds melted into a rich amber sunset, catching my gaze as I paused at the porch rail, tables empty at last, leaning my hips against the railing to untie my apron. Down by the lake Clint and Noah hauled the paddleboat out of the water, laughing about something with the girls, these sounds intermingling with the gentle murmur of voices from within the cafe; Mom and Ruthann sat at table three rolling silverware, along with Gran. Chester and Chief relaxed under the porch swing. I sighed.

"I was so worried about you this morning," Blythe suddenly said, coming from around the side of the cafe, carrying his work apron. He approached to within a foot and a half, then leaned beside me and looked out in the same direction, across Flickertail to the sunset. I, however, could not tear my gaze from his profile. He stood with shoulders hunched slightly forward, curling his big hands over the top railing. It remained stunning to me that less than twenty-four hours ago I'd been wrapped in his arms. My heart beat swiftly; probably he could hear it from where he stood.

It struck me what he'd said, that he was worried about me, and I asked, "You were?"

He angled a glance my direction, though I could sense he was trying to appear nonchalant. I wanted so much to put my left hand over his right, where it rested on the railing. "Of course," he said, sounding as though he couldn't believe I didn't realize. Watching me, he explained, "I got here this morning just when you were heading out to the dock, on the phone with…Jackson." His pause indicated he was hesitant to admit he knew I'd been talking with my husband. He drew a deep breath and continued, "And then it started raining and I could tell you were freaking out, and I couldn't do anything about it. Finally I had to bring you a raincoat, I couldn't stand it anymore…"

He trailed off while I listened, again with open surprise.

"Oh, Blythe," I whispered, a lump of emotion suddenly bulging in my throat. Speaking his name felt so good I almost said it again.

He went on, his voice slightly hoarse, "I know it couldn't possibly do any good, but I would love to knock out that son of a bitch for you, Joelle. Gramps told me the whole story—I'm sorry, but I asked him about it, and I've talked to Jilly about it, too. I mean, after what he's done to you and his kids…"

"Mom! Grandma said I could sleep over with the triplets!" Ruthann called from inside, at that very inopportune moment. Seconds later she popped out the pass-through door, beaming. I turned to gather her into a hug, my youngest, who was always so quick to offer affection. I rocked her side to side, contemplating Blythe's sincere words and yet unwilling to allow Jackie to intrude upon any of my precious, finite time near Blythe.

"When, honey, tonight?" I asked Ruthie, seeing Mom following in her wake, clutching a green tub of silverware against her belly. Ruthie's hair was braided, a couple of clover flowers tucked behind her ear. She appeared so little, my baby in so many ways. I cupped her soft cheek, and her golden-green eyes, the Davis family eyes, shone into mine as she nodded happily.

"Jo, Liz called and asked if Ruthann would like to come over. They're having a bonfire," Mom explained.

"Sure, that's fine," I told Ruthie.

"I was just heading back to town, I could drive you two," Blythe offered, with admirable calm.

Ruthann scrambled from my arms as my heart rate at once increased. My back to the cafe, I studied Blythe's expression; he held my gaze for a fraction of a second and the heat that thrummed constantly between us seemed to pulse.

"That would be great," I said, just as off-handedly.

"But how will you get back out here, Jo?" Mom asked.

Again Blythe was ready with an answer, explaining, "It'll be perfect timing for me to come and pick up Gramps. We drove together."

"True." Mom shrugged, then turned to call after Ruthann, "Be sure to grab your toothbrush, little one!"

Alone again with Blythe my body temperature continued to rise. He let a more self-satisfied grin play over his lips, lowering his chin just slightly and giving me a long look with his smoky-blue, long-lashed eyes. *Holy hell.* I tried to draw a full breath, but could not. He grinned even more deeply, seeing my agitation.

"Thanks," I whispered.

He murmured, "Anytime," and then shoved gracefully away from the porch rail.

Ruthann and her overnight bag shared the space in the middle of the bench seat of Blythe's big truck. We drove with the local country station playing, and Ruthie, excited to be attending a party to which her big sisters were not invited, sang along with Trisha Yearwood, with characteristic gusto. Blythe smiled at me over the top of her head as he navigated Flicker Trail, his right hand at six o'clock on the steering wheel, just like before.

"You're a good singer," he told Ruthann.

"I always sing with the radio!" she paused briefly to say.

"She and Camille are the songbirds," I explained to Blythe. "Ever since they were little. Tish, not so much."

Ruthie giggled, saying, "I'm telling her!"

I laughed at this threat. "She knows she can't sing. It's no secret."

"Mind if I join in?" Blythe asked, and even before Ruthie spoke he sang gamely along.

"Hey, you're good!" she told him.

Blythe turned onto Fisherman's Street and we were close to Liz and Mark Worden's street; not that Landon was particularly difficult to navigate, but I directed Blythe to their split-level. As we parked we could already hear laughter rolling from the backyard, and seconds later the triplets (I still didn't have their names straight) flew around the corner of the house, drawn by the sound of a vehicle. There were two girls and a boy, one of the girls gripping a marshmallow roasting stick. I made a sound of protest just as her father appeared, on their heels.

"Jo!" he called in welcome, catching his wayward child and scolding, "Fern, you'll take your eye out! Not to mention someone else's!"

"Hi, guys!" Ruthie called, immediately swept into their crowd.

Mark Worden, who I'd known since grade school and who we always called Wordo, jogged over and scooped me into a bear hug; he was now married to Justin's little sister Liz, but had two kids from a previous marriage, in addition to his and Liz's triplets; from the sound of things, all of the kids were here this evening.

"Moved home finally, huh, Jo?" Wordo asked, reaching to shake with Blythe.

"For the summer at least," I said, smiling at Liz as she pushed out the screen door, loaded down with chocolate bars and graham crackers.

"You two want some s'mores?" she offered. "Thanks for letting Ruthann come over, Jo, the kids have been begging."

"Oh, it's great," I said. "Tish and Camille have made a lot of friends but Ruthie doesn't have as much opportunity."

"How about a couple beers, you two?" Wordo offered.

Though I knew it would be fun to hang out, I also knew that Blythe and I had very limited time this evening, and I was not about to waste one speck of it.

"Thanks, guys, but Blythe drove us over and we need to get back to the cafe," I said. "Rich doesn't have a ride otherwise."

"Okay, no problem," Liz said. "I'll bring Ruthie home tomorrow after breakfast."

"Sounds good," I told her, and then called good-bye to my daughter.

Back in the truck, the air remained supercharged, as though an electric current radiated outward from my heart.

"We could have stayed for a while," Blythe said easily, the truck rolling slowly along the road. "But I'm glad you said we needed to go."

I was beginning to tremble a little.

"Me, too," I whispered.

"What would you like to do?" he asked then, his voice low and husky. My legs shook so much I cupped my hands around my thighs, lightly, as though that might help. I was suddenly self-conscious of my outfit (cut-off jeans and a green tank top, old tennis shoes) and the state of my hair, still slung back in a ponytail that surely smelled of the fried fish I'd served since afternoon. I hadn't even reapplied any makeup since my rain-drenched fight with Jackie this morning. But Blythe did not strike me as someone who cared about these sorts of things. His admiring gaze remained steady upon me.

"How long have you known Rich?" I asked, biding a little time.

"Since I was little, even though he and Grandma Pam always lived up here in Minnesota. I've lived in Oklahoma all of my life. Dad and Mom split up when I was five or so, and Mom took care of me. You knew her, right?"

"A little," I told him. "The summer I met her was the first year Rich and Pam were married, I think."

"Mom and I didn't visit up here very much," he said, and I watched him without replying, the breath tight in my chest. He went on, "Your mom and Ellen, and Louisa, are such great ladies. I admire their independence, I really do. Louisa really grilled me when she heard I'd been in jail. She didn't think Joan and Ellen should hire me, at first."

"What changed her mind?" I asked, my voice hardly more than a whisper. We had driven back through Landon and were rounding the lake again, but on the opposite side, near the public boat landing. Shore Leave was visible across the lake. Blythe angled onto a side road, one that led into the dense woods, and finally brought the truck to a halt, far off the beaten path. We were in a clearing I knew well, one of the old state park campsites, where I'd spent many a merry summer night in days of old.

Blythe turned the key and the engine quieted. It was dusk, the sky lavender and violet-tinted through the trees. I turned his way and bent my left knee onto the seat, facing him. He angled to face me, too, just barely two feet away.

"She looked at me, really hard, and finally concluded that I was all right," he said, and I remembered we'd been talking about my grandmother. "She said she couldn't see anything dangerous in my eyes."

I laughed a little, saying, "That sounds like Gran."

"That meant a lot to me," he said. "I want you to know that. I was worried that everyone here would judge me, would think I was nothing more than a criminal."

"Gran gives people a fair chance," I whispered.

"I was in jail because I stole my boss's car," he explained quietly, though I hadn't asked. But of course he understood that I wondered. He closed his eyes briefly and said, "I was twenty-one and had been fired. I did three months of a nine-month sentence."

It wasn't exactly hard time, but it couldn't have been easy either. And he would be branded a criminal for the rest of his working career, maybe even the rest of his life. I said, studying his face, "Thank you for telling me."

"I figured you'd be wondering," he said. He did not seem as young the longer we sat here together. His serious voice lent him a maturity that made it far too easy to forget that I was in fact twelve years older. The radio volume was low, still playing softly in the background, and the dash lights picked out the blue of his eyes. His jaw was scratchy with a day's growth of whiskers, his hair held back in its customary ponytail, low on his neck. I drank in the sight of him. He was so good-looking he was beautiful, with his soft lips slightly parted. I almost gulped, slipping my hands under my thighs to stop from touching him.

The silence between us grew ever deeper; my heart fired so hard it was almost painful.

"You are so pretty," Blythe said softly, and touched my jaw with his right hand, cupping it and caressing along my neck. "Your eyes are so green."

"Thank you," I whispered. He moved his hand to my waist and gripped lightly, fingers skimming over my back, almost teasingly. His other hand slipped along my bare thigh and drew me closer.

"I'm going to kiss you," he whispered.

"Yes," I whispered back, trying not to sound like I was begging. He pulled me close and I slid my arms around his neck, pressing my breasts to his chest, moaning softly as his lips parted mine. I knew, I really did, that I should stop this right now, that I shouldn't be arching my back so he could swiftly unhook my bra. But I shut out that voice and broke the contact of our mouths only so that he could slip the tank top over my head.

He breathed lightly against my neck, pressing little kisses, tasting me, hands warm around my hips. My bra joined my shirt, abandoned on the dashboard. I gasped a little as he rubbed his stubbled jaw gently against my skin. He leaned back and I swiftly unbuttoned his shirt, running my hands over the hardness of his bare chest, suddenly flush against him, Blythe claiming my mouth with his hungry kisses. It felt so good to be half-naked with him, so incredibly good. He kissed a hot path down my neck, my collarbones, at last stroking his tongue over my nipples, murmuring appreciatively as I cried out and curled my fingers into his hair.

"I love how you smell," he murmured, resting his lips between my breasts; my heart lashed my ribs even more fiercely at his tender words. He kissed my left nipple, teasing with his tongue as he said, "And how you taste. Oh God, I dreamed about doing this the night we met. I know you didn't know me then, but –"

"I did, too," I whispered, wanting to tell him the truth, radiant with heat and nearly panting as he continued lavishing my breasts with attention. At last he surged upward to possess my mouth and between kisses I confessed, "Oh Blythe, I dreamed about this, too. So much…"

"Will you let me make love to you?" he whispered, his questing fingers moving to the button on my shorts, and I was forced to tell him, "We can't…"

He pulled back immediately, though he kept me in his arms. He said hoarsely, "It'll be so good, just let me show you, Joelle. Please, let me show you…"

Temptation clawed me, surely leaving marks along my flesh, but I had to explain, "I have my period. We can't tonight, anyway."

He let that sink in for a half-second, but then tipped his head slightly to the side and regarded me with a smile tugging at his lips. He said, low, "I have an idea. Come with me, beautiful woman," and moved to gather up my tank top, presenting it to me and then turning the knob to raise the radio volume, just slightly. I watched in surprise as he nudged the driver's side door with one shoulder to open it.

I slipped the top back over my head, my lips surely swollen from his incredible kisses, leaving my bra crumpled on the dashboard. Blythe rounded the hood and then proceeded to open my door, reaching up, like a gentleman at a formal occasion, for my hand.

"May I have this dance?" he asked politely, his unbuttoned shirt parted over his hard chest and knife-blade belly. His tone almost shy, he explained, "I wanted to ask you the other night, but I wasn't sure if you'd say yes."

I felt myself beaming at him, rocked by his tenderness yet again. I whispered, "Of course, *yes*," and slipped my hand into his, allowing him to help me from the truck and into the night. On the local country station the deejay was talking about the weather for the rest of the evening, and then a slow Randy Travis song filtered through the speakers, one from my high school days. My heart thrashed as powerfully as though I'd just sprinted all the way from Shore Leave to be here in Blythe's arms. Which I would have, no question. With wonder in my eyes, I reached my hands up, way up, and around his neck, and felt his strong arms gather me close. His eyes were just visible in the purple-tinted gloom of evening. His long hair hung down his back, thick and with a slight wave, but utterly masculine. I traced patterns against the nape of his neck, frightened by how possessive I felt of him, just how *much* I felt for him.

But it was best not to think about that right now.

"You feel so good in my arms. So right," he said quietly, in keeping with the nighttime.

"You, too," I murmured back, drowning in his eyes. "You have no idea."

We swayed slowly, holding each other close, as the song moved into another. Blythe reached up and gently tugged the band restraining my hair, then spread it around my shoulders with one hand, a sweetly intimate gesture. When he lowered his face to kiss me, two songs later, I pulled his mouth to mine. He responded heatedly and I clutched his head, my fingers in his hair, wanting to take him as completely as possible into my body, even knowing I could not, just now. His tongue swept into my mouth, sending an arrow of heat straight between my legs. With a smooth motion he lifted me on the hood of the truck, not breaking the contact of our mouths. I kissed him back with utter abandon, taking his lower lip between my teeth, licking the cleft in his chin, tilting back my head as he moved to kiss my throat. He slipped the tank straps over my shoulders and bent again to my breasts.

"*Blythe*," I implored, unbuttoning his jeans.

"Joelle," he groaned as I gripped him tightly, shuddering with the pleasure of how hard he was.

"I don't care if you have your period," he said, dead-serious, his voice hoarse. But I couldn't let him, no matter how little I cared about that fact right now either.

Instead, I hopped nimbly from the hood, whispering, "Come here," and led him back into the truck, where the radio still crooned love songs. I shoved him (as much as someone my size could shove a huge, incredibly strong man like Blythe) into the passenger seat, climbing over him and unzipping his fly, feeling my pulse everywhere in my body. It was dark but instinct guided my motions, and I leaned down and took him into my mouth, delighting in the swelling fullness of him, running my tongue around and around, as he cupped one hand against the back of my head and shuddered with a gasp. A long time since I'd done this kind of thing, but it was like riding a bike…I still had it, and almost smiled at the thought as I took him deeply down my throat. His breath grew ragged and I felt the huge tip of him swell even more.

"*Joelle*," he gasped out. "I'm gonna…"

But it was too late and I tried desperately not to gag. I managed rather nicely, I thought, sitting back on my bent legs and surreptitiously wiping my mouth. He sat with his head tilted back and eyes hooded, hands lax on the seat, the picture of satisfaction. I smiled at him, so completely happy in this moment. And rather proud of myself, at the same time.

"Holy shit," he murmured, managing a sweet smile for me. "Next time it's your turn, sweetheart."

Sweetheart. I moved like a magnet into the curve of his beckoning arm and snuggled against his side. He smelled amazing. I ran my right palm over his stomach, bare beneath his unbuttoned shirt, marveling at the hard, smooth texture under my hand. He caught it lightly and brought my knuckles to his mouth, kissed them gently.

"You're on," I whispered.

I felt like the criminal twenty minutes later as we drove back around Flickertail to Shore Leave, though not so much as a hair was out of place on my head, my ponytail back in place, tugged severely tight. Blythe held my hand in his, our fingers linked, his thumb tracing lazy patterns against my skin.

"What are we going to do?" he asked, when we were about a minute from the cafe.

I knew exactly what he meant, but the truth was I had absolutely no idea.

"My girls won't understand," I said immediately. "I mean, if I tried to explain that you and I are…" I fumbled to momentary silence. Did I use the word *dating* here? Is that what we were doing? I concluded lamely, "Everything with their dad is too raw right now."

He glanced over at me and said seriously, "I'm not trying to play you, Joelle. You know that, right? Please tell me you know that."

I was startled that he'd say such a thing—especially when I was probably the one playing him. Using him to feel better about my impending divorce, my cheating husband; spending the last hour with Blythe was like stealing a hit of the most addictive drug in the world. But as much as it terrified me, the truth was I knew far more existed between Blythe and me than just our intense physical attraction. I really, really liked him. And there was no way in hell I could dare to let myself feel this way.

"I know that," I whispered as he turned into the parking lot. "I don't think that. I promise I don't, Blythe."

"I'm glad," he said.

An hour later I sat on the porch with Jillian and Gran, Tish and Camille. The girls were curled on the swing, giggling about something while Gran and my sister played Slapjack with a deck of cards. All the men in our lives, acknowledged or otherwise, had disappeared to points unknown, at least for the night. I listened to the girls with one ear, but I didn't hear Noah's name mentioned. My thoughts were in a snarl; I was alternately giddy with the memory of what I'd just done with Blythe and knotted with guilt for the same thing. The word *hypocrite* seemed seared on the backs of my eyelids every time I blinked.

It's not as though you've hurt anyone, I thought, chewing my thumbnail, reminiscent of my oldest daughter.

But you'll get hurt. Or you'll hurt him. This can't last and you know it, the grown-up, rational part of my mind insisted. *You're rebounding with him and it can't last.*

But I want it to last, so much more than I can even admit.

I pictured the way Blythe's eyes looked just before he kissed me, so smoky-blue and full of want. I pressed a fist to my belly and remembered unzipping his jeans and then...

"Joelle, what's got you so distracted?" Gran demanded, effectively snapping all my attention to her.

"I'm just thinking," I hedged, glad for the darkness that hid my flushed face. Gran flapped a hand at me and I pretended to ignore my sister's speculative gaze.

"No good ever came from that," Gran teased, then motioned for me to join the card game.

I scooted my chair up to their table as Gran dealt me in on the round.

"We're going to have to replace the cordless phone," Gran added, but the glint in her hazel eyes was a merry one.

"Why, what happened to it?" Tish asked from five feet away, hanging upside down off the seat cushion, her feet braced on the back of the swing.

"Mom chucked it in the lake when she was talking to Dad this morning," Camille explained, and I hooked an elbow over the back of my chair and turned to face her, eyebrows raised.

"Grandma told me," Camille explained. She reassured, "I understand though, Mom."

"Well, thanks," I said, irritated at doing such a childish thing, for letting Jackie get me that angry. Partly to change the subject, but mostly because I was wildly curious, I continued, "So, when did you meet Noah Utley?"

"A few weeks ago," Camille said, showing signs of instant retreat.

"Don't you dare get up," I said, though my tone softened the words. I studied my daughter's lovely face, unaccustomed to observing guile there; she was hedging just as obviously as I'd been a few seconds before.

Camille squirmed under my continued steady gaze and specified, "About a week after we got here from Chicago."

"He's from a nice family," Jilly added, fanning her cards and peering at her niece. "We went to high school with his brother."

"Yeah, Noah said," Camille told us.

"Did he graduate high school this year?" I pressed.

"No, last year. He's back from his freshmen year at the university in Madison," Camille explained. "He wants to be a pharmacist."

"Hmmm," I said, turning around to face the card game. Jilly raised her eyebrows at me.

"Five card stud?" Gran asked, and I abandoned the Spanish Inquisition—for now.

Hours later that night, I lay restless in bed when my phone vibrated. I had been expecting it, and yet my heart still turned cartwheels and heated my blood.

"Hey," came his deep, sexy voice.

I snuggled into my pillow, covers over my head and Gran's snores in the background.

"Hey," I whispered, nearly delirious with happiness at just the sound of his voice. I cupped my free hand over my belly and stroked lightly, wishing it was Blythe's hand. And then I giggled a little at the thought of him crammed into the twin-sized bed with me. I explained quietly, "I was just imagining the two of us trying to fit in my tiny bed."

He laughed and asked, "What size is it?"

"A twin," I whispered. "It's the same bed that I slept in as a teenager. It's too small for me alone. You would be hanging off the edges."

"Would you believe I had a full-size bed back home?"

"Did you have to fold in half?" I teased.

"I wasn't always so tall," he said. "I grew sophomore year, like a weed. And yeah, after that I pretty much folded in half."

"How big is your bed at Rich's?" I demanded.

"Full," he admitted, and laughed again. "A pullout couch, actually. Not that I'm complaining. I'd pull you right in here with me."

"I wish I was there," I whispered, my words tinged with wistful regret. "I wish we could watch movies and cuddle in your bed."

"Oh God, and make love," he added, with such sincere enthusiasm that I shivered and then giggled. He said, "Thank you for tonight. I'm sorry we have to hide out."

"Blythe," I whispered, longing to say so many things that I should not. Instead I faltered to a halt.

He understood the pause and said quietly, "I just wanted you to know

I had a great time tonight. I loved dancing with you. I love being near you, Joelle Anne."

"Thank you," I whispered, so very moved by his words. "I love being near you, too."

"Good-night, then," he said, low and sweet.

"Good-night," I told him, caressing the phone. And then I whispered in a rush, "What we did tonight…" I needed for him to know what was in my heart. I wanted him to know that I was not using him, that I cared more deeply about him than he could have guessed. I whispered, "What we did tonight means so much to me. I want you to know that, Blythe. I don't—I've never…what I'm trying to say is, I have never cheated on my husband. I would never have dreamed of it. I'm not…slutty."

"I know that," he whispered, his voice gentle. "What happened tonight was amazing. It was a privilege just to hold you close."

"I want you to hold me close again," I whispered.

"I will," he said. "You can count on it, Joelle."

"I can't wait for tomorrow," I said.

"Me, either," he said, his voice full of feeling. "See you in the morning, sweetheart."

Chapter Twelve

BLYTHE AND I WERE UNABLE TO CONCOCT AN EXCUSE TO go anywhere together in the next few days, and had not been allowed more than a few minutes truly alone since the evening of the bonfire at Liz and Wordo's. The day after, Blythe had found me behind the cafe just as the sun sank, and pulled me around the far edge of the garage. There, in relative privacy, we clung like rain-drenched leaves, kissing with all of the pent-up desire that raged beneath the surface after being all day within the same space but completely unable to touch. Forced to speak politely as we worked, as though nothing existed between us but a casual acquaintance was more devastating and nerve-wracking than I'd ever imagined.

"I missed you," I whispered breathlessly, between kisses.

"I missed you, too, I dream about this all day," he murmured against my lips, running both hands over my ribs, up and down. As he spoke he tasted my mouth, my chin, nuzzling my neck, leaving me weak in the knees, aching with longing, even as a constant refrain screamed in the back of my mind, *It's just for a moment, it's just for a moment…this can't last…*

To shut out that terrible voice, I lined his jaws with my hands and kissed him, deep, reckless kisses. My breath emerged in gasps as he opened his lips in small, suckling hot spots along my neck. He pressed his face to the upper curve of my right breast just as the screen door slammed twenty yards away, and the sound of Clint and Tish thumping along the porch boards penetrated the haze surrounding us. I drew away, reluctance dulling my every move. Blythe understood and let me go with one last, sweet kiss.

"Later," he promised, and smiled into my eyes as my heart reverberated hard enough to send ripples over the lake.

I dreamed about him every night, the kind of dreams where I'd wake near dawn in the middle of an orgasm, sweating and disoriented, back in my twin bed instead of his arms. In my rational moments I understood exactly what was happening, how I was overwhelmed by the incredible wealth of his attention, his sweet affection, his desirability. I still couldn't believe he felt this way about me; if I'd considered myself attractive (which I honestly had at several points in my life) the last few years was not one of those times. Blythe had discovered the Joelle buried away, deep inside. The worst part was I knew she would get crushed away again, because she was not conducive to the responsible mother figure that I must be—there was no choice there—and then I would curl up like a cooked shrimp, cradling my stomach, dreading that day.

Another week slipped past too quickly, like water through a loosely-woven net, during which we stole moments as we could and my guilt grew to alarming proportions. It was not, however, large enough to prevent me from seeking him out. Finally one night he caught me after the dinner rush and said, low, "I'll call you later."

Both of us were tired of being allowed only minutes in each other's company. During lunch, I'd told him that tonight I would sneak out to meet him. I didn't care if this was an offense for which I would ground my daughters, I didn't care that I could get caught twice-over, by my mother *and* my children. I only cared about being with Blythe for hours in a row.

Casually, as though we were discussing the weather, I nodded. His answering grin set my heart clubbing and I worked hard not to smile back, seeing Jillian headed our way with her arms full of silverware.

"See you," Blythe said with impressive casualness, but I couldn't look up at him for fear of betraying everything I felt.

"Have a good night, Bly," Jilly said cheerfully as she swung into the seat across from me.

"That's the plan," he said, again with admirable innocence, and I prayed Jilly couldn't hear my heart clanging. Surely she would see how flustered I appeared. Shit, all my sister needed was one look at my face and she'd know; I swung my hair around my cheeks.

Blythe made his graceful way out the screen door onto the porch. I forced my eyes to remain on the napkin I rolled around a set of flatware, though it was almost painful to do so; I wanted to watch my man as he walked through the dusk to his truck, the truck we planned to make love within in only a few short hours. My hands shook a little and to cover my nerves, I asked Jilly, "So, how's it going with Justin?"

Jillian sighed, sounding as though she wished she held a cigarette. "Shitty," she responded, and my gaze flashed up to find her own fixed winsomely out the window. I studied her dear, familiar face, her pretty lips with so much natural pigment they appeared rose-tinted, her deep blue eyes with their long, thick lashes.

"Why?" I asked softly.

"God, Jo," she said, and her voice sounded choked. I dropped the napkin I held and reached over to clasp her right hand. She closed her eyes, inhaled deeply through her nose, and whispered, "Fuck it, I love Justin. *I fucking love him.*"

"Jill," I whispered. She was serious. All around us the noise of the cafe receded. I sensed the vulnerability and sincerity, the simple truth of her words. Mom and Aunt Ellen, both laughing at the bar with some regulars, seemed a million miles away. The kids, running around down by the lake, might have been on a distant planet. It was just Jilly and me. Her eyes sought mine and I was reminded for the countless time in my life just how much I loved my sister, and wanted her to be happy.

"But I need him to admit it first," she whispered, and her words emerged thick with pain. "I won't have it any other way. He's so goddamn stubborn."

"Jillian, he loves you, too, I'm sure of it," I told her, and I was. "You should see how he watches you when he's here. He totally loves you, but he's acting like a big fucking chicken."

I earned a smile from her at that, a slight one, and she squeezed my hand. She said, "I feel like this is one of those schemes we'd cook up when we were kids, remember? Like, after watching *The Parent Trap*."

I giggled a little, recalling well those long, golden summer days. "We thought we could plot and plan everything into working out. Remember when we talked ourselves into believing we could get Mom and Mick back together?"

"God, yes. What were we thinking? We didn't have any clue where he was."

"We planned to ask Minnie," I said, looking at the counter, almost able to see my great-aunt standing there as she had a thousand times in years gone by, her golden hair tied into a complicated twist, horn-rimmed glasses perched on her nose; she wore these relics on a chain of smooth turquoise beads and was fond of gazing over the top edge of the rims, silently, pinning you with those Davis eyes. Even the most stubborn complainer could be rendered instantly mute by Minnie's stare. I smiled a little, just recalling.

"Minnie would have told us to take a leap off the end of the dock instead of looking for Mick Douglas," Jilly said, following the direction of my gaze and thoughts, both. "She never thought he was good enough for Mom."

"Hey," I said intently, drawing her attention back my way. "But Justin *is* good enough for you. Do you hear me? You deserve to be happy, sister of mine."

Hope flashed in her indigo eyes, bright as a promise.

"What he needs is a little kick in the ass," I mused, thinking aloud, tapping my fingertips against my upper lip. "A good old-fashioned catalyst."

"Grace Sorenson is getting remarried in two weeks," Jillian said, her voice speculative. Grace was Eddie's youngest daughter, and her wedding reception would be held at her dad's bar, like most in the greater Landon area.

"Ask him to go with you," I suggested, resuming silverware-rolling at my usual pace.

"I thought I might ask Blythe and then make Justin super jealous," she murmured, and my hands absolutely froze. Before I could consider reacting she said, her tone sizzling with knowing, "*Gotcha*. You honestly didn't think I would notice? Give me a fucking break. You thought I was too distracted, admit it."

I looked up and into her eyes, and saw there a mixture of certainty and dismay.

"Dammit," I muttered, giving up all pretenses.

"I'm worried for you," she implored, leaning forward. "I see you getting hurt."

"Dammit," I said again, more resentfully this time. I snapped, "You lied about him having a girlfriend, didn't you?"

"That was more for Camille's benefit," Jilly defended. "Remember, before she met Noah she thought Bly was pretty hot?"

I glared at my sister.

"Jo, *seriously*."

I bit my lower lip to keep from responding and Jilly, unwilling to spare my feelings, pressed on, "He isn't sticking around here. You're *married*. Granted, to a cheater asshole, but still. What do you think can possibly happen between you and Bly after this summer?"

And then I turned a little mean, darts in my voice as I observed, "Well, it's not really your business anyway, is it?"

Unruffled, Jillian allowed, "You're right, it's not mine, but it is theirs," and indicated my children, stomping up the porch steps with wet, tangled hair that would smell of lake water, sunburned and laughing, Clint bringing up the rear with a volleyball in his hands.

Jilly nailed me with this point and she knew it; there wasn't one outcome I could imagine which didn't leave both Blythe and me devastated. I closed my eyes and said, my voice a tightly controlled whisper, "I know it won't last, Jillian, but I won't get hurt. I'm just fine."

She said quietly, "You've always been a bad, bad liar, Jo."

It was silent in our house, and perfectly still, just after one in the morning. I lay restless in my twin bed, disguising sexy lingerie beneath an old pajama t-shirt, breathless and yet riddled with doubt, waiting for Blythe to call, as he did every night. But tonight my period was over and I'd committed to meeting him…and longing saturated my soul, turned my stomach into a butterfly garden. Earlier, I spent an hour in the tub, soaking in bubble bath called Perfectly Peachy. I shaved my legs with extra care and smoothed lotion over their newly-satiny length. I brushed my hair until it fell like slippery silk over my shoulders, then slipped into my favorite bra and panty combo, a soft, sheer set purple as wisteria blossoms. And now I waited, only a few feet from my snoozing grandmother.

You know you shouldn't do this, Joelle…

But I want to…oh God, I want to…I want him…

Blythe's cell number flashed on my phone's screen just as it began to silently vibrate on my nightstand, and I snatched it into my hands.

"Meet me by the lake in five minutes," he commanded; I could hear the grin in his voice, and the anticipation.

"I'll be there," I said, my stomach soaring. And my heart. I could feel it, throbbing and pulsing all through my body. I nearly fell out of bed, stumbling over the edge of the mattress in my haste. Five feet away, Gran shifted and stopped snoring; I froze in the act of drawing shorts over my hips, but she didn't wake up, and I hurried from the room on silent bare feet, flying down the stairs and then over the dew-damp grass, all doubt completely erased. I ran, breath coming hard, and then I saw him, striding across the parking lot from the direction of the lake road. We met near the edge of the grass. I jumped into his wide-open arms and he caught me hard and close, crushing me against his huge chest. I felt his nose against my hair, and he murmured, "You're here."

"I'm here," I whispered.

He said softly, "You smell so good, baby."

I loved how he called me baby, and sweetheart, loved it to my core. I smiled, pressing my nose to his neck and inhaling, then commandeering his jaws in both hands and bringing his lips to mine. My mostly-bare legs fit around his waist and he clutched my hips, kissing me absolutely. I could never get enough of kissing him, holding his face in my hands, tipping his head as I would, drawing his full lower lip into my mouth to gently close my teeth around it. I felt drunk, the blood in my veins molten.

"Blythe," I said. His eyes were closed and I reveled in that for a moment, kissing the cleft in his chin, his neck, then back to his lips to savor the taste of him.

"Joelle," he whispered, and his tone was reverent.

"Where can we go?" I whispered, and his eyes opened and flashed fire into mine.

"My truck," he said, and let me slide down his chest to the ground, then captured my hand and hauled me along behind him, a man on a mission.

Inside the cab, he turned the key, shifted into gear and then pulled me against his side, where I went willingly, biting his earlobe, letting my hands seek under his t-shirt as his were so fond of slipping beneath mine, caressing his flat, hard belly and the planes of his chest.

"Don't stop," he whispered, and I smiled against his neck, moving lower and finding him through his jeans, my heart beating ferociously as I imagined what was to come.

Minutes later he parked in what I now thought of as *our* clearing and wasted no time in hauling me against him, working swiftly to remove my lingerie. In the meager light he looked almost slightly menacing, his eyes so intense that an electric desire sliced through my body. Wordless sounds of pleasure flowed from my throat as he made short work of his clothes and then captured my wrists in his huge hands, lightly, taking me back upon the bench seat, moving over me and bracing on his forearms. I was shaking, wanting to beg him to make love to me until I couldn't walk…but there was so much more than simple desire swelling between us. I could tell he also felt the strength of it by the way he stared into my eyes, his beautiful mouth somber, eyebrows drawn slightly together.

"Please," I begged and then he grinned at me and nipped my chin, arranging himself between my legs, still wearing his boxers.

"You got it," he whispered back, teasing me a little now, licking along my neck with unrushed strokes. He released my wrists and immediately

I curled my arms around his neck and untied the band holding his ponytail, digging my fingers into his thick, wavy hair. I moaned as he kissed my breasts with wide-open lips, stroking sensuously with his tongue. I lifted my hips into his touch, feeling the sleek wetness of need between my legs as his fingers slid deep.

"You're so wet," he breathed.

I hooked my thigh around his waist and he grinned and moved lower at once, trailing warm kisses down my belly until he breathed softly against my most sensitive skin. There he pressed a lingering kiss and I stifled cries against my forearm as he opened his lips, tracing his tongue around and around, clutching my hips in both hands.

"Blythe, *oh my God*," I moaned. "Please…*I need you…*"

He moved instantly back above me, breathing hard now, his boxers gone. I reached to caress his huge length, and he shuddered and whispered hoarsely, "I need you, too, baby, come here." He leaned to one elbow and reached into the glove compartment; I realized he was getting a condom, which he slipped in place with record speed. I was ashamed to think that a condom was the last thing on my mind.

He kissed me sweetly, cupping my face in his hands. Studying my eyes, he whispered, "Joelle, I've wanted to make love to you since the first night I saw you. You don't know how much I've longed for this."

"I still can't believe it," I whispered.

He shook his head as if he couldn't believe *me*, gliding a warm hand over my belly, parting my thighs even further, stroking until fireworks exploded behind my eyelids. He whispered, "I want to make this so good for you."

"Blythe," I begged again and he plunged into me at last, taking me almost over the edge right there.

"*Joelle*, oh God, *yes*," he groaned as we thrust together with so much vigor that I saw stars. But I craved it, needed it, didn't care if I would be slightly bruised tomorrow. It was so right. The world ceased to have any significance except for this one moment, and I rejoiced in it as Blythe drove into me again and again, unceasing. I clung to him until a rocketing climax shuddered through me just seconds before he cried out and lowered his forehead to my shoulder, both of us slick with sweat.

Long minutes later, he turned and shifted so that I was on top of his chest, cradled. He stroked my back from tailbone to nape in a soft, gentle rhythm. I pressed my face against his chest, wreathed in the scent of him, my right hand resting upon the steady beat of his heart. Lulled somewhere between waking and sleeping, I imagined I heard him murmur *I love you*, but by morning, back in my own bed and alone, I was sure it had just been part of a dream.

Chapter Thirteen

"Jilly told me you had a girlfriend," I said the very next night as we lay tangled together in the wee hours, same place, same truck, same blissful nakedness. The cramped truck was hardly a first choice for any lovers, unless you counted illicit ones, like us, but I didn't care; I would have gone anywhere to be with him like this.

His chest bounced beneath my cheek as he laughed, and I braced on one elbow to study his face in the faint light. He lay flat on his back on the bench seat to cuddle me, staring up at the ceiling of his truck, and shifted slightly to tuck one forearm beneath his head.

"I did, last winter back in Oklahoma," he said, his voice deep and relaxed. "Her name is Cindy, but we broke up way before I moved here. I must have mentioned her to Jills."

"She told me you had a girlfriend here in Landon," I explained, and he gently tucked a loose strand of hair behind my left ear. "I guess I didn't believe her, even from the first."

"She must have misunderstood," he said. "She's very protective of you, I can tell you that."

"We try to take care of each other," I said, thinking of what Jilly said yesterday, before I'd actually made love with Blythe. My insides curled over on themselves as I imagined how soon I would have to end what we'd only just begun. The thought hurt me like a physical blow.

"Before you got here, all she could talk about was how worried she was about you, what a jerk you were married to." He added, almost bashfully, "And I didn't help any, asking about you all the time."

"How long were you here before us?" I asked, trying to picture him at Shore Leave this past spring, learning about my family, hearing about me from them, all while I wallowed in my own depression back in Chicago. I gently traced over his eyebrows as he answered.

"About a month. Gramps called me around Easter and said he might have a job for me if I'd be willing to move to Landon. I thought about it a long time, I hated to leave Mom all alone, but she insisted I needed a change of scenery. So I came up to Minnesota around the end of April."

I'm so happy you did, I thought, moving my questing hands downward, stroking his collarbones, his chest, falling deeper into this trench of feelings for him…

"I feel like I knew you before we even met," he said. "Jilly couldn't wait for you to get here, you should have heard her. She talked about you constantly, and I loved it. And that first night I got here, Joan and Ellen showed me a bunch of pictures of you guys—"

"What pictures?" I said, cutting him off mid-sentence, and he laughed again.

"Pretty much from the time you were born," he said, and I buried my face against his chest, laughing, too. "All the way to your wedding. God, you were so young when you got married."

"That's what happens when you get pregnant on prom night," I responded, not intending to sound so flippant.

"When did you meet…Jackson?" he asked, pausing as though reluctant to speak his name, running a hand along my back, sending shivers over my ribs. Blythe's touch felt so good, so right, and I didn't want to talk about Jackie. I'd hardly thought about my cheating husband in days.

"I always knew him," I heard myself murmur. "Small town. Both of our families have always lived here. We went to school together since kindergarten. We started dating the summer before high school."

"I hate that he has the power to hurt you so much," Blythe said softly.

"You know, a lot of that has to do with our girls," I said, sliding up his body and pressing a kiss against his neck. He was so warm and strong, and he smelled so good. He smelled like heaven. How would I go the rest of my life without being allowed near him, just like this? I kissed the cleft in his chin next, cuddling closer as I clarified, "If it wasn't for our girls, I wouldn't care what he was doing back in Chicago." Well, that was mostly true. I was still wounded by Jackie picking another woman over me, especially when we'd still been together when he picked said woman. But I was not mortally wounded, like I'd thought back in December, not even close.

"Do the girls know what he did?" Blythe asked.

"I told Tish and Camille before I told Ruthie," I said, cringing at the memory of telling my youngest. "Ruthie took it so much harder than her sisters. Milla and Tish are so distracted by their Landon friends, and by that *Noah*…"

Noah Utley irritated me to no end; he made no real efforts to talk with me, and did not seem to realize that part of dating someone meant getting to know that person's family.

"That's the kid Camille is dating?" Blythe asked. "The one always hanging around waiting for her?"

"That's him," I said, and considered the conversations I'd overheard between my two older girls. I sighed as I said, "And she's really fallen hard for him. She's never had a serious boyfriend and I'm so worried for her."

Listen to yourself, I raged. *You sound like such a hypocrite. Here you are sneaking out of the house and having repeated sex in a truck. You would lock Camille in her room for such a thing.*

"You're close to your kids, be glad of that," Blythe said softly. "Tish talks about you all the time, when she's helping in the kitchen. And they know they can talk *to* you, which is the most important thing. Maybe not as much this summer, right? I remember going through that with my mom, around that age. But Ruthie still hasn't gotten there yet, I can tell."

I calmed a little, resting my face against his shoulder, reflecting how comfortable I felt with him, like we could talk about anything at all. Even though he wasn't my girls' father, technically wasn't a father at all, he noticed things; he understood. I whispered, "You're right about Ruthie. I would die if I thought my girls didn't talk to me about things. I guess I've taken it for granted until now. I never thought they kept secrets from me." I exhaled a small, pitiful laugh, whispering, "*Shit*. I guess I deserve it. When I think back to all the secrets I kept from Mom…"

"Joan seems kind of…" Even though I wasn't looking at him I sensed Blythe smile as he groped for the right word. He finally concluded, "In her own world. Dreamy, I guess."

I giggled, rolling atop his chest to kiss him. He wrapped me close, growling against the side of my neck. I caught his wrists and pretended to pin him on the seat, teasing, "Are you making fun of my family?"

He was already getting hard again as I straddled him, and my grin turned naughty. I demanded in a whisper, "Well?"

"Maybe a little," he allowed, gliding a hand down my belly to cup me between the legs. I shivered as he gently stroked. Holding my gaze in his, he whispered, "Before I actually met you, I had the strangest feeling that we were meant to meet. It struck me right in the chest that first night I got to the cafe, back in April. That was the night your grandma looked into my eyes and decided I was all right, and I saw your picture for the first time. I couldn't wait for you to get to Landon, Joelle. I was honestly counting the days. I know that seems crazy. But still, when you walked around the corner that first night, I felt like you'd punched me right in the chest."

Our hearts were pressed close, beating together, and tears prickled in my eyes. I whispered, "All I could think about was you, Blythe, from that moment on."

He circled me with both arms and I was the one that felt punched in the chest, by his sincerity. Oh God, why now? Why after all this time did I meet someone like him, after I'd already been married and was only growing older, certainly too old to seriously consider a future with him. He was only in his twenties, with years of what should be unencumbered life ahead of him. I was a mother of three children…with no plans to have any more.

"Blythe," I whispered, hating myself for what I was about to say. But the thought of my girls burned in my mind, my responsibility to them. I said miserably, "This can't be."

"Why?" he whispered back, slightly defensive, his eyebrows knitting.

"Why can't it? Don't tell me it's because I'm too young. I've seen a lot more in my life than you'd care to know, probably."

I drowned in his earnest eyes, studying the angles of his beautiful face, his full lips that had touched me everywhere now. He said intently, "I've never felt like this before and it scares me, too."

My chest seemed to cave in, tears washing over my cheeks. He brought a knuckle under my chin, lifting my face and kissing me, with utter sweetness.

"I want you so much," he said, crushing me closer, rolling me to my back.

"I want you, too, Blythe, sweetheart," I whispered, shutting out all my fears even as tears streaked over my temples and to the seat below, spreading my legs around his hips in as natural a motion as anything I'd ever felt, and for the fourth time that night we came together as close as two people can be.

Morning light streaked over my aching eyes; I slept hardly at all after Blythe brought me home. I forced myself from bed but didn't shower, because that would wash his scent away, and I craved that scent all over my body. Aware that I was behaving like a woman deeply in love, or lust, or a startling combination of the two, I avoided the cafe for the first morning since we arrived back in May. Instead I tugged on jeans and a tattered Minnesota Twins t-shirt that once belonged to my husband, and made my way into the woods, away from the lake and along the ancient path worn into the earth by years of animal foot traffic.

Red pines and burr oaks stretched for miles and I was familiar with the way I headed now, a steep path that climbed in a roundabout fashion up the side of the bluff beyond Shore Leave, the sky tinted by the gray of very early morning, the air sticky with humidity. From every direction birds sang and called, heralding the new day; the crickets were silent. I walked with long steps, breaking into a sweat within minutes despite the early hour. By the time I reached the summit my breath came fast and trickles of moisture glided down my neck, but I'd timed my climb pretty well; the sun was just cresting the horizon when I sat on a small outcropping of rock to watch. I curled my arms around my knees and rested my chin on top, able to admire the rippling clouds in the eastern sky despite the agitation in my soul. I watched as they seemed to glow from within, first a deep magenta and then a warm gold. The air was completely static with the dawn, thick with the promise of a hot day, and I sighed, and then sighed again.

I was hiding out here, not just on the bluff. I was hiding at Shore Leave, waiting for something to happen, to change, to fix itself. Hiding from Jackie and what I'd known and avoided admitting to myself for the past decade—the fact that he and I should never have been married in the first place. How could I ever have believed it would work? How could I have stayed away from Landon, and my family, for so very long? And now…now my life had unexpectedly collided with someone else, a man I hadn't realized I was searching for until finding him…

Oh, God…

Blythe. Blythe Edward Tilson.

I hugged myself around the ribs, painfully hard. I could not believe that just two months ago I didn't know him, when my whole world now seemed about him. Which was insane. My whole world was my children, not a twenty-three-year old ex-con…who I was sleeping with, and who I…

In my entire life, I'd only ever been in love with Jackie—unless you counted my girls, who taught me all about the much different and powerfully fierce love that accompanies motherhood. I never imagined that I would be without Jackie, even when I first suspected that he was cheating. I supposed somewhere in the back of my mind I figured he would remember how much he really loved me, his wife and the mother of his daughters, his high school sweetheart, and want me back. I realized now how pitiful that hope was, and that I would not ever take Jackie back, even to salvage our family, not at this point. Aunt Ellen and Gran were right; Jackson the man was lacking, and I no longer believed that he deserved me, no matter what a good father he was to my children.

Could I go back to Chicago? Everything within me rebelled against this thought, but what choice did I have? My daughters' lives, their home and private schools and friends, were all in Chicago. What would I do when summer ended, as summer always did, and my girls needed to return to their regular, non-summer lives? I knew my responsibilities, the role I needed to fill for my daughters. *But what about my heart?* Did I discredit that part of myself entirely? I envisioned Blythe living with us somewhere in Chicago, Jackie providing child support and me getting a job to help support us. Chicago, the sharp-edged city where I spent the past seventeen years…sitting here in the woods, Chicago seemed like a dream. A long, strange, townhouse-living dream, in which I mothered my heart out and then one night walked in on my husband screwing another woman. I tried to picture Blythe as a surrogate father to three teenaged girls. He didn't deserve that strain, the monumental stress of that. He should be free to date, to remain carefree, to find a girl his age and eventually have his own kids.

Tears poured from my eyes at the blade of this thought. I brought my wrists to my nose and inhaled, smelling Blythe on my skin, and loving it, craving it, and craving him. I cupped my breasts and then my belly, skimming my fingers over myself and imagining him. I still couldn't believe that he felt this way for me…that I responded so much to him. He was my man; I recognized this truth, no matter how illogical. But our combined lives could never work, not in any incarnation of my visions of the future.

I wandered back down the trail after the sun rose, jogging the last few hundred yards; I showered with reluctance, washing away Blythe's scent, and then dressed in jean shorts and a green-and-white striped tank, and snapped my hair into a rubber band before heading to the cafe, my thoughts somber. I worked lunch for Mom, a busy one as it was Friday, Blythe within touching distance and yet a million unreachable miles away, with my family present. It wasn't until late afternoon that he managed to get me alone, as I emptied the garbage from lunch in the metal can around the far side of the cafe.

"Joelle," he said, coming up behind me, spreading his hands over my back. He loved to do that, and I loved when he did—I felt so cherished, so precious to him.

I dropped what I was doing, spun around and came up hard against him, wanting to take back what I said last night about us not working.

"I'm so sorry," I said against his neck, breathing him in like a drug I was unable to live without. We'd parted with uncharacteristic silence last night when he dropped me off in the parking lot of the cafe.

"No, I hate this sneaking around," he said against my hair, holding me tightly to his chest. "And I didn't mean to scare you away with what I was saying last night. I just want to enjoy being with you, Joelle. I love being with you, so much. I don't want to pressure you."

I squeezed my eyes shut and held him.

"Can we just have that, for now?" he whispered.

I thought about my first impression of him, the gorgeous, self-confident ladies' man I assumed he was, just based on his physical presence. I would never have guessed what a dear, tender soul lived beneath that exterior.

"Yes," I told him, pressing kisses along his neck, bare above the blue Shore Leave work shirt he always wore. "Yes. Blythe, sweetheart, *yes*. Come here."

"I'm right here," he assured me, rocking me gently side to side. He brought his forehead to mine and said softly, "I have a plan for tonight. Can you get away around nine?"

"I'm going to head into town and hang out with Leslie Gregerson," I told Mom after the dinner rush, stifling the guilt of lying to her as an adult. As a teenager I'd lied with ease to ensure a night out with Jackie. I cringed at the thought, glad that Jilly was outside on the porch—she would see through the story I'd concocted, in point-two seconds.

"You mean Leslie Cooper, now," Mom amended. She offered me a smile and added, "Gran is teaching the girls how to play poker tonight, doesn't that sound like fun?"

I rolled my eyes at my mother, but I was smiling as I said, "Tish told me that today. And Clint is having a sleepover? God, poor Jilly."

"Nah, they're camping out in tents. We won't let them in the house," Mom joked. "And we're having a bonfire. Dodge is bringing Liz's triplets. Ruthann just loves them."

"I'm so glad she's made some friends of her own. She gets left out."

"Bring Leslie out here," Mom invited, tossing a dishtowel over her shoulder. "It'll be a fun night."

"Maybe," I hedged, feeling guilty as hell. I kissed her cheek and then found the girls lined up at the bar, watching as Aunt Ellen made a blender of grasshoppers, a minty ice cream drink that tasted just right when the humidity was up past ninety percent, as it was this evening.

"Hi, honey," Ellen called to me, over the whine of the blender. "You want a sip?"

"Mom, it's called a grasshopper!" Ruthie said.

"But there's no alcohol in ours," Tish reassured me.

Ellen and I exchanged a look, full of amusement.

"Mom, can Noah come hang out tonight?" Camille asked, winding a lock of her dark hair around her index finger. "Grandma said we're having a bonfire."

"That's fine, as long as he doesn't stay over in the tents with Clint's friends. And I'd like it if you stayed here," I said, watching carefully for her reaction; I very much preferred they hang out at the cafe, where there were plenty of other people to keep an eye on them.

You gigantic hypocrite, I thought.

"He won't, Mom, *jeez*," Camille said, rolling her eyes at me like I'd just rolled mine at Mom; I supposed I deserved that.

"Where are you going, Mom?" Tish demanded, sounding like a prison guard. Or like a slightly-frightening litigator. She'd let her hair grow this summer and it fell almost past her ears, no longer a regulation Peter Pan-style.

"Over to a friend's from high school," I said smoothly, hating myself. I'd never purposely lied to my children before, but reminded myself what I would be giving up very soon, and his name was Blythe. I deserved every second with him, until then. For a split second I felt the sharpness of Camille's gaze the way I would a needle pricking my skin, but then she turned away to accept her grasshopper from Aunt Ellen, murmuring, "Thank you, this looks great."

"You aren't sticking around to play poker?" Ellen teased, and immediately I was sure my intentions were as transparent as a windshield. Ellen's expression reminded me so much of Great-Aunt Minnie; all she needed to complete the look was that old pair of horn-rimmed glasses.

"Not tonight," I said quietly. I dearly loved my auntie, whose calm steadiness was a perfect complement to Mom's tendency to blow things out of proportion. Ellen studied me and I was about to confess to everything, no more than an inch away from laying it all out right there on the surface of the bar before my aunt's unwavering gaze.

Yes! I longed to shout. *Yes, I fucking love Blythe Tilson! I am in love with him! Are you satisfied?*

But I only said, "Next time, I promise."

And then I heard Jilly's voice float through the air behind me; we'd been on the outs with each other since our last talk, existing in a modified silent treatment for days now, and I was so happy to hear her sounding cheerful that I chose to ignore the ironic lilt also present in her tone.

"Have fun," she said, bellying up to the bar between Ruthie and Tish. We studied each other somberly as the girls chattered with Aunt Ellen, oblivious to the silent conversation happening between Jilly and me.

"I will," I whispered, telling her about fifty times more with my eyes; mostly I said, *I'm sorry I was such a bitch the other day. I know you were just worried about me.*

I'm sorry, too, she said back, without a word. And then, *Oh Jo, be careful. Shit, please be careful.*

The screen door clacked open and Dodge's booming voice yelled from the front of the cafe, "I've got firewood in the truck, heard we were having a bonfire out here tonight! Clint, get out there and help the boy unload!"

Which meant Justin was here. Jilly's whole posture changed and I could tell she hadn't been expecting him. I smiled a little at this sight of her sudden fluster and said, "You have fun, too, Jilly Bean."

Chapter Fourteen

I DROVE OUR OLD STATION WAGON INTO LANDON AND THEN proceeded to the south end of town, away from Fisherman's Street, parking near the pines and spruce that stood watch over the town for probably close to a century. Blythe was already waiting in his truck but he climbed down immediately. He looked so amazing in the sunset light, so tall and broad-shouldered and handsome, that I was rendered immobile, clutching the steering wheel as I watched him come to me. He opened the car door and presented a bouquet of fresh daisies, his smile just the tiniest bit bashful.

"I just picked these," he explained, ushering me to his truck as I held the daisies to my face and felt a blush seep hotly over my cheeks.

"Thank you," I whispered as he opened the passenger door. *Flowers.* He picked wildflowers for me.

"You look fantastic, Joelle," he said, and his tone was so admiring that I blushed even deeper.

I'd tried to look fantastic, a little worried that everyone might wonder why when I was supposedly just visiting Leslie, but the impromptu bonfire party appeared in full swing as I left Shore Leave, showered and eyelined, shaved and peach-scented, wearing my sexiest sundress and heeled sandals, and no one took particular notice of me. Until this moment, and I was ridiculously glad I'd spent time primping a little.

"Thank you again, so do you," I said, and he did, of course. His thick hair fell loose over his shoulders, the first he'd ever worn down it when I hadn't untied it as we made love, and he reminded me a little of Hawkeye in one of my favorite old movies, *The Last of the Mohicans*. He was freshly shaved, dressed in jeans and a dark shirt that emphasized his shoulders, the curves of his strong arms crisply defined. His lips curved into a smile and I stumbled climbing into the truck, just looking at him.

"I'm taking you out," he told me as he bounded inside the truck and started the grumbling engine. "The fanciest place I could find within decent driving distance."

"You are?" I asked, thrilled. I hadn't been on a real date since…well, high school, really.

"And it's not that fancy, just to warn you," he said, and I giggled.

"I don't mind, it's just so good to be here with you," I said, and he reached with his right hand and caught up my left, his thumb caressing my skin as he pulled onto the highway and proceeded to drive to Bemidji.

We ate dinner on the deck at the Sparkling Waters Cafe, overlooking gorgeous Moose Lake, which lay like soft blue silk in the twilight. I felt light as dandelion seed, buoyed with happiness at being with him on a real date. I asked the server for a glass of water without ice, so my daisies wouldn't wilt; Blythe grinned in pleasure as I situated the bouquet just off-center on our table, so it wouldn't impede our view of each other. I wanted nothing blocking him from my gaze, studying him from just across a small, candle-lit table as we talked, loving the way he grinned periodically at something I'd say, thrilling at his sweet attention. I sipped a glass of red wine, letting the promise for later build within my body. I felt so perfectly matched with him, certainly not like a woman twelve years his senior; then again, Blythe carried himself with a kind of somber confidence that belied his years.

"What would you have done if you hadn't gotten pregnant with Camille?" he asked as we shared dessert, strawberry shortcake, at my insistence.

I scooped a spoonful of whipped cream and berries, considering; we'd spoken a great deal about choices this evening. I finally said, "I would have gone to college, too, but definitely not so far from home. Jackie and

I wouldn't have stayed together. He was so ready to go to Chicago and become a wealthy lawyer. It's what he always wanted, and worked for."

"Did you want to marry him?" Blythe asked quietly, watching me.

I swallowed and said honestly, "I did, at the time, I did very much. But I wouldn't have if not for being pregnant. Jackie's mother was very insistent that we marry. And we did, just after graduation that year. We were so young, like you saw in the pictures from that day. Oh God, we didn't know anything about each other. I can see that now."

Blythe nodded seriously. And then, startling me a little, he asked, "Do you still love him?"

He looked out over the lake immediately after asking, his gaze touching the far shore, where stars sparked to life on the indigo backdrop of the eastern sky. But as I opened my mouth to answer, his eyes came back to my face like a compass pointing to true north, direct and intense. It killed him to think that I still might love Jackie—it killed me that he thought I could possibly still love Jackie after this summer.

I said, slightly breathless, "If you asked me two months ago, I would have said yes."

"And now?" he asked, low, and it was as though we were the only two people left in the world. My knees started to shake a little.

"I realize that I gave up loving Jackie a very long time ago," I whispered truthfully.

"I love that you brought that with," Blythe said as we climbed back into the truck after dinner; I kept one of the daisies from the vase on the table, laying it carefully on the dashboard, and meant to press it between the pages of a book later, in this way keeping a memento of our first date.

"I'll keep it always," I told him, experiencing a sudden pang—for the first time I thought with a sense of fledgling hope, *We can stay together. This does not have to end with summer.*

"We'll put it somewhere special so we'll always look back on this night," he agreed, and the heartfelt promise in his tone buoyed my wild hope. He started the engine and sat with one hand hanging over the wheel. Before I spoke, he cupped my jaw and said softly, "I want to make love to you in an actual bed tonight, and not this old truck."

His words created hot little earthquakes all through my lower belly. I teased, "Just not a twin bed."

"Anywhere," he said. "Any actual bed. Even a sleeping bag at this point."

"I could make that happen," I said, laughing more as he groaned and then tucked me under his right arm. He whispered against my hair, "I would very much love to get us a hotel room right now. What do you say?"

"Yes," I whispered.

Twenty minutes later we were guests at the AmericInn of Bemidji; if it seemed strange to anyone that we didn't have luggage, I didn't notice, too besotted with my lover to make any such observation. Blythe took my hand as we headed down the hall to our room, moving with languid grace, but the second we were inside he wasted no time, shutting the door and turning smoothly to collect me in his arms, cupping my face in his hands and studying me with no grin this time, all seriousness and heat. He bent and kissed me flush on the lips, breathing against me for a moment, inhaling the scent of me just as I did him, a kind of sweet, passionate absorption of the other, before kneeling slowly, watching my eyes every second. I reached to curl my hands over the hardness of his shoulders, just where they met his neck, unwilling to stop touching him even for a second.

"You don't know how beautiful you are, Joelle," he whispered, his eyes blazing in the dusk of the little room. His big hands held my hips, thumbs moving in lazy circles, low on my belly.

"Please," I implored, digging my nails into his flesh, and he grinned at the urgency in my voice, sending a double bolt of lightning streaking through my core.

"Lie down," he whispered, his thumbs moving lower, still circling gently. I did, bracing my elbows against the mattress. He lifted my skirt and slowly removed my panties, kissing these as he set them aside. I gasped a little, so completely aroused by such a simple gesture. Blythe spread my thighs, again with unhurried movements, before lowering his mouth. I cried out his name, repeatedly, coming hard against his questing tongue. At long last he emerged from between my legs and moved fluidly, jeans around his ankles. A hot, hard column of flesh stretched to meet me, a condom already in place. He wrenched free of his shirt and I clung for dear life, our wordless cries caught between hungry kisses. And for a long while after we lay totally motionless, tangled together; at last he stirred and planted soft little kisses all along the side of my jaw, then bit my earlobe, and I squeaked.

"Thank you," I murmured against his neck, where his hair hung hot and wild, and he snorted a laugh at my words.

"Yes, you're welcome," he said. "I got no pleasure from that at all."

I tightened my thighs around his hips and teased, "You didn't?"

His eyes told me the truth and he grew hard again almost instantly.

"You bring me more pleasure than I have ever known," he said.

It had been years since I'd felt this way...maybe never...even when Jackie and I were dating and made love constantly. Because this time I took nothing for granted, understood fully the danger of that.

"Don't stop," I begged, clutching his strong shoulders, sweat trickling between my breasts. His tongue traced the same path in the opposite direction.

"I won't stop," he promised, hoarse with pleasure.

My body was so completely in tune with his, I felt close to flying. He shifted us and I moved on top of him, my hair a hot, humid mass over my shoulders.

"I can feel you...all through my body," I panted, bracing against his chest as we studied each other, his expression of joy burning into my soul. In all my years of making love with an expert like Jackie, I never felt such uninhibited passion. Blythe's big hands moved along my back, his tongue over my nipples. I gasped, arching my spine, slippery with sweat and desire, and he moaned deep in his throat, murmuring, "Come all over me, baby, oh God yes, all over me."

Blythe, Blythe, I love you, oh God, I love you, I thought, wanting to speak it aloud but far too afraid. When he came he cried out against my neck and I fell atop him, never wanting to let go.

"Joelle," he murmured against my skin, and I knew I would never tire of hearing my name on his lips.

"Blythe," I whispered back, clutching his head against my breasts, twining my fingers possessively into his hair. And for that moment, it was enough.

Chapter Fifteen

"I WANT TO HOLD YOU WHILE I SLEEP," I TOLD HIM AN hour and a half later, after we'd reluctantly dressed and loaded up to head back to Shore Leave.

"I want that, too, sweetheart," he said somberly. Our hands were joined on the seat, and my panties had been located and were back in place. My insides, however, were not. I was rattled to the core by his very presence, and by the enormity of my feelings for him. And again, Jillian was right. I was going to get hurt, I was going to hurt him, and I couldn't bear to think about it. He added, "Although Gramps would probably knock me out for taking advantage of a lady this way."

I giggled at that, despite everything. "Rich wouldn't believe the things I want to do to you," I said. "I think I'm the one taking advantage."

"If that's the case then please, by all means, take advantage of me every night," he teased. We were only a quarter-mile or so from the exit to Landon, and I felt the strain of leaving him begin to gnaw at my belly. I tightened my grip on his hand.

"Do you think the bonfire will still be going on?" he asked, pulling into town and parking again by the towering trees at the south edge, where our evening began.

I glanced at the dashboard clock; it was only a little after midnight, so I nodded. My throat was tight now that I needed to go home and pretend I'd been with Leslie Gregerson all evening.

"Come over," I said, unable to face being apart from him right now. "I'll head home, and you take a few minutes, and then show up."

He moved to cup my face and kissed me sweetly. I clung, afraid that I was going to cry and ruin our beautiful night, and he held me, whispering, "It's so hard to pretend there's nothing but friendship between us around everyone else."

"I know," I told him. "I'm so sorry. I don't know what to do."

"I'll come," he told me, smoothing my hair and looking into my eyes. "You look beautiful."

"Thank you for the date," I told him, peppering his face with little kisses. "I've never had a better one."

"Fuckin' right," he teased, as though to coax a smile, and then added, "Me, neither, sweetheart. I'll be there soon, I promise."

I drove alone over the familiar streets, hot with both agony and exhilaration. I checked my reflection in the rearview mirror as I took the car slowly around Flicker Trail, noting that my make-up was mostly gone; at least my hair was combed smooth and sleek, thanks to the brush in my purse. I prayed that no one would pay attention to me before I could sneak to my room and change into shorts and a sweatshirt.

Hurry, Blythe, I thought. *I already miss you.*

I pulled into the parking lot at Shore Leave to see the flames of a four-foot-tall monster in our fire pit across the way, around which it appeared an entire village of primitive beings was dancing and worshiping. I smiled at the sight. The sounds of laughter, shrieks, and the local country station on the radio met my ears as I made my way around the far side of the cafe and paused to free my feet from the heeled sandals. Barefoot, I ran to the house and up to my room, shucking my dress and pulling on the first pair of shorts I came across, then digging around for a sweatshirt. I found a soft turquoise one from my high school years as I saw Blythe's truck pull into the lot, fifty yards away, and my heart began reverberating like a kettle drum.

No one will suspect a thing, I told myself as I ran, literally ran, back in the direction of the bonfire, wanting to wait for Blythe but knowing better. I spied two tents, which looked like ancient pagan structures in the leaping light of the fire, and then came upon my family in their respective chairs. I did a quick inventory, spying Ruthann and the triplets;

Ellen, Mom, Dodge; (Gran had been in for the night); and finally Justin and Jilly (engaged in a conversation of their own). I could hear Tish on the dock, and Clint, and certainly a couple of Clinty's friends, but no Camille, and no Noah Utley. For the first time since leaving for my date with Blythe, all of my mother-activated alarm lights began spinning.

"Hi, honey!" Dodge heralded, waving at me from his lawn chair, grinning, a mug of something probably around 100-proof in his grip; he didn't drink the hard stuff often, but when he did, it could singe your nose hairs.

"How's Leslie?" Mom asked.

"Good," I said simply, tripping around everyone's knees on my way to my sister.

I plopped down on her other side and asked pointedly, "Where is Camille?"

Jilly, who never looked flustered, looked slightly flustered. "Hi, Jo. Swimming, I think."

"Where's Noah?" I asked next.

Jilly gave me a look and said, "He went home about an hour ago, said he had to work in the morning."

Oh, I mouthed.

"You have a good night?" she asked, studying me closely. Beside her, Justin seemed unable to take his eyes from her face; he looked like some kind of devil in the firelight, but an incredibly attractive one…if that made any sense.

"Yes," I said casually, but Jilly heard the depth of feeling in my voice.

"Good timing, Jo," she replied, low but sarcastically, looking past my shoulder.

I spun around just as Mom called, "Bly, hi there! It's about time you joined us! I told Rich to send you over. He wasn't feeling up to coming out tonight, but you're always welcome."

"Hi, Bly!" Ruthann called. She, the triplets, and both dogs were sprawled on a blanket near the fire, along with bowls of popcorn and a bag of marshmallows.

"Hi, Ruthie, hi everybody," he said easily, loping up and grabbing an abandoned chair, settling in as my gaze absolutely ate him up from the other side of the fire, taking in every detail of face and frame, caressing and lingering and adoring. His hair was tied back, his clothes perfectly in place, his lips warm and soft, his eyes the blue of Flickertail in the early morning. He looked totally innocent, and I imagined being in his arms just a little while ago, taking him joyously into my body, my head flung back as he licked the sweat from my skin and took my nipples between his teeth…

Jilly elbowed me discreetly and I snapped my gaze away, but only for a second, because Blythe's skimmed over to me and he telegraphed a private hello with his smoky eyes, before turning to answer Ellen's question about what he wanted to drink.

I love you, I love you so much, Blythe Edward Tilson. Oh God, why do I love you so much? I can't love you this much and recover from it…

I was jerked from my despairing thoughts as Tish ran up from the lake, imploring, "Mom, can we take a midnight canoe trip?"

"Hey, that sounds like a great idea," said Justin, who was obviously not a father and didn't realize that he should always get parental permission before giving the go-ahead. "Talk about old times."

"Dammit, Justin," I nagged, reaching around my sister to smack his shoulder.

"What?" he retorted. "We haven't done that in years."

"You all need life jackets, Joelle," Mom ordered, as though this had been my idea. "All of those boys need one, no matter how great they think they can swim. We'll have Charlie Evans out here giving us all citations."

"Yay, thanks, Grandma!" Tish cried, bending to kiss Mom's cheek. She was a mess, fully dressed but dripping with lake water, her pockets inside-out and an earring missing, my outspoken and often pain-in-the-ass middle daughter, my Patricia.

"Boy, help them get going," Dodge instructed Justin, who rose and gave his dad a crisp salute.

"Jills, come help me," Justin said, and she directed at him a smirk I knew well.

"No way, I'm comfortable right here," she said, but he made as though to throw her over his shoulder and she scrambled to her feet to avoid his teasing.

"Jo, I'm not doing this without you," Jilly complained, draining the last of her beer.

"No way!" I said, curling into my chair and hugging the sweatshirt around me. "I am not ending up in the lake tonight."

Blythe was grinning, watching me from the other side of the fire.

"Mom, we want to stay here," Ruthie said. "We're going to roast marshmallows."

"Grandpa said he'd help us!" added one of the triplets.

"That's right, sweetie," Dodge agreed.

Ellen returned with a couple of bottles of beer and handed them off to me and Blythe.

"Thanks, Ellen," he said, rising to accept it, and then, "Let's go, Joelle, it'll be fun."

"Yeah, c'mon, Mom!" Tish begged.

"Dammit," I muttered again, though I would have gone just about anywhere or been dumped into any lake for Blythe Tilson. I stole a long sip from the beer and then said, "Patricia, get those life jackets from the shed."

My daughter whooped and ran for the shed, just as Clint and two other boys bounded into the light of the fire, all of them wet, carrying sticks that resembled weapons in the flickering flames. Clint, character-istically cheery, said, "Hi, Aunt Joey! Hi, Blythe! When did you guys get here?"

"Is this a *Lord of the Flies* thing?" Jilly teased the boys, who looked blankly at her.

"They must not teach that one anymore," Justin said, grinning at my sister.

"Just in time for a canoe trip, I guess," I told my nephew.

"Sweet! We're going right now?" he responded, voice cracking a little, with pure enthusiasm.

"Honey, take these guys and get the canoes in the water," Jilly told her son, and the three boys ran back in the direction of Flickertail Lake. Jilly hollered after them, "God, don't poke out your eyes!"

Blythe made short work of his beer as Tish returned with her arms full of life vests.

"How many canoes do you guys have?" Blythe asked me, taking two of the vests from Tish.

"Three," I said, lingering a little behind the group with him as we made our way to the water. Once out of sight of the fire, he moved immediately closer to me. The darkness was thick, humming with mosquitoes, and I shook my hair closer around my neck. Down on the lake, Clint and his friends were laughing and insulting one another, but they effectively managed to get our three canoes, plus the paddleboat, into the water.

"Guys, you have to put these on," Tish ordered, passing out vests, and as they all began complaining, something struck me.

"Tisha, where is your sister?" I called over to her.

"She had bad cramps, Mom," Tish said, for the benefit of everyone. "She went back to the house a little while ago."

"Gotcha," I said, as Clint groaned at Tish's words.

"Here, baby, put one of these on," Blythe said quietly, handing me a jacket, and I took it, smiling up into his eyes.

"Ride with me," I whispered to him.

"Just try and stop me," he whispered. He let his fingertips brush my puffy orange life vest, teasing, "You need help tying that?"

"Thanks, I think I got it," I whispered, but dared to steal a quick kiss, and then we headed for Flickertail, which stretched silver and ebony and mysterious under the night sky. Jilly and Justin claimed a canoe, and I was heartened to see how much they were flirting. I was also grateful that the least observant of my children was accompanying us, having a lot of trouble playing it casual around Blythe.

"You riding with us, Tish?" Jilly called to her.

"No, with Clint and Liam," she responded, splashing through the knee-deep water and climbing aboard a canoe. Clint and one of his pals were taking the bow and stern positions, oars in hand. The canoe jerked sideways as Tish clambered aboard, almost taking them all into the water. Clint used his oar to splash her.

"Only three to a canoe, kiddo," Justin said.

"No, Rye's taking the paddleboat," Tish explained, giving Justin a grin and indicating the boat in question, which Clint's friend was already navigating into the night.

"Whatever," Justin grumbled, climbing into the stern of the second canoe. "Grab an oar, Jillian!"

"No way," my sister retorted, settling into the front, fresh beer in hand. "I'm enjoying the ride."

"Do you want to get us arrested?" he asked, but pushed off willingly enough.

Clint, Liam, and Tish paddled away into the night, in pursuit of the paddleboat, and my sister called after them, "Stay on the edge, you guys!"

"Like you're so worried about rules," I teased, helping steady the third canoe as Blythe gracefully boarded, then returned the favor for me with the oar braced on the solid ground under the water as I hopped into the front.

"Hey, if we see Charlie in his tugboat I'll ditch the bottle," Jilly said.

"Funny," I responded, peering over my shoulder at Blythe as he pushed away from shore and began applying the oar to the sleek black water. We moved with considerable speed, following Justin's lead as he took their canoe to the left. It was a clear, diamond-spangled night, and I snuggled into my sweatshirt and lifted my chin to study the sky. The air was quiet without so much as a breath of wind, the stars brilliant with no moon to overshadow them.

"It's gorgeous out here. At all times, really, but especially at night," Blythe said, his voice with a tone of reverence, and I looked back at him as he studied the heavens, the oar braced over his lap and dripping into the water. We drifted along for a time, purposely lagging behind, listening to the night noises of crickets and frogs, mosquitoes and the occasional owl, amplified as sound waves bounced across the water. Maybe twenty yards ahead, the kids laughed about something; somewhat closer to us, we could hear Justin and Jilly bickering good-naturedly.

I muttered to Blythe, "They better have sex tonight," indicating my sister and Justin, and he laughed.

"You should see the way they flirt," he said in response. "Before you got here, I went out with them to Eddie's one night. You could have set a match to the air between them. What's taking them so long to admit it?"

"Stubbornness," I said, with certainty. "They're both stubborn as hell."

"But they're perfect for each other," Blythe said.

"That's true," I said softly, but my eyes were only for Blythe. He grinned the same way he had the first night I met him, slow, easy, smoldering. I bit my lip. It took a considerable amount of willpower not to close the few feet of space separating our bodies, but I remained where I was, content for the moment just to be near him.

"You're so lucky to belong to this place," he murmured.

"I never appreciated it until we would come back here from Chicago to visit," I said, wrapping my hands around my knees and stretching my back a little.

"Did you like living there? It doesn't seem right for you, somehow. I can't imagine you away from Landon," he said, ever perceptive.

I considered the city in which I lived as a new bride, as a new mother, where my girls had each been born, picturing the department stores, the fabulous restaurants, incredible museums and concert halls, my luxurious townhouse…all of the things I was supposed to return to in just a few short weeks. Finally I said, "No, you're right. It's no contest. There are things I like about Chicago, but my heart is here, truly. Landon will always be home."

"I used to feel like that about the town where I grew up in Oklahoma," Blythe said. "But it's lost so much appeal now. I don't think I could ever live there again."

I studied him, trying and failing to picture him as a child, a teenager. I asked, "Why's that?"

He shrugged, resuming paddling with a smooth motion. He said quietly, "Being in jail did a number on my perspective. You get older, see things differently. Or maybe you see them for how they actually are, but you'd never noticed."

For a moment I couldn't respond, struck by the fact that he was so very young…far too young to even voice the phrase *you get older*, especially in that tone, but then again he insisted that I underestimated his life experience. We'd discussed it several times already, in our quest to cut through the thicket of unknown facts separating us. He spoke very little about being in jail; he told me he wasn't ashamed, necessarily, but it was still hard to discuss. He did, however, speak often and with fondness of his mother and the trailer in which he'd been raised, and I tried again to picture him as a boy…for a second my mind truly betrayed me, and I found myself imagining another baby, *our* baby…a sweet, blue-eyed little boy…and then I gulped and looked away from him, because imagining a future without Blythe hurt too fucking much.

In the wee hours of the morning, after checking on Camille (sound asleep in her bed) and getting Tish and Ruthie tucked in near her, I made my way back to the living room to say good-night to my sister, determined to ask how the evening went with Justin, from her perspective. Jilly was curled on our old couch, almost asleep there, and despite my own exhaustion I squeezed next to her, aligning my front with her spine, letting my chin settle between her shoulder blades. She smelled familiar, and like wood smoke.

"You had a good night with Bly, didn't you?" she murmured, sleepily. "He's such a sweetie."

I closed my eyes.

She found my left hand with one of her own and linked our fingers. She knew I was hurting, but didn't comment, only squeezed my hand in hers.

After a time, I whispered, "How was your night with 'the boy?'"

She giggled a little, barely audibly, at Dodge's nickname for Justin. She whispered, "He is such a stubborn man, but we have a date tomorrow night."

"That's wonderful!" I cried in a whisper.

"It's fucking amazing," Jilly muttered. "G'night, Jo," and we dozed there, snuggled together. I didn't recall anything else until Jilly startled awake, somewhere near dawn, and said clearly, "Someone's coming."

I groaned, blinking in the darkness of the room, realizing I was still wearing my contact lenses. They felt like hubcaps attached to my eyeballs. I flopped to the other side of the couch, stiff from being in the same position for hours.

"It's probably Gran getting up," I replied, still groggy, groping for the afghan that covered the back of the couch, desiring warmth and more sleep.

Jilly was only partially awake, but she whispered, sounding certain, "No, it's someone new," before resuming her light snoring.

Chapter Sixteen

IT WAS THE EVENING BEFORE THE FOURTH OF JULY, AN event in itself at Shore Leave. We had long celebrated the Fourth traditionally, in Landon at the parade and picnic, then on the water during the evening, for the fireworks. The night before, however, a huge group gathered at the cafe for a dance and an amateur fireworks display, set off by Dodge and Justin; many more people boated over and stayed on board their vessels, floating in the leisure of decked-out pontoons to watch the show. It was an event that drew a crowd since my childhood.

This year I was a woman torn nearly in two. I spent days working lunch, trying to catch my daughters for a word edgewise. I wasn't sleeping much lately, but I didn't feel tired; lovemaking restored my energy in myriad ways, restored me to *myself,* if I was honest, and despite the fact that I ran across the dewy grass every night to meet Blythe and didn't catch more than five hours of sleep or so a night, I felt more alive than I had in a decade. And yet the effects of hiding and sneaking, lying on occasion, to secure time with him bit ever more savagely into my conscience with each passing day. Blythe, too, was disenchanted with the secrecy, but I told him, quite honestly, that my children could not handle the truth, and he didn't push me any further.

I was crazy in love with him. I'd fallen hard and fast, completely tail over teakettle, as Gran used to say. Every day I lived desperately in the moment, determinedly beating away the entities of Responsibility and Common Sense. Jackie never called back in order to converse with me (when I was being more reasonable and less bitchy, according to his description), though he still communicated regularly with our daughters. I could be grateful to him for that, if nothing else at this point. A divorce was coming and I couldn't claim to be upset by this, not any longer. Instead the stress of what I would do in August, decision time, gouged me. The rational part of me, Joelle the Longtime Mother, knew what I would have to do, which was return to our lives in Chicago; I was deluding myself that there was even another choice to make. I must put my girls first, no matter what. My love for them superseded all else...but it hurt so horribly much to even think about giving up Blythe that I couldn't manage to dwell on it for more than a moment.

"Mom, can I borrow that one white skirt?" Camille asked, snapping me from my absorption. I stood gazing out across Flickertail Lake, watching as a sailboat glided along the horizon, letting the breeze stroke my face. It was late afternoon and in an hour or so a local band that usually played Friday evenings at Eddie's would set up on the porch; Mom and Ellen helped Dodge string paper lanterns from four poles sectioning off a rough square of earth in the flattest part of the yard, near the fire pit, where the kids usually set up the tents. I'd been listening as the three of them gave each other shit as they prepared the dance floor, putting up with Gran as she loudly directed operations from her lawn chair.

"Sweetie, you can have that skirt," I told my oldest, turning to smile at her. "I haven't worn that since high school. I don't think it would even fit me anymore."

Camille offered a genuine smile, looking lovely and tan, and very much like her father; she'd always possessed that same effortless grin as Jackie. Her dark curls were loose and soft on her bare shoulders; my girls all inherited Jackie's enviable mane of hair, thick and cascading and luxurious. Camille's cheeks shone pink and her long-lashed hazel eyes glinted in the mellow sun...it didn't take a genius to see that she was experiencing a case of the First Loves; to be fair, my opinion of Noah improved slightly as I'd spent more time around him. I still considered him a little flippant, even though Camille insisted he wasn't trying to avoid me, and I didn't get the sense that he was insincere. My concern was the unfiltered emotion that shone in my daughter's eyes when she looked at him, the kind of emotion that brims in your heart like a drug, overriding your sensibilities, capable of ripping you limb from limb before you're even aware of the attack.

Oh, my hypocrisy seemed to know no boundaries this summer, but I didn't want to think about that right now.

"Thanks, Mom," Camille chirped, and seemed about to breeze away, but then suddenly her gaze grew speculative. "Are you okay?"

"Sure," I said, forcing a light tone. The last thing I wanted was for my daughter to be worried about me.

"I'm just thinking about Dad and how you threw the phone in the lake," she said, and then asked carefully, "Have you talked to him since then?"

"No, I haven't," I told her. "But you guys have, right? Is he upset with me?"

"No, he didn't say anything about being upset. But he seems worried about you," Camille said, leaning on her forearms beside me. She looked over at Mom, Ellen, and Dodge, and giggled. "They look like they're having fun."

"What do you mean, worried?" I asked, not about to let her drift into a new subject without explaining this statement. "Why would he be worried about me?"

"Tish told him about how you cried sometimes," Camille confessed, apology in her eyes. She started to say, "I told her you'd be—

"I haven't cried at night since the first week we got here!" I snapped, hot with indignation.

"I know," she muttered. "Tish always tells Dad everything. You know."

I nodded acknowledgment of this, my pride stung. Then again, how could my pride hurt any worse after catching Jackie and Lanny on his desk? What were a few tears compared to that? I forced a subject change now, asking, "Hey, did you ever get over to White Oaks? Bull and Diana will be here tonight."

Camille looked immediately in the direction of the lodge, though it wasn't visible across the lake from our vantage point. She said softly, "Not yet. But I still want to."

"Is Noah coming to the dance tonight?"

Her eyes flew back to mine as she said, "Yeah, of course."

I nudged her shoulder, teasing, "You won't mind if I dance with him, right? He knows how to waltz and everything? You know, that dance from when I was a teenager?"

"Ugh, Mom, you're so annoying," she grumbled, pretending to be irritated with me.

"Thanks, that's my job," I replied.

"Milla, come and help me get ready!" Tish called then, from the direction of the path to the house, and I stifled the urge to march over to Tish and take her by the ear. I reflected that Tish had always been a daddy's girl, incapable of keeping things from him; she wanted to follow in Jackie's career footsteps, after all.

"See ya," Camille said, and hurried down the porch steps.

"See ya," I whispered softly, and looked back at the sailboat, but of course it was long gone.

The kitchen was closed for the evening, but Shore Leave was bustling with bodies a few hours later. I managed to sneak a shower in the bathroom at Jilly's, since my own was occupied by three girls fighting for mirror space. I blew out my hair, brushing it into silken softness over my shoulders, which were bare above a strapless, apple-green sundress I'd purchased last spring at Fox's in Chicago. It fit snugly over my waist and then flared into a knee-length skirt perfect for twirling.

I hadn't worn much for jewelry this summer (my wedding band and engagement diamond remained in the cut-glass dish on my dresser back in Chicago) but dug out a pair of slender gold hoops from my high school collection of earrings, spread mascara over my lashes and gloss on my lips, and studied my reflection with a quaking heart, vibrating with anticipation at the thought of seeing Blythe (who I hadn't seen since he left for home around four).

Just enjoy tonight, I told myself. *Enjoy every second.*

Soon enough I would have nothing more than the memory of this beautiful summer, and all flutterings of joy gave way to a desperation that made my teeth clench.

Just be happy tonight, Joelle.

Jilly emerged from the bathroom just as I located my sandals. I glanced over at her and gave a low whistle; she glared at me and then rolled her eyes.

"Hot Mama," I teased my sister. She wore a sundress with a short skirt and three tiers of ruffles cascading over the front, emphasizing her breasts. The color was a blue so deep it was almost purple, which echoed the blazing indigo of her eyes. Her hair was golden as sunlight.

"Thanks, you look good, too," she said. "Let's go boogie."

It was a basic potluck; people brought coolers with beer and soda, bowls of pasta salads, hot dogs, burgers, and all the fixings. Two of our picnic tables were lined up near the makeshift dance floor, covered in checkered tablecloths and overloaded with food. Dodge and Rich manned the grills, everyone eating and drinking, kids running all over (my own included); Gran was stationed on the porch, chatting with the band as they set up their drums. No microphones for this occasion, just a guitar for the lead singer, a local woman named Haddie, her husband Pete on bass, and Pete's twin brother Shawn on drums. I'd known all of them in high school; they'd been seniors my freshman year at Landon High.

Walking up to the familiar scene from a distance, Jillian at my side as always, with the slanting sun casting a soft summer glow that dusted everyone's hair, I felt a burst of contentment in my stomach. It caught me off guard, this sensation that things were right in the world, that I was on the correct path; occasionally I'd felt this way over the years and the feeling always seemed to strike suddenly and melt away almost instantly, allowing me to retain only a little of its force. I didn't know how to interpret it at this juncture in my life, when so many unknowns hung in the balance, when I was faced with decisions I'd been so consciously avoiding...

As though conjured by my thoughts, Blythe strode through the crowd, wearing his customary jeans and a dark blue t-shirt, his hair tied back and a smile on his sensual lips as he joined Rich and Dodge, wrapping one arm around Rich's shoulders, with complete affection. He hadn't spied me yet, but his internal radar was tuned to me (as mine certainly was to him), and he looked up and caught sight of my adoring gaze. He grinned so warmly, so tenderly, and an answering grin overtook my face.

Jilly clutched my arm and warned, "Jo, you've got to turn it down a little, unless you want to tell everyone the big news tonight."

I pulled myself together, though I couldn't look away from Blythe until we reached the crowd and about a dozen people claimed my attention: friends from Landon, the girls (Tish was mad at Camille about something), Mom (who needed me to grab a pan of brownies out of the fridge, and did I know where she'd put that box of sparklers she'd dragged out of the shed for the evening?) Of course everyone talked at once.

"Mom, you look really snazzy," Tish noted, her gaze roving up and down my dress. "Is that the one we picked out back home?"

"Yes, and thank you," I said, attempting to sound unruffled. "I haven't worn it yet, so I thought why not?"

"It looks so pretty with your eyes," Ruthie said, and I felt unduly observed, like a science experiment, which wasn't fair; they were just being admiring.

"Thank you, honey," I told my youngest, and bent to kiss her forehead. "You both look pretty, too. Did Milla do your hair?" Ruthie's curls were pinned into a thick topknot, with tendrils drifting down her neck. I teased, "You look like a lady from another century. Very romantic."

Ruthann nodded, then indicated her sister, saying, "And she made Tish put on a skirt."

So saying, Tish tugged irritably at the hem. She added, "Wow, Aunt Jilly, you look great, too."

"You don't need to sound so surprised," Jilly said. "But thanks, Tisha. Where's your big sis?"

"She's hanging out on the dock with Noah," Tish said in a voice that implied she was tattling. "She's so *annoying* now that he's here all the time."

"I agree," Ruthann added. "It's all 'Noah this' and 'Noah that.'"

"You guys are so harsh," Jilly teased them.

Behind me, Mom called, "Jo, go grab those brownies, will you?"

"I'm going, I'm going," I told her, skirting the crowd, peeking over at Blythe as I did. He stood chatting with Dodge, but his eyes followed as I climbed the porch on the far side, and he excused himself and casually followed me, at a distance. I entered the silent cafe, populated only by dust motes this evening, although the sounds of chatter and laughter from outside were only slightly muted. I pushed through the swinging door into the kitchen as I heard the outer door open once more; I smiled at the sound, as I knew it meant Blythe headed my way. Sure enough, he ducked through the same swinging door seconds later, into the kitchen that was empty of all but me, and I moved into his embrace at once.

He caught me close and brought my mouth to his, kissing me with small, teasing pecks before running his tongue lightly along my bottom lip. I curled my arms tighter around his neck; he was such a good kisser it literally made my knees weak. For a sweet long moment we kissed, growing more and more aroused, until he drew away just a breath and said, "You look amazing, baby."

"So do you," I told him, kissing his jaw, the cleft in his chin, and then his lips again, while his hands slid over my back, caressing, both of us unable to get enough. I said, "I'm so happy to see you. When I was walking over here with Jilly, I had this flash of feeling…not quite like how Jilly gets those feelings, you know, like I was telling you the other night, but similar…"

"What kind of feeling?" he asked softly. "A good one?"

"As though everything in the world was right," I said, clinging to him, and his gaze was tender upon my face. He moved his hands to stroke my hair.

"I've felt that way ever since the night you got here," he whispered.

"I need you so much," I dared to tell him. His eyes drove into mine as we held each other.

"Joelle," he whispered, and I swallowed hard at his tone.

"Later," I promised, pulling his lips to mine for one last kiss.

"Yes, later," he said against my neck. "I'll head back out first."

He did, with reluctance. I pressed both hands to my face, attempting to gather myself together. As I stepped outside, I happened to glance down at the dock, spying Camille sitting with Noah on the glider at the end, their heads tipped close together. I felt a sharp punch in the gut, seeing my daughter with a boy that way; she was seventeen, I fully realized, the exact same age I was when Jackie got me pregnant with her. But Camille was so much more innocent than me, and I could hardly forbid her to see Noah when they were so clearly smitten with each other.

As though you should talk, I admonished myself, harshly. *Oh God...*

I bit the insides of my cheeks, hard, and put that thought out of my mind; the band was picking out the first chords of a John Denver song, and I wanted to dance.

The sun sank and the western sky became rimmed with copper and violet, saffron and gold. The band played mostly up-tempo numbers, which was good because we could all shake it up or line dance without having to partner up. Blythe was a little shy, snagging a lawn chair near Rich (and most of the other husbands, who preferred nursing a drink and talking about fishing to any dancing) and cracking open a can of beer. I wanted him to dance, but was too self-conscious to go and pull him into the crowd in front of everyone. Instead I had a good time with the womenfolk and the few guys brave enough to join us (Clint was one, the cutie), meeting Blythe's eyes once in a while and telegraphing private messages to him.

Stars lit the sky and the lanterns glowed in rich jewel tones when the band finally slid into a slow set, and Dodge appeared to ask me for a dance. I was happy to dance with him, even happier that Justin came to claim my sister, the first he'd braved the dance floor this evening. Jilly slipped into his arms with her eyes like blue sparklers. And so it wasn't until much later in the evening (after I'd danced with Rich, and Clint, and a couple of rounds with Ruthann, who still liked to try and stand on my feet while we waltzed) that Blythe dared to approach. I smiled at him with my whole heart, as people coupled up all around us and Haddie sang a love song. Blythe held out his arms and asked, "May I have this dance?"

I slipped into his embrace, where I understood I wanted to be more than anywhere in the world, taking his left hand in my right, formally, as his right arm curved around my waist.

"Have you been having fun?" I asked as we swayed along to the music, Blythe gently stroking my back. If I rested my cheek upon him, it would have been in exactly the same spot where I pressed my face when we made love, and it was so difficult to act as though there was nothing between us but friendship.

There was no way I could continue refusing to acknowledge what I felt for him.

"Of course," he said, his deep voice caressing like a touch along my skin. "But this is the best part of the night…so far."

"For me, too," I whispered.

"I wish I could kiss you," he said, grinning down into my eyes. "You have no idea how fantastic you look. I love feeling you in my arms. I love it so much."

My heart ached at the sincerity of these words. "Thank you," I told him, tightening my grip on him. I said, "I will kiss you later, you can count on that."

After the song I took a break from dancing, joining Blythe as he reclaimed his seat near Rich. Rich sat chatting with Bull and Diana Carter, owners of White Oaks, and a younger couple, the co-owners of a nearby Rose Lake campground. I sat on Rich's other side, wishing I didn't have to put space between myself and Blythe this way, when everything inside of me wanted to be holding his hand, at the very least.

I'd known Bull and Diana Carter forever; they were the parents of three daughters and a son, longtime residents of Landon. The Rose Lake couple, who I'd met once before, last summer, were obviously very happy; I felt an intense pang of jealousy as I observed, though I would never dream of letting it show. The man, named Matthew Sternhagen, held his wife loosely around the waist as she relaxed on his lap, her dark eyes on his face as she laughed at a story he told. She was pregnant, probably about second trimester, their fingers lightly linked over her round belly.

"Jo, your girl asked about White Oaks earlier this summer," Bull rumbled in his familiar gravelly voice. "I'd be happy to show her around, anytime."

"She would love that," I told Bull, whose given name was Brandon; both his build and personality had long ago earned him his nickname. "Camille's just been busy this summer. But she loves history."

"Then she'll love the original homestead cabin, where Mathias used to camp out," Diana added, referring to their son, and I smiled. I knew their kids pretty well; their oldest daughter, Tina, was Jilly's age, and once upon a time we'd all partied together. I hadn't seen Tina or her younger sisters much this summer, but likely they were busy with their own families. Bull and Diana's son, the baby of the family, had probably graduated high school this past spring.

"How is everyone? Mathias must be headed to college this fall," I speculated.

"He's already finishing up his second year at the U of M, can you believe it?" Diana asked. "He didn't get back this way for summer break, though, since he's working in Minneapolis. Business major, you know. The girls are all in Landon, though, thank God. I'd go crazy if they all moved away from me. Tina and Sam might head over later, with their kids."

"We'll get our boy back up here someday," Bull said. "Even if I have to head to the city and fetch him by an ear."

"You need a drink, honey?" Rich asked me, and I seized the opportunity with both hands.

"That sounds great. But I can get it," I said, and then asked the group at large, "Anyone else?"

"I'll help," Blythe said.

I led him through the crowd, feeling conspicuous and not really caring about that anymore, but no one paid us any mind, too busy enjoying themselves to notice. Instead of heading for the coolers and the drinks, we made our way around the back of the cafe and into the hot July darkness, where we could be together and blessedly alone.

"Come here," Blythe commanded, his voice melting over me like the humid night air itself, and I went, up and close where we kissed and kissed, until he was breathless and I was nearly panting. A sense of desperation was beginning to jam itself into every moment alone—the end of summer, looming like a gaping hole before us, the threat of our time together ending.

"The house," I said urgently, my lips a fraction of an inch from his, and he wasted no time, hauling me along as we ran over the lake path, drunk on each other. The house stood silent and dark, the sounds of the party now distant and sweet, like a movie playing at a drive-in theater across the way. I pulled him inside, where he'd never yet been; too afraid of getting caught to take him upstairs to the twin bed in my room I ordered, "Kitchen."

It was incredibly dark here in the house, with no moon or streetlight available, and though we were well away from anyone, I was too worried about someone noticing any lights on over here to click any into existence. But I was very familiar with this space, and pulled him to the center island, where I made short work of discarding my panties before hopping up to sit on the counter. Blythe moved between my thighs with a throaty sound of appreciation, skimming his fingers under my skirt. I created a perfect space for him there, working hard to get his jeans undone.

"Come here," he murmured against my lips, clutching my naked hips and plucking at my lips with his incredible mouth. I shivered with the joy of being close to him, my Blythe, and he shifted his hips and let his boxers fall. It wasn't until later, my head on his chest, that I floated slowly back to myself. Blythe made a throaty sound, then kissed my left temple and murmured, "You don't know what you do to me."

But I do, I wanted to say. *I do know, because it's the same for me.*

He gently shifted me so he could haul his jeans into place, simultaneously collecting my panties, kind enough to slip them as far as he could, to about my knees.

"Thank you, sweetheart," I whispered.

From a foot away he grinned, bending to kiss my bare thighs one after the other, and then replied, "I love when you call me that."

"Come here," I demanded, hugging him as hard as I was able. Despite the fact that he'd only just left my body, already I craved him back inside. It was like a torch that flamed hotter the more we touched. He brought my knuckles to his mouth and kissed them, softly.

He whispered, "We better get back there, baby, before someone misses us."

And I knew he was right; I already missed him more than words could express.

Chapter Seventeen

JULY BURNED SWIFTLY ALONG, THE HOTTEST MONTH OF the year, the humidity up past ninety percent most days. Blythe and I met every night that I could sneak away, his old black truck our sanctuary. There we would talk and make love, make love and talk, listen to the radio and snuggle together. It was an insanity of living in the moment, and as much as I craved and hoarded our precious time together, each passing night brought August closer. And I dreaded August, tried my best not to accept its inevitable arrival, put off conversations about what I planned to do then, until one night near the end of July when Blythe, who'd seemed on edge all day, would no longer allow evasiveness.

"I want to tell everyone about us," he whispered against my hair. I lay sprawled on top of him, listening to his heartbeat beneath my left ear; I lifted my head to see him regarding me with serious eyes, one elbow tucked beneath his head.

"My girls won't understand," I said for the countless time, but for the first truly wondered if I was conveniently hiding behind that excuse.

"Why not?" he asked immediately. "They love you and they want you to be happy, don't they?"

How to explain this to someone who was not himself a father? Though I knew he would try, for my sake, he couldn't possibly understand the subtleties, the intricacies, the stress of the parent-child relationship. I said, and my heart was already coming undone, "It's not that."

"Then what is it?" he asked, and there was a layer of anger in his tone, one I'd never heard before this moment.

I floundered for a response. I said hoarsely, "It's everything. They're still adjusting to being away from their dad, and our separation."

"They seem pretty happy to me," he contradicted. "I've never seen such happy kids, Joelle. They worship you, and they have their grandma, and Ellen, and Jilly, *and* Louisa."

"That's true, but—"

"But what?" he interrupted. "When were you planning on telling them anything?"

"I don't know, I…" I was ashamed when, again, I couldn't justify myself. *Not yet, oh God, not yet*, my heart pleaded. Not yet, when there was no good place for any of this conversation to go.

"Joelle," he said, and his voice quavered just slightly, with emotion. He shifted and drew me gently with him, until we were sitting, my knees bent over his lap. He demanded quietly, "Where do you see us going? Be honest with me."

"I don't know," I said, agonized, tears filling my eyes as his grew tortured. I wanted to bury my face in my hands, but I wouldn't look away, not now.

"What have I been to you this summer?" he asked heatedly. "Sex, nothing more? A good lay?"

"You *know* that's not true," I whispered, a sudden husk wedged in my throat, aghast that he would think that.

He drew a determined breath and took my hands into his. "Well, I love you, Joelle, in case you couldn't tell. I fell in love with you the moment we met, even if I didn't realize it until later." It was the first time he'd actually spoken what I knew burned between us.

Tears streaked over my cheeks and I held fast to his familiar hands, his hands that caressed me with such passion, such tenderness, at last telling him the truth, "Blythe, I'm so in love with you, oh God, sweetheart, I can't tell you how much I love you. You have to know that."

He closed his eyes and drew a deep breath through his nose. I released my grip on his hands and cupped his dear, beautiful face, whispering, "I am so scared to lose you, but I don't know what to do, Blythe. I honestly don't know what to do."

His eyes opened instantly and flashed into mine. "Don't go back to Chicago, Joelle. Stay here. You *belong* here. Stay here with me."

My heart constricted.

"I mean it," he went on, fire in his voice now, conviction.

"Blythe," I said, closing my eyes as tears gushed over my face. "You don't know what you're asking."

"I do know, you think I don't because I'm too young, but I know what I'm asking you. I love you, Joelle, and I won't let you go. Hell, I can barely make it through the day waiting to be with you. I want you, woman, do you hear me? I love you and I want you to stay. Don't go. It would break my fucking heart."

I hugged him, burying my face against his shoulder as his arms crushed me close. He went on, his voice low and passionate, "Give me a chance. You'll see."

My heart seemed to crack along a jagged fault line as I said, "I wish I could, Blythe, you don't know how much I wish I could. But I have to think of the girls first." I gulped, throat aching as badly as if I'd swallowed broken glass. I whispered miserably, "I *have* to put them first, there's no other choice, and that's not fair to you. Don't you see?"

He grew totally still. We were both naked, clinging to each other, and I was breaking up with him. But I must do it; I was older, and wiser, and the bottom line was I loved him too much to let him do something he would come to regret when he was older, after he'd been through the strain of a relationship with someone who had three children, the stress that is inherent in *any* relationship with kids in the equation. I couldn't do that to him, and my heart shattered into pieces in my chest.

He spoke earnestly, insisting, "We can make this work, Joelle. I know it. I will not let you go."

I held back the sobs that wanted to rip into existence. I managed to say, my mouth bitter as rust, "You don't know, Blythe, you *couldn't* know what it means to be a parent. It's so much hard work, it will drain you dry. And I love my girls, I would do anything for them, and I still feel that way. How could I expect you to take on all of those responsibilities when they're not your own? I won't do that to you, I won't. You'd end up hating me."

His eyes blazed into mine, fierce and blue. "Don't say that. *Never* would I hate you."

"You could be with anyone you wanted," I whispered wretchedly. "Anyone, Blythe. Not just a woman with three kids of her own."

He stared at me as if I'd just stabbed him. And then he said roughly, "I don't *want* anyone but you, aren't you listening to me? I want you, Joelle, I want to be with you. I want us to have a family."

I couldn't stop the sobs now, even though I tried. The sounds huffing from my chest made it seem like I was choking. Blythe pulled me back against him and said, "Don't cry, please don't cry, baby."

I pulled away abruptly, so angry at myself I could hardly stand it. I groped around for my bra, my shirt, my hands shaking.

"I'm sorry, I'm so sorry," I said, again and again. "Please take me home."

"Joelle, don't do this," he begged, and the pain in his deep voice sent razors into my heart.

"I'm sorry," I whispered, trying and failing to hook my bra with such trembling hands. I left it, pulling on my shorts instead.

Blythe seemed to turn to stone; I couldn't handle the expression in his eyes. Without another word, he tugged on his boxers, his t-shirt, with movements tense and short. He turned the key and shifted into gear, and I sat with my face in my hands as he drove me back to Shore Leave in complete and horrible silence.

Less than five minutes later we pulled into the parking lot and he put the truck into park with careful, deliberate movements. He sat motionless, his hands hanging on the steering wheel and gaze fixed out the windshield into the darkness beyond. *Oh God, this was it.* This was the moment I was leaving him behind. My stomach heaved; just as I wrapped my fingers around the door handle he looked my way. The expression in his eyes punched a hole straight through my chest.

But as I hesitated, he bit his bottom lip and turned resolutely away. I clung to my conviction and forced myself to climb out of his truck. For a moment I thought he would peel out of the parking lot, waking the entire family, but he drove away slowly, and I watched until the red glow of his brake lights disappeared around the lake. Tears assaulted my face as I stumbled down the shore to the lake, barefoot, my bra unhooked and my shorts unbuttoned. I probably looked like the victim of a crime, with my mascara-streaked face, half-dressed. I knelt because I needed to throw up.

You knew this was coming, Joelle. You knew it.

But it's wrong. It's so wrong to let him go...

Blythe, come back. Oh God, Blythe Tilson, come back to me...

I made it about three steps onto the dock boards before I saw Jilly, sitting on the glider with a cigarette. At my approach she turned and said quietly, "I'm sorry, Joelle, I am so sorry."

"Oh, Jill," I moaned, and sank alongside her, tipping forward at the waist until my forehead was on my knees. I sobbed so hard my head pulsed. Jilly rubbed my spine with her left hand, over and over; I kept repeating, "I love him, Jillian, I love him so much." Her empathy transferred to me through her gentle touch, though she wisely said nothing. But then again, there was nothing left to say.

Morning dawned gray and cheerless. Tish, Clint, and Ruthann took out one of the canoes under a heavy sky; Camille hadn't emerged by ten, and was sleeping soundly when I poked my head in to check on her at ten-thirty. I knew this exhaustion meant late nights with Noah Utley, though I was hardly one to talk, despite the fact that my own late nights were very much over. Right now, I could not think more than a few hours ahead; somewhere in the back of my mind I was planning and packing our gear, loading our car and preparing to drive home to Chicago. We'd leave a week earlier than I originally intended, and I was well aware that I was running away. If I stayed here I would not be able to keep myself from Blythe, of that I was certain.

I spent the day hiding in the house, watching reruns (I hadn't actually turned on the television once all summer), sprawled on the couch, listlessly flipping channels. We'd never had a cable network in my high school days, but Gran enjoyed it now. I stared at show after show, having no idea what I was seeing. Around one in the afternoon Camille came down the steps in a long t-shirt and fuzzy slippers, shadows blooming under her eyes. She took one look at me and asked curtly, "What's the matter, Mom?"

I straightened up immediately at the suspicious edge in her voice, and said, "I just have a headache, sweetie."

She bought this (or at least pretended to), and continued to the couch, while I reoriented my focus upon her face. I asked, "Are you sick, honey?"

She shook her head and immediately got back up, though she'd just settled into the cushion. Without another word she made for the kitchen, leaving me to stare after her and wonder whether I should follow and feel her forehead, as I would have years ago. She was prone to headaches, I knew, just as I used to be at her age.

"There's aspirin in the cupboard beside the stove, Milla," I called to her, and then buried my face in my hands.

Evening rolled around, and I felt like fucking hell. My head throbbed. My eyes resembled bruises. I concocted an excuse to get out of dinner, even though Dodge and Justin were grilling steaks for us. I curled into a ball of self-pitiful torture in my twin bed, covers drawn over my head to shut out the mellow, peach-tinted light that streaked in through the window.

Blythe, I didn't mean it, I thought yet again, pressing against my eyes, willing him to hear me. *The last thing I want to do is leave you behind.*

Tomorrow would be July 28. I planned to take a few days to pack, say our good-byes, and then drive back to Chicago. The girls would be disappointed that we were leaving early, and I was devastated, but I couldn't stay any longer, even though everything within me rebelled against leaving, both Shore Leave and Blythe, but especially him. He hadn't called, nor been out here, though Rich's car arrived earlier in the afternoon.

I curled around my stomach and bent my forehead to my knees, thinking of last night, of the way his eyes looked when I ended us. *Oh God…*

If only I were unmarried, and twenty-three, how different things would be…he would understand in time, I must believe this. There could be no other choice. I thought back to May, arriving here crushed by my husband's betrayal, and how much my viewpoint about Jackie had altered since then. I felt happier in the last two months, despite everything, than I'd felt since I was young and unfettered and hopeful. And Blythe was the reason. Tears stung my eyes as I cried again, until there was nothing left, until I was hollow.

It was fully dark when I woke, though a quick glance at my cell phone indicated only a few hours passed. My mouth tasted parched and I sat up slowly, wincing as my temples pounded in response. I pulled shorts over my pajama shirt and ventured downstairs, and then outside, where the air was sticky with humid warmth under a still mostly-overcast sky. The crickets seemed to be a million strong and I strained to listen over their singing for the sound of voices on the porch. I couldn't hear anyone, but the parking lot was empty except for our vehicles, so at least Dodge and Justin were gone for the night, and Rich was nowhere to be seen. My shoulders relaxed incrementally. I could see the candle lantern burning as I walked closer, and then saw Gran and Jillian sitting around one of the tables; Jilly's face was lit with the glow, the light falling over Gran's at a right angle. Chief and Chester galloped over to greet me, tails wagging, and Gran turned to study me as I climbed the steps to join them.

"Joelle, what the hell is going on?" my grandmother demanded as I wilted into the chair opposite my sister. Jilly took a long swallow of her beer, regarding me with somber blue eyes.

I couldn't speak, unable to look away from the candle flame. I longed in that moment to tell Gran everything, longed to confess my love for a much-younger man, to own up to my feelings. I was so tired of hiding what I felt.

Gran observed, "You're as blue as I've ever seen you."

"Where's everyone?" I hedged, hoarse with despair. Jilly slid her beer across the table for me.

"Gone to bed," Gran said, and then asked bluntly, "It's Blythe, isn't it?"

"Goddammit, Jillian," I muttered, but simple relief also descended, the recognition that my relationship with Blythe was no longer a secret.

"Don't go blaming me," my sister all but yelped. "Like it wasn't as obvious as the nose on your face at the party!"

"Well I ended it," I hissed. I curled both arms around my torso, where it ached and pulsed at just the thought of what I'd ended. I whispered miserably, "I'm doing what I *have to do*."

"Joelle, it hasn't been a secret all summer, doll," Gran said, taking no mercy now. She thumped the butt of her cane on the porch floorboards and studied me with unflinching eyes. "You love him?"

I met her gaze steadily as I whispered, "Yes, God help me, yes. I love him."

Gran sighed then. "I knew it. I can see it all over your face, Joelle. Joan and Ellen knew it, too. You got it bad, as bad as Jilly here for the boy."

Jilly huffed a little, drawing her hooded sweatshirt more firmly around her shoulders and grumbling, "Why must everyone insist on calling Justin that?"

At the same time I sputtered, "Even *Mom* knows?"

"Oh, for heaven's sake, Joelle, she's not blind," Gran said.

And then suddenly, from out of the darkness, came Camille's voice. My shoulders jerked in surprise as she spoke from the edge of the porch, where she certainly heard every bit of our conversation. She said, "I knew it, Mom."

My head jerked her direction as she emerged slowly from the shadows, wearing an old sweater of mine over her shorts, hugging herself in the old-fashioned way she had, when things were tough and she needed the reassurance. Just like me. My heart sank onto the porch floor. Camille walked to within a few feet of us, her face lit from below by the lantern light, and stood totally motionless, appearing much older than her seventeen years. The candlelight picked out her delicate features, her pretty lips and long eyelashes, the freckles a summer's worth of lake time exposed. Her hair was soft on her shoulders, her arms clenched around her midsection. I felt for a moment that some sort of judgmental guardian angel rather than a child to whom I'd given birth stood over me.

"Camille," I said softly, on the thinnest of ice. "I didn't mean for you to find out this way. And it doesn't matter anyway, I ended it last night." Never mind the pain that seized my insides as I spoke those words; my entire body ached at the remembrance. I moved almost unconsciously into a pose mimicking my child, hugging myself harder.

"Blythe is so much younger than you," she observed, her voice quiet and strained. "How could you…*how could*…"

"Camille, I love him," I justified, heart clubbing against my crossed forearms. Gran and Jilly might not have been there, so silent were they, observing as though watching characters in a play.

Camille bent her head and I realized she was crying, softly and almost silently, and I was snagged, caught somewhere between concern and resentment. Was it that reprehensible to her, that I could possibly have such feelings? Tears flowed over her cheeks as we remained frozen in our respective places, until I relented, stood, and moved to gather her close. But Camille lifted a hand, a wordless request to halt, and I froze, blinking in stun. She gasped a little, as though in pain, and suddenly whispered, "Mom, I'm pregnant."

An invisible mushroom cloud seemed to morph over the porch, enveloping all of us in the numbing shock of the aftermath of that statement. As though through a long tunnel, I heard myself repeat, "Pregnant?"

The years melted away and I was suddenly swept back into the afternoon of my own confession; Gran and Jilly were present for that one, too. I'd confronted Mom while she sat peeling potatoes in the kitchen, mid-May, the trees outside in full apple-blossom splendor. I suffered through morning sickness for a week before finally working up the nerve to confess to her; only Jackie and Aunt Ellen knew at that point. Ironically, I spoke the exact same words to Mom that my daughter, whose tiny body I'd carried within my own, so full of shock and wonder and terror, just spoke to me. I remembered how Jilly, slicing the peeled potatoes for potato salad, froze and looked up at me, her blue eyes wide with surprise. Despite everything, she hadn't predicted my first pregnancy.

"Milla," Jilly said now, moving to her when it was apparent that I could not. I turned and curled my hands over the top rung of the porch rail, bending forward at the waist as though I might be ill. It wasn't that I was attempting to be melodramatic; I just needed a moment to absorb this news, which effectively trumped my own. I studied the lake, collecting myself, drawing a sense of peace from the familiar water, cloaked now in the darkness of a July night. Behind me, Camille clung to Jilly, sobbing now, rough, frightened sobs. My heart clenched like a fist and I moved instinctively to wrap my arms around them both, pressing my lips to my daughter's long, loose hair, her beautiful hair I'd combed into a top curl when she was just months old.

Oh Camille, oh Jesus. No, please no. Not this. I wanted to clench her shoulders and demand, *How could you? How could you do this to yourself, and your future?* But of course I did not. There was no use, not now.

My beautiful, smart, sweet eldest child, who was supposed to begin her senior year of high school in a few weeks, and then attend college and live in a dorm, earn a degree and obtain a fantastic job, befitting her intelligence and charm...no, no, no. She couldn't be pregnant. This wasn't how it was supposed to be, not for her. Not for Camille. All of those plans washed away now, as sticks in a strong current. I knew that better than anyone. She was exactly the same age I was with her. This, all of this, was my fault. Unequivocally, I blamed myself.

"Does Noah know?" Jilly asked quietly.

I felt Camille's nod. "Yeah, but he..." Here her breath hitched and she began weeping noisily again. When she was able to speak she continued, "He wants me to get an...abortion. He said he'd pay for it."

"That little bastard!" I yelped.

Jillian, who was the calm force I could not be at the moment, asked, "What do *you* want, honey?"

Camille moved from our dual embrace and sank to the chair beside Gran. Gran, sitting in unruffled silence, reached and curved her hand over Camille's, palm up on the tabletop. Jilly slipped her arm around me, holding me close with one slim, wiry arm, and I drew a deep breath in an attempt to regain some balance. Not much luck there. At last Camille spoke, whispering, "I want to keep the baby. I could never do something like that."

"Noah will have to support that decision," Jilly said. "Even if he doesn't want to."

"How long have you known?" I asked my daughter.

"For about a week now," she said, keeping her eyes downcast.

"Does Tish know?"

"No, Mom, of course not. I just told Noah a day ago."

"Did you take a pregnancy test?"

Camille lifted her gaze at this question, leveling me with a scathing look. "*Of course* I did, I'm not stupid. I have the pee stick if you want to see it."

A trickle of anger seeped into my belly then, burning away some of the shock, and I lamented, rhetorically, because I didn't exactly expect an answer, "How could this happen? Weren't you protecting yourself?"

"I did, we used a condom all of the times," she said, somewhere between a hiccup and a sob. "Mom, I'd never even had sex before last month. Seriously." And she began weeping again. I hurried to her side, wrapping an arm around her as she sat, my shoulders drooping with exhaustion and concern and a hundred other things that mothers consider when their daughters admit to being pregnant at seventeen. This time she allowed my touch, resting her head against my stomach, holding me around the waist.

From a few feet away Jilly said, "I *knew* someone was coming, I had that dream last month, remember, Jo?"

I shot her a look that asked, *Is this really the time?* But then a gut-instinct sensation rocked over me, unexpected and undeniable. I knew in that moment that we were meant to stay here in Landon, and not return to Chicago this week. I shuddered a little at the intensity of the feeling, realizing maybe I'd known this all along, and only now acknowledged the truth.

Camille misinterpreted my shudder and sobbed, "I'm so sorry, Mom, I didn't mean for this to h...h...happen..."

I hugged her harder, aching for her, and yet some ulterior satisfaction at coming to a decision was fulfilled in the same instant.

"Some things are just meant to be," Gran said, speaking my thought, and I reached across the table to squeeze my grandma's hand.

Chapter Eighteen

"WELL, SOMEONE IS GOING TO HAVE TO TELL JACKSON," Mom said over coffee the next morning. She, Ellen, Jilly, Gran and I were crowded around table three, a pot of strong black coffee taking center stage. Camille was still in bed, or at least she'd been when I left the house, and Tish, Clint, and Ruthann were outside somewhere, full of a breakfast that would have satisfied ten lumberjacks. Mom tended to turn to the stove when confronted with any sort of calamity.

"Oh God, I'm not telling him," I groaned, trying not to eyeball the kitchen where I'd spent so many hours studying Blythe this summer. The cafe was still and quiet this early Monday morning, filled with the scents of fresh-perked coffee and cooking oil, cheerful beams of sun slanting in from the east-facing windows.

"Joelle, he has to be told, and sooner than later," Mom badgered. Gran made a small motion with her coffee cup and Mom backed off, slightly. She added, in a gentler tone, "You haven't talked to him since you tossed our telephone into the lake."

"Mom, really," Jilly said. "It's not like he won't find out soon enough."

"Honey, I'm just so glad that you're staying here, I can't tell you," Ellen put in, squeezing my hand in hers, and I shot my auntie a silent *thank you*. She said, "I hoped you might decide to stay since the moment you got here."

"But surely you can't expect the girls to keep on being crammed into that loft," Mom went on, ignoring Ellen's pleasantries, her brow furrowing. She wore her feather earrings this morning, her hair in one long braid down her back. I studied my mother's familiar face with an age-old combination of deep love and utter frustration.

"Mom, of course not," I replied. "I was already telling Gran and Jilly before you got here that I'm going to talk to Liz about looking for a place to rent, at least for now. Jackie will have to pay child support, and I'll look for another job."

"Liz will hook you up," Jilly said. She was delighted at this turn of events. After Camille went to bed we sat on the porch with Gran and talked until almost three; I hadn't slept more than about four hours, and couldn't believe that Gran was up and about, but she looked as chipper as ever, clad in a hot-pink shirt featuring a rainbow trout leaping for a lure. She was the one to remind me that Justin's little sister was a real estate agent.

"And you'll have to get the girls registered for school," Mom said. "When is Camille due again?"

"Late February," I said. I felt as though I was reacting just as well as could be expected, given the circumstances. "She can go to school at least until what, January?"

"Oh, this is such a shock," Mom said, putting one hand to her forehead. "I can't believe I'll share a grandchild with Curt and Marie Utley. I would never have guessed. And Camille might not want to go to school in her condition, have you thought of that?"

"Joanie, this isn't the 1950s," Ellen said. "She's got nothing to be ashamed about."

"That is not what I meant," Mom said, sounding affronted. "It's just that—"

"I managed just fine," I interrupted, then sipped my coffee, meditatively. "Though I will never in a million years make my child marry that little bastard. After what he suggested." I was still quelling the urge to drive over to the Utleys' dairy farm and punch Noah in the face. If he thought he was getting away that easy…as though Camille got pregnant on her own, or to spite him.

"Jo, 'little bastard' is not the most tactful expression under the circumstances," Jilly pointed out, as the bell above the door tinkled and the kids came into the cafe. I regarded my two younger girls, thinking that there was no time like the present; Camille requested that I break the news to them.

"Mom, we're hungry," Clinty announced, flopping down at his customary spot. He slouched back against the chair frame and regarded her with his big blue eyes.

"Already? Then go raid the fridge, my little eating machine," Jilly said, winking at her son.

Tish perched on the tabletop near my right elbow, jingling the bangle bracelets on her arm; she'd found my old jewelry collection and those in particular proved a big hit. I studied the old metal bangles, silver and pink, blue and turquoise, mesmerized for a moment before Ruthann blocked my view as she came to give me a hug. I clung to my littlest girl, my sweetest child, though as a mother I could never acknowledge that thought aloud. Ruthie's warm arms around my neck fortified me to say, "Hey girls, I have a couple of things to tell you."

Both of them regarded me with somber expressions. Ruthann asked, quietly, "Are you and Daddy getting divorced?"

I'd spoken with Ruthie about mine and her father's separation, omitting the facts about Jackie's desire to remarry Lanny. Ruthie took the news much harder than Camille and Tish, as I'd known she would, and cried for an hour before calming down. I'd held her, stroked her hair, and answered all of her questions, but since then she'd avoided the subject, though I knew she talked about it with her sisters, as Tish informed me. But now my youngest faced me without flinching. I could certainly do the same in return.

"Yes, honey, we are, but the news I have is about Camille," I said. The room seemed to grow huge and silent, but I shouldered on, saying, "Girls, this isn't easy to tell you, but we're excited no matter what, and we support your sister—"

"Ugh, Mom, spit it out!" Tish groaned.

I narrowed my eyes at her and finished, "She's having a baby. She's due next February."

Tish gaped at me. I might as well have produced a hammer and bounced it off her head, so stunned did she appear. Ruthann frowned in confusion, even though she'd been delivered the whole birds and bees talk at age ten, like her sisters before her. When it was apparent they weren't going to speak, I continued, "She's still pretty surprised by all of this right now, so give her a big hug this morning when you see her, okay?"

Tish flung her hands into the air, ever my drama queen. She demanded, "That's *all* you're saying about this?"

"What do you think I should say?" I asked her. "I just found out last night myself, kiddo. I was pretty shocked, but what else can we do but more forward, huh?"

"Does this mean I get to be an auntie?" Ruthann asked, a certain amount of wonderment in her voice.

"Yes, sweetie, that is exactly what that means," Ellen said, winking at her. "It's a big job."

"I think it'll be a boy," Clint chimed in, taking things in stride, as was his fashion. Then he asked, "Who's the dad? Noah? You want me to kick his ass, Aunt Joey? I'll do it, you know I will."

I rolled my eyes at my nephew and said firmly, "No. Thanks though, Clint."

"I'm sure Milla would be flattered you thought of that," Jillian teased, eyeing her son over her coffee cup.

"And girls," I went on, this time watching Tish even more warily. "I've decided that we should stay here, in Landon."

"And not move back to Chicago?" Ruthann asked, and my gaze flickered to her. "But what about all of our friends? What about Daddy?"

"Sweetie, you can visit him anytime you like," I was quick to reassure. "But I think we belong here, don't you?"

Ruthann's lower lip looked in danger of protruding, but she rallied and then nodded. Tish shrugged and said, "Yeah, that's cool, Mom."

And I managed the first smile since breaking up with Blythe.

Later in the afternoon I escaped my family to take a walk. The sky was a fanciful blue, Flickertail Lake glimmering like a polished stone, no significant wind to mar its surface. I ambled barefoot, reconsidering everything about my life as I followed the lake path. The leaves were so thick on the trees, the grape vines so profuse and wildflowers blazing with such abandon, that I seemed to be in a jungle rather than a temperate deciduous forest. My favorites, the tiger lilies and the daisies, were in full splendor in the sunny ditches. Beneath my feet, the path was dusty and pitted with rocks. Looking at the daisies only reminded me of the one I kept pressed between the pages of our old *Webster's Dictionary*.

Could I change my mind, relent to what my heart so desperately wanted? We were going to live here now, and maybe Blythe and I could date openly; we could see where things would go. I walked with that thought beating at my breastbone, pretending it could happen, that he wouldn't eventually go insane being a surrogate father to three teenagers and now a brand new baby. I did the right thing by not letting our relationship go any further, I knew that.

But it hurt so sickeningly much.

You love him. You are in love *with him. Don't throw that away, Joelle.*

My heart sobbed, rattling my ribs, and I folded my arms over it, walking for several more beats with my head lowered.

But he's so young. What if he doesn't want to stick around this little old town? And then my certainty responded with, *But he loves you. You know he does. And you've never felt this way, not even for Jackie.* I drew in a lungful and held it, knowing this was true. But I couldn't make decisions based on what I wanted alone. I hadn't that right. *So what will you do tomorrow, and the day after that? Next year, and the next?*

The only thing I knew for sure was that I was going to be a thirty-six-year-old grandmother.

⨾⨾

On Tuesday I met Liz in town (conveniently keeping me from the cafe and the chance of running into Blythe), and we looked at houses for rent, though I didn't make any decisions. I was still in a state of stun as I drove back to the cafe hours later, from the amazement of settling permanently in Landon. And I could not deny my deep desire to see Blythe's truck pull into the lot; when I worked, I could not keep my eyes from the wide front windows, dying for just such a sight. I was afraid the moment I saw him I would bolt into his arms and never let go. When Liz dropped me off at Shore Leave, I noticed immediately that his truck was not in sight, though Rich's car was in its usual spot. I entered through the porch door and was intercepted by Jilly, on her way out. She held two cigarettes in her hand, and a book of matches clamped in her teeth. She transferred these to me by sticking out her chin, and then said, "Jo, we've gotta talk."

I followed her down to the dock, asking, "Is Camille all right? What's up, Jills?"

She plopped onto the glider bench and lit both smokes at once, then handed one to me. She squinted up at me and said quietly, "Fuck, I can't say this to you."

"What?" I demanded, flicking ash though I hadn't taken a drag.

"Blythe is moving back to Oklahoma," she said, and studied me with worried eyes. "Rich was telling Mom and Ellen just now."

I swallowed hard, keeping my face neutral with effort. I realized I was also gritting my teeth and stopped at once, though my heart seized like a fist inside of my chest.

"Jo, say something," she begged.

I shook my head, compressing my lips.

"He's leaving this weekend. Poor Rich is all confused. Fuck, Joelle, I'm so sorry."

"What did I expect?" I whispered. I sank beside her, my knees giving out. Tears were coming fast now, and though I never once in my life littered into the lake (unless you counted the phone) I flung the burning cigarette and clamped both hands over my face.

Wednesday and Thursday passed without a word from Blythe. Mom and Ellen hired a new cook, an older guy that Rich knew from the trailer park. Noah Utley showed himself on Thursday, finally, looking ghost-pale and drawn, and though there were a great many things I wanted to say to him, I refrained from any commentary and instead allowed him to join Camille in the living room, where they talked for no more than fifteen minutes before Noah emerged, alone, and made for his car like a bat out of hell. I could only imagine what occurred—I wanted to race over to the house and make sure Camille was all right—but I knew her well enough to know that she needed a moment alone. But I ached to imagine the pain this conversation with Noah had surely caused her.

We were all spying from the front windows of the cafe, of course, and as Noah rushed to escape I marveled, "I can't believe doesn't even have a word for any of us." Even Jackie didn't shirk his duty back when, despite his numerous other failings; he spoke to Mom the same way he would have approached my father, politely and with respect, to ask permission to marry me. Never mind that his mother forced that on us. At least he didn't abandon me back then, when I was pregnant with Camille. I spent plenty of time reflecting on what my life would have been like without moving to Chicago, and long ago concluded that it was right at the time, and most importantly of all, gave me both Tish and Ruthann; I knew in my heart that I kept the best of my husband with me at all times, in my daughters.

I called Chicago after Noah left, knowing there was no use putting off telling Jackie the news—all the news, no flinching, including Camille's pregnancy and my decision to stay here in Landon. I called our townhouse after Jackie's cell phone went directly to voicemail and was surprised to hear a woman answer, a woman with the kind of smooth, sexy voice that could only belong to a slutty coworker named Lanny.

I needed to let that bitterness go.

"May I speak to Jackson?" I asked, trying with some effort to keep my own voice polite and neutral.

"He isn't here," she informed, sounding just the slightest bit confrontational. "He's driving up to Minnesota, actually." I was more than a little shocked to hear this news. Probably it was my surprised silence that compelled her to continue, "He's bringing divorce papers for his wife to sign."

Again I was floored, not so much that Jackie would take something like this into his own hands, but that Lanny, who must realize that his wife was the one to whom she spoke, would take such glee in informing me. I refused to give her any satisfaction, and only said softly, "Thanks," before hanging up.

By Friday evening I was sunk into a desperate panic; I knew from Rich that Blythe planned to leave in the morning. I paced the dock for an hour before I worked up enough courage to call his phone, and held my own with a shaking hand as the line rang once, twice…and then at last he answered, his warm deep voice igniting everything within me, closing off my throat.

"Joelle," he said, and I knew I was going to cry.

"Don't go," I whispered.

"I can't stay here," he said, his voice husky with emotion. "And I won't force you to make a choice you can't make."

"Please don't go," I said, terror at the thought of never seeing him again overpowering my resolve.

"Joelle," he begged. "Don't say that if you don't mean it."

I suddenly realized that he was pulling into the Shore Leave parking lot for the first time since he'd dropped me off last Saturday night. I watched, from fifty paces away, as he parked and asked, "You on the dock?"

"Yes," I whispered, and I didn't hang up as he made his way across the lot, skirting customers' cars, and then moved with deliberation down the hill from the cafe to where I stood, watching. I felt vulnerable, ill with longing, my heart begging me to run to the arms that would have certainly crushed me close and hard against him. The sun skimmed along his hair, tied back in its usual ponytail. He was wearing dark jeans and a dark t-shirt, and his shoulders shifted as he walked, so wide and strong it made my breath catch, as always. He studied me as he approached, his dear face unreadable, and I couldn't help myself, drawn instinctively to him, meeting him just where the dock touched the grass. Beneath my feet, the lake softly lapped the shore.

His eyes were blue and steady on mine, and so full of pain. I pressed both hands hard against my thighs to stop from reaching for him, the phone still clutched in my right.

"I just wanted to say good-bye," he said, low and soft.

My heart felt stabbed, rebelling against this. With just a few words I could turn this moment into heaven, but I was not that selfish. My lips trembled as I whispered, "I'm glad you came."

He looked intently into my eyes, as though memorizing every detail, and I couldn't bear the thought of never seeing him again, because surely when he left that's what would happen, so I blurted, "Camille is pregnant."

His mouth softened a little, and he said, "I heard from Gramps. How is she?"

"All right," I whispered. "We're all here for her."

"How are you, with it?" he asked. "I was worried for you when I heard…"

"Taking it a day at a time," I whispered. *Oh God, Blythe…*

"And you guys are staying here," he continued. "Gramps is happy about that. I'm glad you decided it. You belong here."

"You don't have to go," I said, and my voice shook, no use hiding it.

His lips compressed and twisted, as though he was trying not to cry, but his voice was steady as he said, "I can't stay here, Joelle, not if we aren't together. Call me a coward, but I can't handle that."

At that moment Mom appeared on the porch and called down, tactful as always, "Blythe, you get up here and say good-bye to all of us before you go! We miss you bunches around here already!"

He turned and forced some cheer into his tone, responding, "I will, Joan, and I'll miss you, too."

We walked together, close but not touching, and my mind screamed wildly at me, telling me to stop this, to keep him here. I felt dizzy and panicked, slightly detached from reality as I followed him into the bustle of Friday night at the cafe, where Mom, Ellen, and Jilly were working, along with Sue Kratz, who'd filled in on weekends since I'd been in junior high. Clint and Tish sat at the bar chatting with Justin, drinking tonics with cherry juice, and they were the first to hurry over as Mom spread the word that Blythe stopped out to say good-bye.

My middle daughter hugged Blythe, quickly and intensely, as she did everything. I reminded myself that she had no idea about our relationship. Tish insisted, "I will really miss you," and Blythe roughed up her hair. It was taking all of his effort to act normal, I could tell.

"I'll miss you, too, kiddo," he said, and then put one arm around Clint's shoulders for a hug. "You too, little buddy."

Camille sat at a booth across the room with Ruthann, both of them rolling silverware but looking in our direction. Gran sat with them, a mug of coffee at her elbow, and she waved for Blythe to come over there. He did; no one disobeyed Gran. I remained rooted, even as Tish and Clint followed Blythe, watching as he bent down to talk to Gran; she spoke intently to him, before kissing his cheek.

Jilly stayed at my side, and she watched with me as Blythe spoke to the girls and our grandmother. She hooked an arm around my waist, whispering, "We'll get through this, Jo."

I didn't agree, and moved my gaze away, out the window, pain biting into me. And suddenly, lo and behold, there was Jackson Gordon, my husband, striding across the parking lot as though he owned the place. He looked fantastic, of course, even if he no longer retained the power to move me in that way. His dark curls were trimmed but still managed to fall slightly over his tanned forehead; his clothing was impeccable; his shoulders wide and his movements exuding typical confidence. He was in his home territory, the beloved former football star, now turned wealthy lawyer, moving as though through a crowd of adoring fans.

"Holy shit," Jilly uttered, following my stricken gaze. "What's *he* doing here?"

Tish, also facing the window, happened to notice her dad at the same moment, and her face split into a grin. She poked Ruthann and they both fled the noisy cafe, running to meet him. They intercepted him about ten feet from the porch and for a second Jackie looked sincerely glad, catching Ruthann into his arms as she shrieked, "Daddy!"

Camille, still rooted to her chair, observed with wary eyes, certainly wondering just how much her father knew. Blythe realized who Jackie was and even from across the room I sensed everything about his posture change in an instant. With no hesitation he made his way back over to me, but I hardly had time to register this before Jackie climbed the porch steps; the bell above the door tinkled as he entered. He gave the familiar space a quick perusal, locked on me and headed my direction, our younger two daughters in tow.

"Hi, Joelle, you look great. Jillian, hello to you, too," my husband said smoothly, coming to a stop a mere two feet from us, but then his eyes flashed to Blythe, confused as he intuitively sensed both the protectiveness and animosity emanating from this stranger. Jackie hated it when anyone was taller than him; he was too accustomed to being the peacock in the room, the one everyone admired.

"Hi, Jackie," I said, finally finding my voice. I lifted my chin a little, determined that I would handle this on my own, though my insides churned like the lake in a late-summer storm. I reminded myself that Jackie didn't know about Camille.

"Mom, Daddy's here!" Ruthann chirped, and I forcibly bit back the rude things I would have loved to say to him. I would not sink low in that fashion in front of my children.

"Yes, honey, I see that," I told her. "Would you go and tell Camille to come and say hi to Dad?"

"Sure," she agreed, and scampered away.

"Why are you here, Jackie?" I asked, though I knew (thanks to super-classy Lanny), unable now to keep the edge from my tone. Tish began to look a tad bit concerned, shifting from one foot to the other, her gaze lighting between myself, her father, and Blythe, standing, ironically, in a triangle.

Jackie narrowed his eyes at Blythe and ignored my question, instead asking, "Have we met?"

"No," Blythe said curtly, his voice tightly controlled, but I could hear the tension and slight edge of menace beneath the surface.

Jackie suddenly turned possessive, curling one arm in a familiar way around my waist, tipping his face near my ear and saying, "Jo, I need to talk to you privately."

I tried to move out of Jackie's annoyed grasp, saying, "Give me a minute," but he was not to be deterred, and insisted, "No, *now*, Joelle. I didn't drive all the way here to—"

Blythe's hand was like an iron trap closing around Jackie's forearm. I felt Blythe clamp hold, as Jackie's arm lined my back, and Jackie let go of me immediately, swinging around and facing Blythe, emanating anger now. Beside me, Jilly frantically signaled Justin.

"Take your hands off of her," Blythe ordered, and I shivered a little at the tone of his voice, simultaneously moved that he was standing up for me, ill-timed as it was (there was nothing to fear from Jackie), and wary of my husband's response.

Sure enough, he was livid. "Back the hell off," Jackie said, not bothering to keep his voice down. "This is my *wife*."

Justin, thank heavens, was suddenly there, and my shoulders sank with relief as he clasped an arm around Jackie and said, as though with no idea there was any tension between us, "Buddy, long time no see! How the hell are you?"

Tish grabbed my arm and yelled in a whisper, "Does Dad know about Camille?"

"I don't know, honey," I said, and then with my eyes implored Blythe to keep calm. He was on a razor's edge, I could tell by the set of his shoulders and the black expression in his eyes, but I did have to talk with Jackie, little as I wanted to, now or ever again. Justin succeeded in catching Jackie off guard, at least for the moment, and I redirected my soon-to-be-former husband away from my former lover, taking Jackie outside into the evening light of our hometown, pulling him around the far side of the porch.

The instant the outer door closed, leaving us relatively alone, Jackie wasted no time accosting me, spitting out the words just below a yell, "Who *the hell* is that guy?"

I was ill with the stress of everything that was happening, but controlled my voice enough to insist, "It's none of your business, Jackie, so let's get back to why—"

But he interrupted swiftly, condescension dripping in every word as he demanded, "Are you fucking this guy, Jo? Is that it?"

Apparently he did still possess the power to rouse me to anger. Heat flashed into my eyes and cheeks, and I drove my pointer finger into his chest, hard. He didn't back off, but instead glared at me with his own eyes sparking. Familiar eyes I'd gazed into countless times from across the breakfast table, on vacation at the beach, during sex.

"How dare you!" I yelled. "You *hypocrite!* If anyone deserves to—"

"Don't you have any respect for our girls?!" he raged, interrupting me again, and really boiling now. "It's no wonder that our oldest is knocked up when—"

"How do you—" We couldn't get a word in edgewise over the top of one another. My hands were planted on my hips to keep from strangling him. I yelped, "Who in *the hell* told you?"

"Your mother!" he shouted. "She thought I deserved to know! When were *you* planning on telling me? Or were you too busy getting laid by some guy with a *fucking ponytail*—"

Without thinking, I hauled off and smacked Jackie straight across the face, with a wide-open palm. I was no wimp, and all of my frustration and anger drove the thrust of that motion. Neither of us ever before raised a hand in anger to one another.

Jackie, obviously stunned, yelped and caught me by the forearms and then backed me up against the wall, hard. It didn't hurt, exactly, but I was caught off guard and it must have looked pretty bad, because in the next second he was plucked away from me as though he was a rag doll and absolutely flung to the floorboards, where Blythe towered over him like a superhero enraged.

"No!" I gasped out as Blythe moved as though to finish him off. Jackie rolled to one side and suddenly Jilly, Justin, Mom, Aunt Ellen, and my girls flooded out of Shore Leave and onto the porch, crowding each other to see what was happening. Camille was in a tizzy, sobbing.

Blythe seemed to come to his senses and backed off, but not before issuing a warning to Jackie, "If you ever touch her again you're a *dead man*."

"Fuck you," Jackie told Blythe, getting to his knees, not seeming to care that our children were right there.

Blythe moved swiftly to me, ignoring Jackie's bait, cupping my upper arms with both hands and stroking gently. He asked, "Did he hurt you?"

I wanted to laugh and cry, overcome by near-hysteria at the insanity of the situation. "No, I'm fine," I reassured. "I'm just fine." I was terrified of what my girls thought of all this more than anything. I hurried first to Camille, who leaned against Ruthie, and gathered them close, rubbing Camille's back.

Tish yanked at my elbow and demanded, her voice astonished, "Did Dad *hit* you, Mom? Are you okay? Is that why Bly knocked him down?"

"Holy shit, Aunt Joey," Clint was saying from the other side of Tish, excitement in his tone, and Jilly wrapped an arm around my waist, her grip secure and comforting. She leaned in and whispered, "Wow, that was *so* satisfying, I'm just saying."

"Patricia, your dad didn't hit me," I told her, firmly. "We were having a disagreement and Blythe misunderstood."

Blythe inadvertently blocked my view of Jackie, and so I didn't see him move until it was too late. Mom suddenly shrieked, and I turned in time to see Jackie launch himself and drive into Blythe from behind, knocking him forward and into me. Blythe spun around and took a solid punch in the chest, but he clamped both arms around Jackie in a sort of ferocious bear hug, amid the gasps and shouts from everyone assembled on the porch.

I yelled, "Stop it, *both of you!*" to no avail.

Grunting, they stumbled down the porch steps, Justin on their tails, where Jackie managed to dislodge himself from Blythe's grasp, swung again, and was taken down for a second time by Blythe's hard right.

Jackie crouched forward, going to his knees, and Justin dodged between the two of them and ordered, "Enough!"

"*Joelle!*" Mom yelled, as though I could do anything. Customers poured out of the cafe now, others gathered at the wide windows, practically pressing their noses to the glass, and the air was lively with excited chatter and speculation.

Blythe was furious, steaming with rage, and I raced down the steps in time to observe as Jackie groaned, heaved a little, and then spit out a tooth. On the porch, Ruthann sobbed along with Camille. Jilly and Aunt Ellen were doing their best to herd everyone else back inside, but this was by the far the most entertaining thing going on this evening in the greater Landon area.

"Jo, get back up there," Justin ordered, but I ignored him and bent down to see to Jackie, concerned despite everything at the blood flowing over his chin.

"Get the hell away from me," Jackie snapped, and then winced.

"Don't talk to her that way!" Blythe ordered, outraged.

"You need to chill the fuck out!" Justin's voice cracked like a whip and he manhandled Blythe's shoulders, pushing him away from Jackie and me.

"You need an ice pack for your mouth, come on," I insisted despite Jackie's vicious gaze. "Come on."

"Get away from me," Jackie growled, rising unsteadily to his feet and elbowing around me, none too gently; Blythe made a low, furious sound and Justin finally surrendered him to me. Instinct propelled me into Blythe's arms, which collected me close and hard. His heart was going like a jackhammer and I let myself cling, trying to shut out everything else. At least for this moment, Blythe held me.

I didn't ever want to let go.

"I'm sorry, Joelle, I'm so sorry," he bent to whisper in my ear, and he was shaking, too, post-fight nerves on high.

"It'll be all right," I whispered, my fingers widespread on his back, even though I sharply suspected it would not be all right; Jackie's face was messed up and my girls had observed the entire fight, as well as a good dozen customers.

"Shit," I heard Jilly say from up on the porch, and her tone conveyed true concern. I moved out of Blythe's arms to see Charlie Evan's cop car rolling into the lot, blue top light swirling.

"Oh no, oh *shit*," I echoed, as the bulky officer who'd patrolled Landon since my high school days made his leisurely way to the shifting, babbling group of people congregating in the parking lot.

"Joan, Ellen, I had a call there was a fistfight out here," Charlie said, scanning the crowd with his gaze even as he addressed Mom and Aunt Ellen. The downside of having a law enforcement officer only a half-mile away at all hours.

"Charlie, it's all right now," Mom insisted. "Just a misunderstanding."

"I was assaulted," Jackie said in his lawyer voice, moving decisively through the crowd. He held a bar towel to his bleeding mouth.

"*Coward*," Blythe muttered. I hurried forward, shoving people unceremoniously out of my way.

"Jackson Gordon?" Charlie asked in surprise, assessing the man before him. "I haven't busted you for fighting since you were in high school, boy. Who roughed you up?"

"Charlie—" I began, imploring him, but Blythe was just behind me and said forthrightly, "I did, sir. He was in the process of harming a woman."

"I was in no way harming Joelle!" Jackie yelped. "Charlie, you know my wife."

Charlie nodded politely at me. "Of course. Evening, Joelle. You back to claim her now, Jackie?"

Jackie had the grace to look slightly ashamed.

My grandmother's voice suddenly cut through the crowd; even Charlie's spine straightened a hair at her tone. She came slowly out of the cafe, relying heavily on her cane, and looked down imperially from the porch.

"That's enough of this nonsense," Gran said. "Everyone clear out of here, right now! Show's through for the evening."

Charlie began again, saying, "Now, Louisa," but Gran, not about to be placated, interrupted Charlie and addressed Jackie.

"I've known you since you were a boy, Jackson Gordon, and you've had nothing more hurt than your pride this evening. Now, you have a right to see your daughters, but you leave Joelle alone. She's come a long way this summer and she doesn't need to deal with your selfishness right now."

"Lou, don't talk to me like I'm a child," Jackie snapped, his tone cutting.

"Then don't behave like one," she threw back at him. She continued, unfazed, "Charlie, you know Blythe Tilson, he works for me at the cafe. He was just defending Joelle because he thought Jackson was hurting her. It looked like it, too. I seen everything out the window."

"Is that true, Joelle?" Charlie asked.

I nodded, vehemently.

"Tilson, you say?" Charlie confirmed, and Blythe nodded. Charlie grunted under his breath and said, "Give me a minute," returning to his car. Jackie looked as though he might have more words for me, but took one glance at Blythe's expression and wisely moved to comfort his daughters.

"Thanks, Gran," I said. She rolled her eyes at me.

Blythe at my side, we watched Charlie climb into the driver's seat and fiddle around with his two-way radio. Blythe seemed unnaturally still, but maybe I was imagining that. Up on the porch, Mom was clearly angry, Ellen sympathetic, Gran unflappable, and Jilly, bless her, hustled Clint and the rest of his buddies back inside, at least for the time being; I could see her peering out the window. Finally Charlie emerged from his car, which was still flashing its light, unnecessarily, as if Charlie wanted to create as much drama as possible. This time Charlie's approach was more clipped, less friendly, and sudden fear splashed through me. I expected him to ask more questions, maybe interview a few people, but instead he stopped abruptly before Blythe and said formally, "Blythe Edward Tilson, you have the right to remain silent."

I stared at Charlie as though he'd produced a mallet and clocked me in the face.

"What's going on?" Gran demanded, disbelieving, as Charlie prattled through Blythe's rights. It was surreal, happening to the cast in a television show, certainly not to us. I couldn't move until Charlie unhooked a pair of cuffs from his belt and ordered, "Hold out your wrists."

"No!" I gasped, putting out my hands as though I could possibly stop a police officer. Beside me, Blythe stood grim and stone-faced; he offered his wrists with no resistance.

"I checked you out. There's a live warrant for your arrest, young man," Charlie continued. "State of Oklahoma seems to think you've violated parole."

Jackie was smirking, but I allotted zero time for him, terror coursing through me.

"No, you can't take him," I babbled, as Blythe allowed himself to be cuffed, his eyes begging me to understand.

"Gran, do something!" I cried, desperate now, as Charlie led Blythe to the back of the squad car.

"Joelle, I'm so sorry," Blythe said as I followed directly on his heels. His voice bore the sound of strain, of barely-discernible fear, and I started to cry, inexplicably terrified. Charlie ignored me completely, loading Blythe into the car, and I pressed both hands to my mouth as the door clicked shut. Charlie resettled his bulk in the driver's seat, all without a word for me. Jilly raced out of the cafe and caught me around the waist, everyone staring, and again the crowd surged outside; this was by far the most entertaining event in Shore Leave's history in decades.

Gran muttered, "I'll be damned," and I leaned on my sister, watching as the car turned and drove out of sight.

Chapter Nineteen

I STARED AFTER THEM, DISABLED, BEFORE ENERGY SEIZED me, replacing the terror. I broke free of Jilly and sprinted up the steps, ignoring the questions that everyone tossed excitedly in my direction, pausing only to gather my girls. The three of them stood together in a tight bunch and I ordered, "Come in here," holding the door as they obeyed without question. I led them back into the kitchen, where Rich was already on the phone, plucking at his white hair, as was his habit when distressed.

"Christy, it's Rich, call me as soon as you get this," I heard him say, and realized that he was leaving a message with Blythe's mother.

The kitchen smelled strongly of the fish fry in full swing just earlier this evening. I was breathlessly anxious, fearful for Blythe, and stood momentarily rendered mute, studying the three expectant faces of my girls; Tish's eyes shone with the excitement of events outside the usual routine, in contrast to Camille's and Ruthann's, red-rimmed with the aftermath of tears. I gripped my hands together and opened my mouth to speak just as Tish demanded, "Mom, what's going on?"

"I'm sorry that Blythe hit your dad," I said first, trying not to think about how much I wanted to be following that car with Blythe inside. First things first. I explained, "He only thought Dad was hurting me, which he wasn't. Dad and I were in the middle of a fight."

"Mom—" Camille began, but I held up a hand and she bit her lower lip.

"The thing is, girls, I fell in love this summer." I spoke the words and waited for the outbursts to happen, although Camille already knew.

Tish actually asked, "With who?"

"It's Blythe, isn't it, Mama?" Ruthie said at the same exact second.

I nodded and Tish started laughing, in pure disbelief. When she realized I wasn't kidding, she choked back her laughter and managed to peep, "You did?"

"Yes, and I'm going to go to him now, to see what's going on. I just wanted you guys to know."

"I like Blythe," Ruthie said, although she sounded bewildered more than anything.

"Me too, but Mom, are you *serious?*" Tish asked, her blue eyes wide with wonder.

"*God*, Tish, yes she is," Camille finally spoke, her voice crackling with disdain. "Why do you have to act like such a moron? Yes, I'm having a baby and yes, Mom is having an affair with Blythe."

"Shut your face, Milla! Why do you have to act like such a *bitch?*" Tish flung back at her sister, fists on hips, and I didn't have time for this right now.

"Girls!" I thundered, but then throttled my voice down to about second gear. "We'll talk when I get back tonight, all right? Why don't you guys go find your dad, you haven't seen him all summer."

I bent and kissed Ruthie, and she clung to me to whisper, "We'll be all right, Mom, don't worry."

I left the kitchen at a jog; people were staring, but I didn't give a damn right now. I banged out the screen just in time to catch the tail end of an argument between Jackie and Gran. Hoo boy.

"Joelle, I am not about to put up with this," my husband groused, detaining me with one hand on my upper arm.

"Jackie, I'm sorry about your mouth, really," I said, and I really was, impatience causing me to hop from foot to foot.

"Forget my mouth. What about your relationship," and on that word he hooked his fingers into sarcastic quote marks in the air, which he knew I hated, "with some goddamn *criminal?* I won't have our daughters exposed to that."

I stared hard at him, into the familiar eyes in his tanned face, and realized afresh that he was missing a tooth. It was the one to the left of his perfect white incisors. I knew he was probably only concerned for his children, and that he did not have any clue what an amazing person Blythe truly was, but petulant jealousy was also present in his tone. I drew the line at putting up with that.

"Listen, I know I owe you an explanation, all right? But not right now. Leave the divorce papers, I'll sign them gladly. "

"How did you…"

"Your fiancee," I said, with a certain amount of satisfaction. "She was kind enough to let me know when I called yesterday."

Gran snorted, leaning on her cane. Mom and Ellen were back in the cafe, doing damage control. I didn't see Jilly or Justin anywhere, but the girls emerged slowly back outside, Camille bringing up the rear, dark eyebrows knit, her expression riddled with anxiety. Jackie's gaze softened at the sight of his daughters, and I took advantage of that to dart down the steps, calling good-bye to the girls and Gran over my shoulder.

"We'll be here," Gran called after me.

I grabbed the keys to my car but Justin's truck sat idling in the lot, he and Jilly inside. She caught sight of me and hollered, "Come on, let's go!"

I climbed in, displacing Jilly closer to Justin, where she hooked her left hand around his thigh and patted him twice. Despite everything, my heart smiled to see that gesture, and I buckled up, saying, "Thanks, you guys."

"No problem," Justin responded, clearing the lot and signaling right to head back to town. "It kinda takes me back, you know, getting in the middle of a fight, having to bail somebody out."

Jilly and I both laughed, and my sister speculated, "Who'd you ever bail out of jail?"

Justin said, "Well, Dad for one."

"Oh shit, that's right," I remembered. "Back senior year."

"He got cited for drinking and operating a speed boat," Justin laughed, although it was a pretty serious offense, and his third. Nowadays Dodge did his drinking on shore.

We drove in silence after that; Jilly kept one hand on Justin's leg, and he threaded the fingers of his free hand into hers. I leaned forward, as though that would help us get there faster; as we pulled up to the government center, my heart rate increased exponentially.

It was twilight by now, the western sky laced with mackerel clouds, through which the setting sun beamed in bright magenta. I tried to interpret this as a good sign, a light show from the heavens that meant Blythe was not in serious trouble with the law. What could Oklahoma want with him these days? Hadn't he served his term two years ago? He'd never mentioned parole…for a second I felt a twinge of fear that I didn't know him as well as I thought, but that melted away the moment we were inside and I knew he was nearby.

Justin and Jilly knew the cop working the counter and chatted with him for a few moments, while I surveyed the otherwise empty waiting room with nervous eyes.

"We're here to see Blythe Tilson," Justin said. "He was just brought in."

"Big guy, with Charlie?"

"Yeah, that'd be him," Justin agreed.

"Can I see him?" I asked, trying not to sound as desperate as I felt.

"They're booking him right now," the cop told me, not unkindly. "I'll see what I can do after that." He indicated a handful of orange vinyl chairs and a coffee table holding a couple tattered magazines.

So we waited, a good half hour, and I was so grateful that my sister and Justin stayed with me that I could have cried; instead, I sat and bit my thumbnail while Jilly sipped coffee and Justin flipped through a *Car and Driver* that was probably twenty years old. When Rich joined us, I jumped to my feet and ran to hug him. He explained that he'd talked to Christy, his stepdaughter.

"Apparently Bly punched out a guy that Christy was fighting with. This was just last March, and he's been on parole since then. He should have known better than to leave the state," Rich said, his eyebrows drawn inward and his mouth drooping. "Christy said she didn't think it was a big deal because he was moving up here for a job. But Bly never waited to get confirmation from his parole officer. And now this, another fight."

"Hey, at least he cares about the women in his life, stands up for them," Jilly pointed out.

"He has a hot temper that he needs to watch," Rich said, shaking his head and studying me with open concern. "Jackson wasn't hurting you, was he, Jo? I can't imagine he really would."

"Well, it looked really bad," Jilly said, either the coffee or her nerves contributing to her faster-than-normal speech. "I was right at the window, spying, and Blythe came up just behind me, and we could see Jackie's face but not yours, Jo, and when you stabbed your finger at him, Jackie looked ready to spit nails, and Bly goes, 'I'm going out there,' and I said, 'No, don't, it's okay,' but then you slapped him—nice move, by the way—and Jackie whirled you around really fast. It did look bad…your head sort of flew back as you hit the wall, and Blythe moved like lightning. One second he was standing by me, and the next he was flinging Jackie around like a puppet."

"I can't believe he did that," I agonized. "Jackie lost a tooth and he'll probably try to sue for everything he can, just to be a dick."

"We'll talk some sense into him," Rich assured me. "But, honey, why did Blythe get in the middle of all of this?"

I blinked.

At that moment, thank heavens, another cop appeared through a door and said, "You can see him now, for a few minutes."

I sprang to my feet, heart fluttering like a trapped bird. Behind me, I heard my sister heave a sigh and say, "Rich, there's something we need to talk about…"

I blessed her and followed the cop down a yellow-painted concrete hall, past an office full of crap, a couple of vending machines, and then we took a right and came upon two cells, one of which was empty. In the other, Blythe sat with his forearms braced on his thighs, hands dangling and head bent, but when he heard me from across the room he flew to his feet. I ran to the cell, reaching for him through the bars, and fisted my hands around his shirt, clinging as much as I could. He caught my elbows in his big hands, lowering his face and burying his nose in my hair. I was shaking again, but his touch comforted me, and slowly the trembling subsided. Behind me, I heard retreating footsteps as the cop I'd followed went back the other way.

Blythe drew away enough to look at me, strained and full of concern; tears had recently been in his eyes, I could tell, and this knowledge hurt like a fist to my heart. He said, "I'm so sorry, Joelle, about all of this. You don't deserve this."

"Stop that," I said, moving my hands to cup his face, awkward as it was through the cold iron bars. "I wanted to tell you that I don't want you to go. Stay here. Please, Blythe, stay with me." Tears swam in my eyes and he gripped my waist, the bars between us rigid and unforgiving.

"Joelle," he whispered.

"I love you," I said, tears spilling over now, and he exhaled in a rush, tipping his forehead to my hair. I implored, "I'm *in love with you* and I want you to stay. Please don't go away from me."

His voice thick with emotion, he said, "Oh God, I love you so much. So much, Joelle. But you don't deserve this."

"Don't deserve someone who loves me, who defends me? You are a good man, the best, and I don't want you to run yourself down like that, do you hear me?" I was reprimanding him and crying at the same time, and my words didn't sound as stern as I intended.

"Baby, don't cry," he pleaded, thumbing my tears away.

I caught his right hand and kissed the palm, and held it to my face.

"This is about my mom's old boyfriend, back home," he explained. "He was a piece of shit, and I got home in time to catch him throwing my mom around, last spring. He had her by the hair."

"Then it was self-defense. You were defending her," I insisted.

"Mom told the court all of that," he said. "But I shouldn't have left town."

"What will happen?" I whispered, hollow with fear. I would not let go of him, and a cop was going to come in here and make me, any second.

"No doubt I'll have to go back there and face the music," he said, and my heart pulsed with determination; I would go to Oklahoma with him.

But of course I couldn't go with him, couldn't leave my daughters behind here in Minnesota.

Oh God, Joelle, Joelle, Joelle.

"Time's up!" announced a voice from down the corridor. My heart seized.

"*No*," I insisted. Blythe's eyes were agonized as he studied my face.

"Joelle," he said hoarsely, cradling my face in his hands. He whispered painfully, "There are things you don't know about me."

"Then tell me," I begged him. "What don't I know?"

"I can't explain right now," he said, as the cop reappeared and cleared his throat. Stubbornly, I didn't release my hold. Blythe said roughly, "I love you with all my heart. But I'm not good for you."

"Blythe—" I said, desperation closing around my throat. He closed his eyes for a second, and then released his grip on me and stepped away, back into the cell. His smoky eyes begged me to understand, and I could see what stepping away from me was costing him. I curled my hands around the bars.

He whispered, "You should go now."

"*Blythe*," I implored.

His throat bobbed but he whispered, "Go."

I gathered my strength, hugging myself around the waist to keep my heart from shredding further. I whispered, "Okay."

And then I followed the cop out of the room.

We drove back to Shore Leave in silence. Jilly kept her palm on my back while I sat with my face buried in both hands, wordless with anguish. Justin rolled down his window, allowing the comforting night sounds into the cab of his truck, but I was beyond being comforted by anything. I didn't understand how things went so quickly astray.

Rich stayed behind to post bail and promised to call us later. As we approached the cafe I lifted my face and inhaled deeply through my nose; Shore Leave glimmered with lights and should have been a warm and welcoming sight as we rounded Flicker Trail. I climbed numbly from the truck and was at least glad to see that Jackie's car was no longer in the parking lot. I hadn't walked more than ten steps before Ruthann bounded out of the cafe and caught me in a hug. I rocked her side to side.

"What took so long, Mom?" nagged Tish, hanging over the edge of the porch, peeling apart a piece of string cheese.

"Did you see Blythe?"

"Is he still in jail?"

"Did Rich talk to him?"

"Is he all right?"

"Was he wearing a black-and-white striped jumpsuit?"

I raised one hand to stop the flood of questions, which I was not equipped to handle at the moment, the last from Tish, who was kidding. Jilly filled the void with, "It sounds like he'll have to go home to Oklahoma, to face the charges there."

"Dad is staying at his uncle's," Camille informed me from a porch table, where she sat munching a bowl of popcorn. "He's going to call you tomorrow."

"Great," I muttered. I joined her, cupping a hand around the back of her head as I asked, "Did you guys get to talk?"

"Yeah, and he's not mad at me," Camille said, and I reached and gently squeezed her hand.

Ellen appeared with a glass containing ice and what I guessed was gin and tonic, from the scent. I took a long drink, winced a little, and then took one more. "Thanks, Ell."

"This will all wear out in the wash, you just wait and see," my aunt told me, patting my shoulder, and I wanted so badly to believe her.

"Thanks," I whispered.

"Is Blythe in trouble, Mom?" Tish asked, plopping onto the third chair at the table. She regarded me with somber eyes.

I drew another deep breath, but it came back out like a gasp. I said, "I don't know, honey, I don't know what will happen."

"So, is he like your boyfriend, then?" Tish pressed.

"I don't know," I told her again. My vision swam in the fashion of someone about to pass out. But I would not create more drama for my children tonight.

Jilly said gently, "Girls, enough with the questions right now, okay?"

"I think I'll head to bed," I managed. "You guys are all right?"

"Don't worry, Mom, we're just fine," Camille reassured, gripping my fingers, squeezing me for assurance.

"I love you," I told them, bending to kiss each of their heads. Then I made my way back over the lake path, not allowing tears until I was out of sight. And they came hard, striking me like fisted knuckles to the gut. Despite everything else that occurred tonight, I couldn't stop thinking that I'd left the jail without telling Blythe that I knew he didn't mean it when he asked me to leave. He asked me to leave and I left, without any sort of a fight. Without telling him that I was not about to give up on him.

Hours later, after sleep would not come, I rose and wrapped Gran's robe around myself, leaving her snoring in her bed. With aching eyes I made my way out to the dock, where the wee-hours sky glinted with stars. I wasn't even surprised to find my sister and Justin sharing the glider. Jilly scooted over to make room for me without a word, and I sat beside her and let my head fall against her shoulder.

Justin, from her far side, said softly, "Rich got Blythe out of jail, but they left for Oklahoma tonight. Rich is taking him down there."

"Rich will bring him back," Jilly whispered, catching my left hand in her right. "He will, Jo."

"No, I don't think he will," I whispered. "And that's why I'm going after him."

...The story continues in *Second Chances*

Excerpt from Second Chances

"GO AFTER HIM?" JILLY REPEATED, DISBELIEF RAISING HER voice about a half-octave.

I lifted my head from her shoulder and curled my arms defensively around my bent legs. I wore our grandmother's robe, my feet bare and chilly in the predawn damp, unwilling to be swayed by my little sister's incredulous tone. Instead, resolute in my decision, I rested my chin on one knee and studied the smooth, inky surface of Flickertail Lake, bathed now in muted starlight. The eastern horizon bore a slim stripe of pale saffron, slowly brightening. Though not normally unwilling to voice his opinion, Justin Miller, seated on Jilly's far side, wisely held his tongue.

Finally Jilly could stand my stubborn silence no longer and prodded, "Joelle, what in the hell are you thinking? You can't possibly follow them to Oklahoma. You have to let him go, for now, anyway."

At that I found my voice, ragged though it was from tears and exhaustion. "I won't."

I sensed my sister softening slightly; her next question emerged more gently. "Jo, what did he say when you talked to him?"

It stung me to my core to repeat Blythe's words, but I did, whispering, "He told me that he wasn't good for me, that there were things about him that I didn't know." And then, realizing that Jilly certainly possessed information I did not, I demanded, "What did Rich say earlier? You must have talked to him."

Jilly shifted and raked her right hand through her short golden hair, creating a spiky mess. From the corner of my gaze, I saw Justin curve his hand around her thigh and pat her twice, a calming gesture. For a moment I didn't think she was going to elaborate, and I dropped my feet to the dock and turned to implore her.

"Jilly, please tell me," I whispered, studying her familiar profile.

My sister bit her lower lip and then turned to face me, the blue of her eyes evident even in the meager light. She said, "Rich called about two hours after you'd gone to bed. Mom talked to him. He bailed out Blythe and then told Mom he was taking Bly back to Oklahoma. No ifs, ands, or buts. It was part of the condition anyway, since Blythe has to face charges there. Now, if Jackie decides to press any here, then Blythe will be in extra trouble."

I curled my hands together and pressed against the ache in my belly. Jackie could most certainly decide to take that option; Blythe not only knocked him down twice, but Jackie now also sported a gap in his toothy grin. I closed my eyes, better to block out that image. Instead I saw Blythe's eyes, deep blue-gray and wounded, as he told me he loved me, but that he wasn't good for me. That there were things I didn't know about him. I struggled to draw a deep breath, my heart thumping painfully; I was the one to end our relationship just a week ago, believing I was doing the right thing.

Jilly paused, studying my face now; I sensed more than saw her concern. She added, even more softly, "I think—and Jo, I promise I'm only saying this because I love you and I am fucking worried about you—I think you should stay here. I don't think it will solve anything if you try to go there. What can you do?"

"Show him that I love him no matter what. I let him down, don't you see?" I whispered fiercely, not caring that Justin was hearing all of this, too. To his credit, he didn't clear his throat and excuse himself, didn't so much as shuffle his feet. Instead he quietly studied the lake, keeping his hand wrapped gently around Jillian's leg.

Jilly asked, not unreasonably, "Wouldn't a phone call accomplish that?"

I shook my head, unable to respond through the emotion clogging my throat. I couldn't convey to Jilly just how much I needed to find Blythe, to see this through. He needed me, it was that simple. I finally whispered, "I won't stay long. I'll be back before school starts." Necessity would pull me home before long anyway, the necessity of motherhood. But I understood what I must do, which was go after Blythe, even if it meant he would send me away for good. I needed to know the truth, for better or worse; otherwise I would forever torture myself with the wondering.

"Jo, sleep on it, at least," Justin finally ventured, his tone gentle.

"I will," I whispered, again bending my knees and threading my hands together around them. I didn't mention that it wouldn't change my mind.

The three of us made our way back up the shore a minute later, me in the lead, Jilly and Justin a few yards behind, walking with fingers loosely linked. I climbed the porch steps and then turned to watch them amble along, so glad for my sister's happiness that I spent a moment soaking in it. They continued on past the porch, where I stood with my hips pressed lightly to the top rail. Jilly called over her shoulder, "Stay there, Jo, I'll be right back."

I stayed on the porch, obeying her, watching as sunlight tinted the sky with amber hues. The birds were very much awake; the shore echoed with their lively chatter and conversational chirps. The lake itself remained secretive in the last of the silvery dimness of dawn, level as a mirror with no wind to mar its surface. I studied the familiar sight in all its clear-morning beauty, thinking about what happened since yesterday evening.

Blythe was in trouble. I didn't know all of the details, but I vowed to find out. Just over a week ago, I'd told him that we had no future together. Despite everything my heart was screaming to the contrary, I felt as though it was wrong to ask him to stay, to bind himself in any permanent way to a mother with three girls of her own, one of whom was expecting a baby in February. For the countless time, my heart seized with the realization of Camille's pregnancy. My oldest daughter, conceived when her father and I skipped the last half of senior prom to have sex in his car. No protection, just heat and desire and crossed fingers; roughly nine months later we were legally wed, living nearly a thousand miles from our hometown of Landon, Minnesota, and in possession of a newborn.

As though my thoughts conjured her, Jilly bounded back from the direction of the parking lot, where she'd spent a few minutes bidding farewell to Justin. I sank onto a chair at one of the porch tables, propping my bare feet on the opposite seat. Seconds later Jilly lifted my ankles and claimed the space; I settled my feet comfortably in her lap. She braced her elbows on the tabletop, chin on one fist, and regarded me with somber blue eyes.

"What?" I demanded. I didn't have to sigh.

"You might be able to placate Justin, but not me," she said. "Sleep on it, my ass. You're set on your decision, I can see it in your eyes." She tipped her head slightly to one side and then asked, "Do you want company? You know I'd go with you in a heartbeat."

It was tempting, but in the end I knew it was something I must do alone, and Jilly sensed this truth.

"Don't worry about the girls," she reassured me. "They'll understand. And I'll keep them out of trouble."

I shook my head. "It's not that," I whispered. "I'm counting on you to explain why I have to do this."

She was about to ask me why, to explain it to her, too, but then she sensed the depth of what I was feeling, and asked, her voice very soft, "You really do love him, don't you?"

I closed my eyes, seeing only Blythe, and then I reached across the table and gripped my sister's already outstretched hand. I squeezed it, and she returned the pressure.

"I guess so," she said finally.

We sat for another few minutes in companionable silence, watching as the sun crested the treetops on the eastern horizon and spread its wings over the lake. The sky was powder-blue in the dawn's wake, cloudless, and voices traveled to meet our ears from the direction of the lake path, which wound back to our house and the detached garage with its second-floor apartment that Jilly shared with her son, Clint. My own girls were crammed, quite literally, into the upstairs loft in the house, the same home in which I'd lived my entire life in Landon, and of late they began to voice complaints about the situation; they would just have to live with it a little longer, until I found us a place to live in town.

One thing at a time, Joelle, I reminded myself, scraping a hand through my tangled hair. Right now the first thing on my list was coffee, then a shower; at the moment I was certain I looked more than a little depraved, my eyes red and swollen from weeping, my hair in snarls, dressed in an old bathrobe, the hem of which was far too short for my legs.

Mom and Aunt Ellen climbed the steps on the far side of the porch, Mom reaching behind herself as she walked to braid her long hair, its blonde length now liberally streaked with silver. Ellen always wore her own curly yellow hair short, and it currently resembled a flower gone to seed, fluffy and errant despite her best efforts. Ellen was just a year older than Mom and I thought of her as a second mother. To be truthful, Ellen's stoic demeanor and ability to listen quietly led me to her side more often than my own mother's over the years. She was the first person besides Jackie to know about my prom-night pregnancy, and coached me on how to break the news to Mom, all those years ago.

That thought stuck in my mind as I watched them, two slightly plump middle-aged women with freckled skin and wide hazel eyes, wearing jean shorts and Shore Leave t-shirts, Mom decked in hot-pink hoop earrings with circumference enough to be bracelets. They caught sight of Jilly and me at the same moment; Mom hesitated, but Ellen marched ahead and joined us at the table, setting down the large stainless steel bowl she'd been carrying. It was loaded with a whisk, two clean towels, and a pepper grinder.

"What're you powwowing about, girls?" she asked, no hint of teasing in her voice.

"Jo is going after Rich and Blythe," Jilly told her without preamble, and I rolled my eyes in exasperation, though obviously they'd have to know sooner or later.

Ellen didn't respond, only turned her concerned gaze to my face; stubbornly, I kept my eyes on my hands, folded over each other on the tabletop. Mom overheard this, of course, and I sensed more than saw her lips purse in disapproval.

"But what will you tell the girls?" Mom continued, and I struggled not to rub my temples, feeling the light headache I'd suffered since last night intensifying, but Ellen saved me.

"Joan, she's in love and she's taking this chance," my aunt said quietly. "Do you think life offers chances like candy?"

"Like jellybeans," Mom muttered sarcastically, but she backed off, and Ellen touched my hand briefly before gathering her cooking supplies and heading into the café.

⁂

The Shore Leave Cafe Series

The Shore Leave Cafe series celebrates the joys of a simple life, featuring love, family, friends, and small-town living. We hope you've enjoyed getting to know the Davis women and their café on Flickertail Lake. Read about them all in the nine books in this series; available in 2016 & 2017 from Central Avenue Publishing.

Thank you for reading!